Praise for the work of K

Table for Two

I have never read anything from Kate Gavin before, but she has shot up my must-watch list. I loved this book and all the fantastic tropes that the author packed in. I loved the storyline and how the author built the relationship between the main characters, Jill and Regan. I adored every minute and every page of this book. I wouldn't change a thing, and I really hope that Kate Gavin uses her wonderful secondary characters in future novels. She has jumped on my must-watch list. Can't wait to see what comes next.

-Les Rêveur

Table for Two has almost everything a good romantic story must have. Believable and complex protagonists with good chemistry, a few good supporting characters, well-written emotions, a plausible conflict, and an interesting plot. A combination of an ice queen from a dysfunctional family and her complete opposite worked quite successfully and with Gavin's technically good writing made this novel very well worth reading. If you are a romance fan, I very much recommend it. I had a hard time putting it down, and will read it again. -Pin's Reviews, *goodreads*

Table for Two is just fantastic! Kate Gavin delivers a beautiful story full of real-life situations a lot of us can relate to. Reagan and Jillian meet under very trying circumstances. Reagan is going through a personal hell and somehow this pierces Jillian's cold exterior. Kate Gavin shows that two characters can come from different worlds, but that all roads lead to love. I truly love this book and highly recommend it to readers. It offers a pure of heart journey and leads us to hope.

-Emma A., *NetGalley*

Full of Promise

This was a sweet young adult romance. This is a solid debut for Gavin with a very readable story. One of the mains is a lesbian where the other main is coming to terms with her bisexuality. This is a classic coming-of-age, coming out story, but with much more good feels than bad. I enjoyed the pace and feel of this book. Gavin's writing felt easy and smooth and didn't really have any of that choppiness that you sometimes find with new authors. If you are looking for a YA book that is a feel-good romance, this would be a perfect pick.

-LezReview Books

Full of Promise was a very sweet young adult romance novel about discovering one's sexuality and the emotional turmoil involved...This was a very well-written, captivating read. I believe young adults will definitely embrace Cam's journey and hopefully realize that there are others like themselves who are also finding their way to their own true self.

Highly recommended!

-R. Swier, NetGalley

I have to say... I'm not normally a huge fan or reader of YA/NA novels, but this one really worked for me! Even better yet, it seems to be a debut novel for Gavin, so my hat's off to her!

This one was a very sweet YA read where our MCs Cam and Riley are both high school seniors. They meet when Riley moves to town and joins the soccer team that Cam and her best friend Claire are already a part of. Cam's struggling with home life, taking on extra responsibility of caring for her younger brothers while her mom works more hours after a divorce. Riley is new to town, and she's already an out lesbian, but she's struggling to make friends and be accepted. When Cam befriends Riley, she begins to question her feelings for the new girl and realizes that she might not be as straight as she thought she was.

The relationship between Riley and her mom was beautiful, everyone deserves a mom like this, especially questioning

LGBT teens. It was refreshing to see this POV. Best friend Claire's reaction was a bit over the top, but provided a bit of needed angst to the novel.

All in all, I enjoyed this one and was never tempted to skim ahead, which is my norm in a YA novel. It's a well-written, low-angst read, and I appreciated that Gavin didn't make the younger characters quite so... young. They were intelligent and had level heads instead of being over the top dramatic.

I really enjoyed this one, and think that many others will also. Recommended! I'm looking forward to Gavin's next novel! Solid 4 stars.

-Bethany K., *NetGalley*

We meet Cam at her summer job in the library, rolling her cart past the cute girl she's been sneaking peeks at and who she's been exchanging small smiles with. The hitch is that Cam has a boyfriend and is straight. Later, she meets this new girl, Riley, at school and gradually forms a friendship that has an underlying tension of something more, eventually building into an actual romance.

Full of Promise is a sweet story, smooth reading with all the heart tugs you'd expect from two young women falling in love. But rather than being a straight to gay tale, it was more about Cam recognizing and giving light to another part of herself. There were some emotional bumps but nothing harsh like other coming out books. Good, solid YA story.

-Jules P., *NetGalley*

Three's
a
Crowd

Other Bella Books by Kate Gavin

Full of Promise
Table for Two

About the Author

Kate Gavin is a native Midwesterner, currently living in Ohio. When not staring at a computer screen for her day job or this writing gig, she spends her time retrieving items from her thieving dog, chasing after her kiddo, and bingeing TV shows with her wife.

Three's a Crowd

Kate Gavin

BELLA
B O O K S

2022

Bella Books, Inc.
P.O. Box 10543
Tallahassee, FL 32302

Printed in the United States of America on acid-free paper.

First Edition - 2022

Editor: Cath Walker
Cover Designer: Kayla Mancuso

ISBN: 978-1-64247-385-8

PUBLISHER'S NOTE

Acknowledgments

Book three! Never thought I'd be able to say I've written one book, let alone three. Having a baby in the middle of writing this seemed to make it all ten times harder, but I was lucky to have amazing people in my corner throughout the entire process.

As always, the Bella crew is absolutely incredible and I'm grateful every day that I'm part of the team. Jessica and Linda, this book never would have happened without your support and patience. Thank you times a million!

Cath, so many thanks for your guidance and making this story so much better. Next time, I promise not to be on vacation in the middle of edits.

Em, there are never enough words, pal. Even when I felt like I'd fallen off the face of the earth, you were always there with encouragement and reminders that I needed to be gentle with myself. Thank you for all your beta reading awesomeness. Sorry it was so last-minute... All those hours of CoD helped too!

Tagan, thank you for always answering my "Quick question..." messages even when you had so much going on yourself. You are a rockstar, my friend!

Claire, you are always the best cheerleader. Your excitement for my books gets me excited for them even if it's one of those days where I want to throw my computer across the room.

Andy, I don't know where I'd be without your support and love. You are my rock and the absolute best plotting partner. Erin, getting to be your mama brings me all the joy in the world. I love you both so so much!

CHAPTER ONE

"Almost home?"

Switching to speaker, Zoe Tyler tossed the phone on her bed. She groaned with delight as she lifted her sweater over her head. Between the groan and the fabric muffling her ears, she missed her boyfriend's response.

"Sorry, Jake. What was that?"

"I said I'm running late." He let out a sigh. "Ian needs to approve some materials for a pitch to a client tomorrow and I need to wait around until they're printed and take them to him. I might be able to meet you at the bar for round two."

Ian, Jake's boss at the firm Wexler Investments, had been an almost unending source of tension between Zoe and Jake for the past four months. Working as Ian's second assistant he had come home late more evenings than not and had missed a few too many dates. Jake typically made an effort to take Zoe out to their favorite local bar for weekly trivia night, but it looked like he was canceling on that tonight too.

Zoe gripped the jeans she was about to change into and held them in her lap as she collapsed back on the bed, disappointment washing over her. "It's fine."

"Well, when you say that, I know it's not actually fine," he replied, his voice holding a hint of sharpness. "I am sorry, babe."

"We can just go next week."

His voice brightened as he replied, "Definitely. I love you."

"Love you too," she murmured. He'd already hung up and probably hadn't even heard her reply. She tossed the jeans across the bed, covering her eyes with her arm. *Another night of Jake bailing on plans. Joy.*

She sat up and looked down at her mostly naked body. The black underwear with a hint of lace contrasted starkly with her pale skin. Zoe figured she had two choices. Get into comfy clothes, open a bottle of wine, and binge-watch some TV. Or she could make different plans.

Both options were appealing, but she had been in the mindset to go out, so going out was what she'd do. She texted her best friend, Mia.

Let's go out. Corks...meet in 15 min?

Within a minute, Mia replied with several wineglass and smiley-face emojis followed up with, *See ya there!*

Zoe quickly dressed by putting on the discarded jeans and a black and red flannel shirt. She checked herself in the bathroom mirror and then was on her way to their favorite wine bar, Corks.

After a quick but chilly ten-minute walk, Zoe entered Corks and found Mia sitting off to the right at a high-top table. Her curly, dark brown hair was pulled into a loose bun high on top of her head, a few strands escaping at the base of her neck. The pendant light above the table cast an orange-red glow on Mia's warm brown skin. A glass of dark-red liquid was set in front of the empty chair. "Pinot noir?" Zoe asked by way of greeting.

Mia smiled widely, showing off a dimple on her left cheek. "Of course. What else do you ever order?"

Zoe chuckled. "True." She shrugged off her coat and hung it on the back of her chair before sitting.

"I've also already ordered hummus and a margherita flatbread."

"Oh, that sounds delicious. I love you."

"Again, of course," Mia said with a wink. Then she leaned forward and lowered her voice. "Before we get into things, do you see that woman sitting at the bar, two seats from the corner?"

Zoe turned to the woman in question. She looked to be in her fifties with bright, obviously bottled blond hair. She had dark-rimmed glasses and was drinking white wine. Zoe could only see her profile so she wasn't sure whether she should recognize the woman or not. "Yeah. What about her?"

"Doesn't she look like Mrs. Silver?"

Zoe furrowed her brow at the unfamiliar name. "Who?" she asked.

"Mrs. Silver. Junior year English teacher."

Zoe had known Mia since they were sophomores in high school and had sat next to each other in chemistry class. "Oh," Zoe replied, dragging the word out. She glanced over at the woman again, and now that she had the idea in her head, the woman did kind of look like their former teacher. "She does, a little at least. Has that big mole on her cheek though. Mrs. Silver didn't have one."

Mia gave the woman another look, squinting as if that would make her figure it out quicker. "Yeah, you're right. Wouldn't it be awkward to drink at the same bar as a teacher? I hate running into people that you kinda know and should probably say hi to, but you always know those conversations are awkward as fuck."

Zoe chuckled. "Remember how she always had the radio set to a classical station and played it in the background? Like listening to that would ever make talking about *Romeo and Juliet* better."

"True," Mia replied, holding up her glass.

Zoe clinked her glass with Mia's and took a sip of her wine, enjoying the hints of cherry on her tongue.

"So what's up? What's with the last-minute invite? Not that I'm upset by it or anything," she said with a grin. "I'll always say yes to wine."

"Jake and I were supposed to go out tonight."

"Oh yeah, it's Wednesday, trivia night. What happened?"

"He was stuck at work. Didn't think he'd make it in time. I told him to just forget about it. Didn't want to sit at home alone again so I hit you up instead."

"Well I'm flattered."

Zoe replayed what she'd said in her head and cringed. "Sorry. That kinda came out like you were my last resort or something. I totally didn't mean it that way."

Mia chuckled. "It's okay, really. Besides, I was just going to restart that sweater I'm trying to knit for like the fourth time. You saved me from spending a night of wanting to tear my hair out. I thought knitting would give me a relaxing break, but, honestly, sometimes I'd rather study instead."

The waitress placed their food and plates at the center of the table. "Here you go. Can I get you two anything else?"

"No thanks," Mia replied, already reaching for a plate and a slice of flatbread. When the waitress walked away, Mia said, "This looks so good. You better grab some for yourself before I hog it all."

"Don't have to tell me twice," Zoe replied with a smile. She grabbed a carrot stick and swiped it through the hummus. It gave a satisfying snap as she took a bite. "So how is school going?"

Mia had just started her doctoral program in clinical psychology, which had added to Zoe's appeal of moving to Indianapolis for Jake's job. Zoe and Mia hadn't lived in the same city since they graduated high school in Evansville, Indiana, about three hours' drive south.

"Oh, it's fine. So far. Trying to enjoy the calm before it all gets too hectic. First semester is never a good indication for how things are gonna go."

"Especially if you consider how your first semester of college went," Zoe said, her eyebrows lifting as she took a sip of wine.

Mia held up her hands. "So maybe I enjoyed the freedom of being away from home a *little* too much."

Zoe cleared her throat. "You mean partied a little too much? So much that you came close to failing a class?"

"In my defense, I didn't fail it. And you have to admit, I got my shit together after that."

Zoe nodded. "You did. Mama Pat would've given you a talking-to if you hadn't." Mia's mom had always been a stickler for getting good grades and not slacking off. But not in the super-overbearing way, but in the wanting-her-kids-to-do-well-and-succeed kind of way. She had even taken a hands-on approach, more than Zoe's parents ever had, helping Zoe and Mia study for tests, and editing their papers.

"Oh yeah. She probably would have marched on over to Cincinnati and sat with me in the library until I got all my work done."

They shared a good laugh at that image and finished off their wine. The waitress stopped by to confirm another round. Once she brought their drinks, Zoe took a sip of hers while Mia just spun hers around by the stem and stared at the glass. A sign that something was definitely up.

Zoe moved her plate to the side and put her elbow on the table, resting her chin in her hand. "Okay, hit me with it. What's wrong?"

Mia opened her mouth but closed it just as quickly. She squirmed in her seat, sitting up a little straighter as she continued spinning her wineglass. She licked her lips. "I don't want to upset you, but I hate to see you so disappointed. And...well, I'll just come out with it. Do you think something else is going on?"

"Something else like what?" Zoe asked, her mouth turning down in a frown.

"I'm sure it's not the case so don't get upset. But...do you think that maybe...Jake is seeing someone else?"

Zoe dropped her arm to the table and stared at Mia with wide eyes. "Like cheating on me? What? No way. Why would you think that?" Zoe sat back and crossed her arms over her chest.

Mia held her hands up. "I'm not saying he is. But you've told me about all the times he's gotten home late or skipped out on plans. I was just throwing it out there." After taking a sip of wine, she sighed. "I know he loves you and I don't really get that vibe from him. Just...be careful."

Zoe's stiff posture relaxed and she uncrossed her arms. "I appreciate that, but he's never done anything to make me think that." She leaned forward and ran a hand through her hair. "Yes, he's been a little flaky about date nights. And he comes home late more nights than I'd like. But his boss truly sucks. He's an ass. I met him at the company picnic on Labor Day. Jake never got to enjoy himself or spend time with me because his boss always had him getting him something or writing down details of any prospective clients."

"Ugh. I don't know how he deals with it."

Zoe knew there was more. "But? Don't leave me hanging on what you really want to say."

Mia reached across the table to take Zoe's hand. "But, honey, when is enough enough?"

Zoe sighed and squeezed Mia's hand in return. "I know. I've brought it up a bit before, but I don't want him to think that I don't support him or his work. He says working for this guy could really open doors for him and that if he can get through a year, then he can easily get promoted or move on to someplace better."

"I get that. I really do. But I don't want you to keep giving and giving and getting nothing in return. If he makes you feel shitty sometimes, you need to talk with him and tell him that."

She smiled at Mia, always grateful for her protective side. "I'll try."

"Do more than try. Do it."

"Aye, aye, captain," Zoe replied, giving Mia a mocking salute.

"Smartass." Mia rolled her eyes. "You know I'm always here if you need to talk. Especially if it's here," she replied as she grinned and took the last carrot.

Zoe chuckled. "I'll keep that in mind."

After finishing their wine and parting with a hug, Zoe began her walk home. The wind had picked up so she pulled up the collar of her jacket and wrapped her arms around herself. She replayed the last bits of her conversation with Mia. She had never even thought about the possibility of Jake cheating, but Mia had planted the seed. What if he was though? Would she even recognize the signs? He wasn't being secretive and he never tried to hide his phone. She knew he still wanted her, if yesterday's quickie before work was anything to go by. She shook her head at the thought. No way. He couldn't be cheating.

Still, he was absent and consumed by work. Each time he bailed on their plans, whether they were scheduled date nights or just dinner at home, it hurt. It made her feel like maybe she wasn't enough for him. That no matter what she did—cooked for him, gave him gifts, let his career guide their life—he'd never make her needs a priority. If she was honest with herself, she had given thought to what her life would be like if she ended things with Jake.

But she loved him. She just needed to talk with him. Let him know how she was feeling. Admittedly, not her favorite thing to do or something she was good at. If she had to talk to someone that was in anyway confrontational, she'd mentally rehearse exactly what she wanted to say. But when the time came to say it, did she say any of her important points? Nope. Her mind would just go completely blank.

As she stood in front of their apartment door, she took a deep breath before putting the key in the lock. The lamp in the living room was off, but she thought she had turned it on before she left. Maybe she'd forgotten since she had rushed out to meet Mia.

She took off her coat and shoes before calling out, "Jake?"

"In here," he replied, sounding like he was in the kitchen.

She turned the corner and let out a breath. The sight before her brought a smile to her lips and a warmth to her chest. Candles flickered on their small kitchen table, and plates, silverware, and an open bottle of her favorite wine were set out. Jake was taking out food containers from their go-to Thai restaurant.

"What's all this?"

Jake looked up with a wide smile and set a container onto the counter. He walked up to Zoe and gave her a soft kiss. "Hey. I wanted to make it up to you for bailing on trivia. You haven't eaten, have you?"

"Not really. Mia and I just had appetizers at Corks."

His blue eyes shone with relief. "Awesome! I got you pad thai and a double order of shrimp rolls."

Zoe wrapped her arms around him and melted into his embrace. "You always knew the way to my heart was with shrimp rolls."

"Well, when you ordered them on our first date and refused to share, I kinda got that idea." He hugged her tighter and whispered, "I am sorry."

She kissed him below his ear and pulled back, stroking her thumb across the stubble along his chin. "I know. But let's talk about that later. I'm ready to eat."

"No surprise there," he said with a chuckle.

Zoe shoved him away and sat down. "Oh shut up."

Jake put the containers on the table and Zoe immediately snatched up the one with the shrimp rolls. She put a couple on her plate and handed the container to Jake. She almost wanted to say, "See. Sometimes I can be good at sharing." As she added the pad thai, Jake piled his high with red curry chicken.

They ate and talked about their day, and Zoe found her frustration softening. It wasn't gone completely, just hanging around in the back of her mind. Surprises like this always reminded her how thoughtful and sweet Jake could be. That had been one of the things that had drawn her in when they started dating in their junior year of college at Ball State in Muncie. When she was stressed out by tests or big presentations, he'd show up to her door with something to make her smile. It wasn't even the food or little presents themselves that made things better. It was that he was able to read her moods and know she was struggling. And then knew exactly what she needed to brighten her day.

As they cleaned up, Jake explained his boss's ridiculous demand earlier in the night. Guess this would be as good a time as any to talk to him, Zoe thought. The plates were loaded in the dishwasher and leftovers stowed in the fridge. Zoe leaned back against the counter and crossed her arms. "Can we talk about that?"

Jake straightened, wiping his hands on a towel before tossing it on the counter. His slight frown told her he had anticipated this conversation. "Of course. Go for it."

Zoe dropped her arms and started fiddling with her fingers. She would be a horrible poker player—her anxiety was always front and center, manifesting in some form of fidgeting. "You know I support you and I know that this job could give you so many opportunities later on." She sighed. "It's just…getting a little tiring that you come home late so much. It feels like you cancel plans all the time now."

Jake stood in front of her and rested his hands on her hips. "I know. And I hate that that's what's happened, especially the last couple of months. It's like Ian gets this perverse joy out of knowing he can make my life as miserable as possible because I'll just suck it up and do what he wants. This morning he had me get him this huge bag of trail mix and I had to take out all the raisins and almonds."

"That sounds like a great use of your time," Zoe muttered. How was doing petty tasks like that going to open doors? She lightly gripped his forearms and looked down at her hands as she rubbed the sleeve of his button-up between her thumb and forefinger. She had bought it for his birthday last year and she loved how smooth the fabric felt. Clearing her throat, she asked, "Can't you just tell him that it's putting a strain on your personal life?"

He scoffed. "I wish, babe. He'd just say I don't have the drive for the job and tell me to quit. Hell, he would maybe even fire me on the spot."

"He's such a dick. I don't know how you can stand it."

"One year. I just need to stick it out for one year. Then I can get the analyst job and I'll be set. I can make my mark with that team and just keep moving up. I told you they mostly promote from within. This is my chance."

Jake's favorite professor at Ball State had hooked him up with this job at Wexler, the best investment firm in Indianapolis. Professor Freeman had assured him that working as Ian's assistant would then secure him a spot as a portfolio analyst within a year. Zoe hated the fact that Ian seemed to completely take advantage of Jake, but she tried to stay quiet and support him. Bad-mouthing the situation would take away some of Jake's excitement for the future.

"I get it. I really do. It's not just the canceled plans and late nights though. I feel like I have to do everything around here. Cooking. Cleaning. Laundry. Shopping. You say you'll help on the weekends, but then you end up telling me it's your only time to relax and none of that shit gets done. It's hard."

"I'm sorry. I've been an ass letting you pick up my slack. I'll try to do better," he murmured. "I promise."

"That's all I ask." Only time would tell if he would keep that promise. Her initial, albeit weak, attempts to get him to help more never seemed to result in him pulling his weight for long. Maybe this time she'd stand up for herself a bit more if she didn't see a change.

"Adulting sucks," he said with a sigh.

Zoe snorted. "You got that right."

He cupped her face in his hands, forcing her to maintain eye contact. "I love you."

And there it was. Proof to Zoe that he wasn't cheating and never would. The soft yet intense look in his bright blue eyes. Eyes that always revealed what he was truly thinking. He loved her and only her. He had never given her any reason to think there would be someone else. And she hated that she had questioned it for even a second. His recent behavior was all due to work and nothing more. Now they would just have to work through that and everything would be right in their world.

The corner of Zoe's mouth quirked up. "I love you too."

Jake smiled and leaned in for a kiss, hesitating right before their lips met as if checking to see if she was still upset with him. Zoe closed the distance for a slow kiss and wrapped her arms around his waist. Before either of them could deepen it, Jake pulled her into his body for a tight hug and rested his head on the top of hers. Zoe closed her eyes as she listened to the comforting sound of his heartbeat.

After a few moments, Jake pulled back and met her gaze. "Let's go to bed. I can make it up to you even more," he said with a grin.

Zoe chuckled and let him guide her down the hallway.

CHAPTER TWO

Padding into the kitchen, Paige Newbanks rubbed her eyes and yawned so widely that her jaw popped on both sides. Even though she'd spent the last week working as a barista at a local coffee shop, Craft Café, she still struggled with the early morning shifts. She didn't hate mornings. Hate was such a strong word, wasn't it? She tolerated them and knew they were a necessary evil in the world of coffee. And until she could find a more permanent job it would be a necessary evil in her world as well.

As she pulled a box of cereal off the top of the refrigerator, her roommate, well more like acquaintance from college that was letting her crash at her place, cleared her throat behind Paige. She turned and shook the box. "Hey, Liz. What's up? Want some cereal?" she asked before grabbing a bowl from the cupboard.

Liz's eyes darted around the room and landed everywhere but on Paige. Liz shook her head as she sat on a stool at the breakfast bar. "We need to talk."

Paige's arm stopped in midair as she poured cereal into her bowl. The phrase everyone dreads. Setting the box on the counter, she braced herself for what Liz was about to say. She ran through anything that could be wrong, but she drew a blank. *I clean up after myself, buy food, and give her money for rent. I even pack up my sleeping bag every morning before I leave for work.* Yes, she slept in a sleeping bag in the den because Liz's apartment had only one bedroom. She usually laid it on the floor between Liz's desk and the bookshelves. She knew it probably wasn't ideal for Liz that she was staying here, but she couldn't think of anything that would cause a huge issue.

"Okay. What's up?" Paige asked.

"I'm sorry to do this, but you need to move out. Brandon's lease is ending and instead of him finding a new place, I asked him to move in." Liz picked at a crack in the countertop with her thumb.

Paige felt the blood drain from her face. *Shit. I wasn't expecting that. At least not this soon.* She didn't know the city well at all. Or anyone in it. Well, she knew one other person but she couldn't just show up on his doorstep. "When?" Paige whispered.

"End of the month."

Fuck. Fuck. Fuck. She checked the date on her watch. "But it's the twenty-third," she choked out. Paige gripped the counter, trying to keep herself steady. She felt the sting of tears but willed them away. She racked her brain for places she could look and wondered if she'd be able to find something so last-minute. Then she remembered the time of year. "And Thanksgiving's tomorrow. Do you know how hard it's going to be to find a place?"

"I know it sucks. Honestly I didn't think you'd still be here."

Okay, ouch. It had only been a couple of weeks. When she'd asked to stay, Liz had been sympathetic and told her she could stay as long as she needed. She thought she'd have more time. At least a month or two. Not just two weeks. Her heart beat faster as her mind spiraled. How would she find a place that quickly? The only reason she had to crash with Liz in the first place was because during her initial search so many apartments had waiting lists. Or she just couldn't afford them. Not with her current job and lack of savings.

Fuck. What if I don't make enough for an apartment? Stupid requirements to make three times the rent. She might need to job hunt before she could even think about apartment hunting. She could live in her car if necessary, but it was November and already close to freezing overnight. Her stomach churned as her mind played negative thought after negative thought. But she really had no choice. It was Liz's place after all. "Fine. I'll start looking after work today."

"Great. Well I need to head out. Let's get pizza for dinner tonight," she called out over her shoulder as she walked out the door.

Pizza? Who wanted to think about pizza right now? Paige stared at the cereal in her bowl. She had completely lost her appetite but knew she needed to eat something. Starving and thinking about food for an entire shift was never very fun. She sat on the stool Liz had just vacated and mindlessly ate, each spoonful feeling like she'd swallowed a rock. *What the hell am I gonna do?*

Her shift at the coffee shop started just as her morning had—shitty. She had gotten two out of her first five orders wrong and she'd just dropped a gallon of skim milk, splashing it onto her feet and all over the floor.

"Paige. Meet me in my office. Now," her manager and owner of Craft Café, Rebecca, said firmly.

Her shoulders slumped as she stood after wiping up the last of the milk. Great. She's probably going to fire me, she thought. After tossing the soaked rag into the dirty linen bag, she stepped into Rebecca's office.

Rebecca closed the door behind her and crossed her arms in front of her chest. "Tell me what's going on. It's like your head's in the clouds today. You've been doing great since you started. Until today that is."

Paige's eyes widened and she held up her hands. "I'm so sorry. This isn't like me. It's just…I…I had a rough start to the day is all. I promise to get my focus back. Please. Please don't fire me. I need this job. I swear I won't mess up again." Tears pricked at her eyes but she refused to let them fall. Not in front of her boss. She could break down later. Now wasn't the time.

Rebecca stared at her without saying a word, as if wondering if Paige was worth her time or if she should just fire her on the spot. She relaxed her arms at her sides and stepped closer to Paige, her expression softening as she met Paige's gaze. "I'm not firing you, Paige. Is everything okay?"

Paige swallowed against the lump in her throat and took a deep breath. "Yeah. Everything's fine." She tried smiling, but she was sure it was coming across as more of a grimace. "Can I go?" she asked as she gestured toward the door. Paige needed to get out of there before she let her emotions get the best of her.

Rebecca nodded. "Yep. Get back out there."

Paige let out a long breath. "Thank you."

"And Paige?" Rebecca called out as Paige stepped into the hallway. Paige's grip tightened on the door handle. "If something is going on, I want you to know that you can talk to me about it. I like to think of my employees like they're family. Keep that in mind, okay?"

Paige nodded and left the office. Instead of making her way to her spot behind the counter, she made a detour into the staff bathroom. She leaned back against the door and closed her eyes at the bright, fluorescent lights. Taking several deep breaths, she forced any hint of tears away. Once she was certain there was no longer a chance of crying, she splashed her face with cold water, wiping her face with a paper towel. Paige stared at herself in the mirror, noting her red eyes and the perpetual frown. She practiced a few smiles until they felt a little more convincing. Customers didn't tip baristas that look miserable. And she needed all the tips she could get.

As she walked back behind the counter, she revisited Rebecca's parting words. It was a nice idea to be treated like family by her boss, but she wasn't comfortable telling Rebecca her problems. She didn't want her to think Paige was irresponsible or impulsive for moving to Indy without much thought except for knowing she wanted to reconnect with her brother. She didn't need to bother her with her own family drama. No, Paige would figure things out on her own. Like she always did.

With each passing day of Paige looking for a place to stay, Liz's boyfriend kept bringing his things over to the apartment and storing them in the den. Each additional box felt like a giant "Fuck you, get out" message from him. Every night after work she had spent her free time searching the Internet or going in person to view apartments or rooms for rent. Everywhere either had a waitlist, was too expensive, or the people she'd be sharing with seemed creepy. So far, nothing was working out so it looked like she was destined to either stay in a hotel or in her car that night. She would gladly stay in her car for a while if it meant she didn't have to feel like she needed to keep her bedroom door locked at night.

The morning of the thirtieth, Paige trudged into the kitchen and dropped her backpack, sleeping bag, and duffel next to a stool. She stood at the counter as she watched the toaster, waiting for her bagel to pop up. She was in a daze after spending the night tossing, turning, and crying, nauseated with dread. She still hadn't figured out what she was going to do. She would probably have to find the cheapest hotel she could. Paige jumped as she heard Liz's voice behind her.

"Found a place?" Liz asked brightly.

Paige gritted her teeth as she spread peanut butter on her bagel and wrapped it in a paper towel. There was no reason for her to tell Liz the truth. She wouldn't care anyway and would still kick her out no matter her answer. "Yeah. I did," she muttered.

"Oh, awesome. I was worried when you hadn't said anything about it yet."

Paige held back an eye roll. *Sure you were. So worried that you helped me find a place? So worried that you let your slimy boyfriend practically overwhelm my small sleeping area with all of his shit?* Liz was worried all right. Worried that Paige would still be there when Brandon officially moved in later that night.

She stuffed her bagel in the outer mesh pocket of her backpack before reaching into her pocket for her keys. She took Liz's spare key off the ring and placed it on the counter. "Thanks for letting me stay." She threw her bags over her shoulder and headed for the door.

Liz called out, "See you around."

Yeah right, she thought. Paige walked outside to the parking lot and tossed her bags into the trunk of her silver Honda Civic. She slammed her door after collapsing into the front seat. Resting her elbow on the door, Paige bit her thumbnail and stared out the window. Sunlight was just starting to illuminate the roofs of the buildings around her. If she didn't get going soon, she would be late for work. But she couldn't make herself move. She felt frozen in fear and uncertainty.

Paige unlocked her phone and logged in to her bank's app to check her balance. Six hundred bucks. That's all she had. She could find a hotel or a super-cheap Airbnb, but that wasn't sustainable. Plus, she would need to save as much money as she could for the deposit on an apartment.

She only had two free options. She could sleep in her car. But the temps were going to be below freezing for the foreseeable future. So that held very little appeal. That meant she was left with reaching out to the only other person she knew in the city and the reason she had moved here—her brother. They hadn't talked in years. Since she was five to be exact. She'd had the plan of getting settled in the city and reaching out to him when she felt confident and ready. Now she was going to find herself on his doorstep by the end of the night, asking for help.

It'll be great, it'll be fine. There's totally no way this could end badly, she thought sarcastically.

CHAPTER THREE

Zoe let the door to the apartment building swing shut behind her with a loud thud. Her arms were weighed down by bags of groceries and she struggled to lift an arm to press the button for the elevator. Sure, she could've split her haul into two trips, but she prided herself on getting all of her groceries inside in one go.

Exiting onto the fifth floor, Zoe's stomach grumbled at the aromas in the hallway as she passed by her neighbors' apartments. Something rich, like a stew perhaps. Maybe even fresh bread, she thought as she took another whiff. Whatever it was, it smelled like the perfect meal on this cold, late-November night. As she continued down the hallway, she even smelled cookies baking. *Can I just say screw it and have cookies for dinner?* But of course she wouldn't. She had to feed Jake too.

Her shoulders slumped as she finally reached their apartment at the end of the hallway. She shifted the grocery bags as she fished for her keys. The Christmas wreath with a smiling Santa in the middle brightened her mood for a moment as she unlocked the door. Kicking it closed as she walked through, she dropped her keys on the table just inside the door.

"Jake? You home?" Zoe deposited the bags on the kitchen counter. When no answer came, she sighed and shrugged out of her coat. Tossing it onto the living room armchair turned out to be a bad idea as it fell to the floor because of the overflowing pile of clean towels already there.

Groaning in exasperation, she bent over to pick it up and dropped it on the back of a stool instead. "First, you said you'd be home early and now I find out you didn't fold the towels like I asked," she said, as if her boyfriend was standing right in front of her. She made a mental note to fold them later, but she needed to attend to the groceries first. Feeding her growling stomach was also a priority.

She put away everything except a box of spaghetti and jar of pasta sauce, which she set on the counter. *Dinner. Real food. Not cookies.* She grabbed her phone and sent a quick text to Jake. *Where are you? I thought you were coming home early tonight? Dinner will be ready in thirty.* She received no immediate reply, so she clicked the screen off and put the phone on the counter next to the sauce.

Opening a bottom cabinet, she crouched down to take out a large pot and small saucepan. Her knees creaked as she stood, reminding her that she should spend a little more time on the spin bike and a little less time in front of the computer. After setting the pot of water to boil, she walked down the hallway to the bedroom.

She stripped out of her clothes and turned on the shower. As she stepped under the spray, she leaned her head back to wet her hair. Closing her eyes, she let herself enjoy the high pressure of the water and imagined that one day they could move into a bigger place with a jetted tub.

Before she lost herself in that daydream, her eyes snapped open as she remembered she had a pot of water on the stove. She finished her shower and toweled off. She didn't care if it boiled over, but that meant she'd have one more thing to clean.

All she wanted to do tonight was eat something and curl up on the couch under a blanket.

She threw on sweats and a T-shirt, then reached into Jake's drawer for one of his hoodies. She loved drowning in the soft fabric, and an added perk was that it still held his scent even after being washed. It helped ease her annoyance with him.

The water had just started to boil as Zoe entered the kitchen. She sprinkled in a generous amount of salt and added the spaghetti. She dumped the sauce into the smaller pot and turned on the burner, ignoring her mom's voice in her head that sauce made from scratch was far superior to anything from a jar.

"Maybe if you wrote down your recipes for me, Mom," she mumbled. Zoe hadn't developed much skill in the kitchen yet and typically had to rely on following specific recipes even if she'd made a dish several times. Her mom's "add a little of this and a little of that" way of cooking was never super helpful.

She checked the phone to see if Jake replied, but was unsurprised she didn't see any alerts. She rolled her eyes and put the phone back down. While dinner was cooking, she decided she might as well fold the towels. And once she finished with those, she figured she'd earned a reward—a nice glass of wine.

Jake wasn't much of a wine drinker so he didn't have any wineglasses in the apartment, and she didn't bring any with her when she moved in because those in her last place were her roommate's. So, she stood on her tiptoes to grab a pint glass from an upper cabinet and filled it halfway with a cabernet she had opened with Mia a few days ago.

After taking a sip and returning the glass to the counter, she scooped up a piece of pasta with a fork and tossed it in her mouth. Trying to ignore the temperature of it, she chewed and deemed it perfect. She drained the spaghetti and added the bubbling sauce to the pot. She went to reach for a bowl from the cabinet but stopped when she heard her phone ding.

I'm gonna be late. Don't wait for me.

"Yeah, no shit," she said, dropping the phone to the counter without replying. Fine, she'd eat without him.

She dished up a bowl of pasta and sprinkled some parmesan cheese in her bowl. She and Jake had been bingeing *Dexter* together, but she wasn't petty enough to watch without him. Maybe she'd catch up on some of the *Station 19* episodes she had recorded since Jake didn't like it.

Just as she was about to sit down, she heard a knock at the door. Sighing, she set her bowl and glass on the coffee table and looking through the peephole, she saw a woman shifting from foot to foot.

She opened the door enough to poke her head through. "Can I help you?" Zoe asked, noticing dark circles under the woman's eyes.

"Is Jake here?"

Zoe straightened and opened the door a little more. *Why is another woman asking for Jake? Was Mia right? Could he be cheating?* "No, he's not. I'm his girlfriend," she replied, emphasizing the last word. "Who are you?"

"I'm his sister."

Zoe narrowed her eyes as she shook her head. "No you're not. I know his sister and you're definitely not her." She stepped back and started closing the door until the woman pushed out her hand to stop her.

"Wait. I promise. I'm not lying. I am his sister." She fiddled with a silver ring on the middle finger of her right hand. "Well, half-sister," she replied with a slight shrug.

Zoe let go of the door and folded her arms across her chest, taking a moment to look more closely at this woman. Her eyes were red and puffy, as if she had only stopped crying just before knocking. She was dressed casually in jeans, sneakers, and a gray sweater underneath a navy peacoat. A duffel bag lay at her feet and a backpack was slung over one shoulder. Her posture was slumped forward and her full lips were curled down in a frown. She looked tired, worn down.

The woman reached into the pocket of her coat, pulling out her wallet and holding her driver's license out to Zoe. "Look. My last name is Newbanks. My...well our dad is Brian. Jake has a sister, Sarah, and brother, Derek—both older. I promise I'm not lying. Please. I need to see him. I'm desperate."

Tears filled the woman's eyes and she raised her hand to her quivering lips to bite her thumbnail. Zoe's heart clenched. Whether this woman was telling the truth or not, she clearly needed help. That or she was a really great actress. But why would someone lie about something like this? She seemed to know about Jake's family. And she didn't look like a serial killer. *But weren't serial killers supposed to draw you in and get you to trust them? Boy, I really need to stop watching true-crime documentaries.* She mentally shook herself from the ridiculous thought. It wasn't very helpful at a time like this.

Zoe glanced back into the apartment, seeing her dinner on the table. Something in her gut told her this woman wasn't lying and that she wasn't a threat. A certain resolve came over her as she turned her attention back to the woman. "Are you hungry?"

The woman dropped her hand from her mouth and let out a breath. "A...a little."

Zoe pulled the door open fully and gestured inside. "Come on in. Jake's still at work. I was just about to eat and there's plenty of pasta."

"Thanks," she murmured, stepping inside the apartment and clutching the strap of her backpack.

Zoe watched as her eyes darted around the room, curious yet cautious. She tried to find any similarities to Jake, something to help confirm the fact that they were related. Her nose was pretty similar—they both had a small bump on the bridge. Her eyes were a bit more gray-blue than Jake's bright blue. There definitely was a resemblance.

Awkward silence filled the space, and Zoe cleared her throat. With a small smile, she held out her hand. "I'm Zoe, by the way."

The woman set her duffel bag on the floor next to the TV stand and dropped the backpack on top of it before shaking Zoe's hand. "Paige. It's nice to meet you."

Zoe returned Paige's firm grip with a quick shake. "Take off your coat. You can hang it up in the closet behind you."

Paige opened the closet, pulling out a hanger and wrapping her coat around it. Zoe gave Paige a brief up and down glance while she was turned away. She saw the outline of Paige's cell phone in the back pocket of her jeans. As Paige turned back around, Zoe quickly lifted her eyes, hoping she hadn't been caught giving her a once-over. The slight upturn of Paige's lips said otherwise.

Zoe wrung her fingers together. "So, want some pasta? It's nothing special, but it is edible, I promise."

"That'd be great."

"Would you like a glass of wine?" Zoe pointed to her own glass on the coffee table.

"No thanks. I don't drink," Paige replied, fiddling again with the ring on her finger.

"Sorry. I can put it away. It's not—"

Paige stopped her with a raised hand. "No, I don't mind if you drink. Just a personal preference."

Zoe wanted to ask why, but she didn't want to pry. "Okay. Well, have a seat and I'll dish it up."

When she walked into the kitchen, she kept an eye on Paige. Not that Zoe thought she'd do something. It was just a bit unnerving having a stranger in her place, even if that stranger was possibly related to her boyfriend.

Paige toed off her shoes and sat on the couch, bringing one leg up with her foot curled underneath the opposite leg. She continued to look around the room, and even picked up a framed photo from the side table. It was a picture of Zoe and Jake at the top of the Ferris wheel at Navy Pier.

"That was during a trip to Chicago for our two-year anniversary."

Paige jumped a bit and set the frame back down on the table. "Sorry," she said as she turned and settled back into the couch. "Your hair was longer."

Zoe ran her hand over her hair, which ended just below her chin and had a bit of a wave to it. In the picture her hair had been down to the middle of her back. It had always been such a hassle to deal with so she made the impulsive decision on a particularly windy day to cut most of it off. "Yeah, I got it cut while on that trip actually. Just wanted a change."

"It looks good short. I mean it looked good when it was longer too. It, um, looks good both ways," Paige muttered, her cheeks reddening.

Zoe smiled as warmth spread through her cheeks too. "Thanks. Here you go," Zoe said as she handed over a bowl of pasta and glass of water.

"Thank you."

"You're welcome." Zoe picked up her bowl and cradled it against her stomach as she sat on the other end of the couch.

Paige set her glass of water down next to the picture frame and held the bowl in her hands, stirring the pasta but not taking a bite. They sat in silence and looked anywhere but at each other. Zoe had no idea what Paige was thinking, but the thoughts inside Zoe's head wouldn't stop.

And those thoughts quickly turned to emotions that she hadn't let herself feel just yet—anger and betrayal. If it was true that Paige was Jake's sister, then why had he not told Zoe about her even once? How could he do that? Did he think so little of Zoe that he didn't trust her with whatever family secret was sitting next to her? Or did he think so little of his sister that she didn't warrant a mention in any conversation they'd had in the past? What if he didn't know? And if he did know, then what was she doing here now? Where had she been all these years? What did she want now?

Glancing at Paige, Zoe found her chewing on her thumb again and looking around the room. The uncertainty on Paige's face dampened Zoe's anger. So she took a breath, hoping to calm and center herself. "I was about to catch up on some *Station 19*. Do you know the show?"

Paige turned toward Zoe with a small smile. "I love that show. Where are you at?"

Zoe relaxed into her seat and pulled her legs up onto the couch to sit cross-legged, but slightly grimaced as she confessed, "I'm only starting season three. Have you seen it?"

"Oh yeah, I think I'm all caught up. Get ready for some drama."

"Can't wait." Zoe snagged the remote from the coffee table and scrolled through the list of recordings until she found the right episode.

They sat in silence, watching the show and eating dinner. Occasionally, Paige would make some comment about a character or a scene. Zoe had to admit she wasn't paying much attention to the episode but was thankful that it provided noise to fill the rather awkward tension between her and Paige. Zoe's mind kept going back and forth between wanting to ask Paige questions and fuming at Jake. She needed to know more, but her brain was still trying to catch up with the fact that Jake had a sister she didn't know about. Bombarding Paige with questions about why Jake didn't talk about her or why she wasn't in his life seemed rude. Besides, Zoe needed to direct those questions to Jake. He certainly was in for a treat when he got home.

As the credits rolled on the episode, Zoe heard a key in the door. *Good...Jake's home and can provide some answers.*

Paige took a deep breath and sat up straight.

Jake's focus was on locking the door and kicking off his shoes. "Hey, babe, whose bags are...Paige?" His brows furrowed for a moment before a smile spread across his face. "Holy shit! Paige!" He quickly pulled her up for a hug. "What are you doing here?"

Paige returned the hug but she just patted him on the back rather than a tight grasp. Zoe caught his gaze as he hugged Paige, hoping she conveyed her confusion and anger. Jake's face paled and he pulled away from Paige.

"Well I moved to Indy a few weeks ago, and the place I was staying kinda fell through. I was just wondering if I could stay here for a night or two." She looked nervously between Jake and Zoe.

Jake answered immediately. "Totally. You're in luck, we have a second bedroom that we haven't rented out yet."

Zoe clenched her jaw. *Hello? I live here too. Don't want my input?* It wasn't that she had a problem with Paige needing a place to crash, but it would have been nice for Jake to ask her if it was okay first.

"Thanks. I appreciate it," Paige said.

"No problem." He paused, staring at her with a soft smile. "It's been a while. I can't believe you're here. I'll just go get the room ready for you." He moved to Zoe's side and kissed her cheek. "Hey. Sorry I was late."

Zoe's lips pressed into a thin line. *But not sorry that I just found out about your half-sister you never told me about?* Looked like she didn't know Jake as well as she had thought. Or maybe he didn't love her enough to let her in. Expletives raced through Zoe's mind, but it would be rude to say what she wanted to in front of Paige so she just added, "There's some leftover pasta on the stove."

"Great." He started undoing his tie as he walked down the hallway.

Zoe stared at his back until Paige's voice pulled her out of her thoughts. "Thank you for letting me stay," she murmured. "Hopefully I'll find a place and be out of your hair by the end of the week."

"You're his sister. Of course, we'd help you out." She clenched and relaxed her fists at her sides. "I'm just gonna heat up his food. Need anything?" Paige shook her head but the hesitancy she'd displayed earlier reappeared. Zoe felt a weird need to calm her unease so she gave her a small smile and gestured to the TV. "Turn on whatever you want. And, um, make yourself at home."

She entered the kitchen and divided the rest of the pasta between a plate for Jake and a container she then put into the fridge. As she waited for Jake's portion to warm up in the microwave, she gripped the edge of the counter and dropped her head, taking slow, deep breaths. How could she not know about Paige? And how could Jake not ask her if she was okay with Paige staying?

Zoe straightened when Jake came up behind her and wrapped his arms around her waist. She stood stiffly as he whispered in her ear, "I'm sorry."

"About which part?" she asked, turning her head to meet his gaze. She wanted to scream at him or cry. She felt almost claustrophobic in his embrace. It no longer felt comforting. It felt oppressive. She wanted to push him away. But she couldn't do any of that. Not now. Not in front of Paige.

"All of it. I promised to be better about getting home on time. And…I should've told you about Paige a long time ago. I just haven't seen her since I was a kid. Our dad—"

"You can tell me about it later," she ground out. The microwave let out three shrill beeps and Zoe handed the plate to Jake. "We need to get back out there. She probably knows we're talking about her."

Jake took over Zoe's seat on the couch and sat cross-legged with his back against the armrest, settling the plate in his lap. Zoe sat in the armchair off to the side and felt a little like a third wheel in her own home.

"So what made you move here?" he asked, taking a bite of pasta.

Paige cleared her throat. "You," she replied. "My mom got married last year and her husband was getting transferred for work so I didn't really feel there was a reason to go back to Detroit after graduating from Western Michigan. So...I thought maybe I could move here and we could get to know each other again."

"Oh wow. That'd be great. How'd you know where I live though?"

"Don't be mad, but I got your address from Br...your...um, our dad."

"You've been talking to Dad?" He furrowed his brow and set his plate on the coffee table.

"Yeah. Um, it's a bit of a long story that I really don't want to get into right now. But I got in contact with him after I graduated. We chat every couple of weeks or so."

"No shit. Why didn't he ever tell me?" he whispered.

Zoe watched as hurt flashed across Jake's face, and her anger faded. She really had no reference for what was going on or what had happened in their family. She couldn't help but feel sorry for Jake and Paige and their obvious pain from the past.

"I asked him not to," Paige said.

"Why?" Jake asked.

"I just thought it'd be better if no one else knew. I know how much my mere existence is an issue for your family."

Jake sat in silence for a moment, as if trying to let Paige's words sink in. He let out a short but bitter laugh. "That's an understatement. But that's a topic we also don't need to get into right now. So what all have you been up to?"

They chatted while Zoe cleaned up all the dishes from dinner and then zoned out to some random reality show playing in the background. She should probably listen and try to interact but she didn't have the energy. Once the clock hit ten, Zoe decided she'd had enough. She needed some space. "I'm going to head to bed. You two stay up and talk as long as you want."

Paige stood and stretched her arms above her head. "No, I should get to bed too."

"Yeah, I'm gonna go shower. Night, Paige," Jake said, kissing Zoe's cheek before heading to their bedroom.

I guess showing her around is my job, Zoe thought. She quickly double-checked the lock on the front door and shut off the lights in the living room as Paige picked up her bags. "Let me show you your room."

"I'm sorry you have to go through all this trouble," Paige said as she followed Zoe down the hallway.

"You're not the one who needs to apologize," she mumbled.

Paige's brow furrowed. "What?"

"Nothing." Zoe cleared her throat as she grabbed a fresh towel and washcloth from the bottom drawer of the vanity and put them on top of the sink. "Here's your bathroom. We have our own so this will be all yours." Then she turned on the light to the guest bedroom across the hall and gave it a once-over. The bed was made and there were none of her or Jake's belongings that would be in the way. They had rented a two-bedroom in hopes of having a roommate to offset the costs but had found they liked living together with just the two of them. *Guess that's changing for the night. Or week.* She turned back to Paige, taking in the uncertainty on her face and her white-knuckled grip on the strap of her backpack. Zoe pulled the sleeves of her hoodie over her hands and folded her arms across her chest. "And here's your bedroom. Um, good night."

"Night," Paige whispered.

Zoe closed the door to her bedroom. She'd been tempted to slam it, but didn't want Paige to know how upset she was. Jake was the one who needed to know how she felt. Her body was vibrating with anger.

Sighing, she leaned against the door and closed her eyes until she heard Jake open the door to their en suite. He walked in wearing only a pair of boxers, his wet hair sticking out at all angles. Most nights Zoe would walk up to him and wrap her arms around him as she took in the familiar scent of his body wash. But tonight was anything but normal. She abruptly pulled the hoodie off and tossed it on top of the dresser and then did the same with her sweats.

She brushed past him as she headed for the bathroom, ignoring his soft call of her name. Zoe wanted time for herself as she got ready for bed. After switching from contacts to her glasses, she sat on the closed toilet lid with her elbows on her knees and her head in her hands. With Paige there and all of Jake's attention on his sister for the rest of the night, Zoe had felt out of sorts sitting there in silence. Paige seemed like a nice woman, but her barging into their lives was the last thing they needed. Especially now, with all their relationship issues.

When Zoe emerged from the bathroom, she found Jake sitting up in bed with the sheets pulled up to his waist and his hands nervously tapping out a rhythm on his leg. Zoe climbed into bed on her side and mimicked his posture, except her arms were folded across her chest.

She ended the tense silence as she asked in a low voice, "How could you not tell me about her? She's your sister."

"Well, technically she's my half-sister."

"Like that fucking matters," Zoe replied, her voice rising with each word. She relaxed her arms, closed her eyes, and took a calming breath. Paige didn't need to hear them fighting. When she spoke again, her voice caught in her throat as she asked, "Do you think you can't talk to me about things? Don't you trust me?"

Jake reached for her hand and cradled it in his lap, brushing his thumb across her knuckles. His eyes widened with desperation. "I do trust you. Of course I do. And you have every right to be hurt and angry and anything else you're feeling right now. I don't really know what to say except that she just hasn't really been part of my life."

He took a deep breath as if bracing himself for what he was about to say. "My dad cheated on my mom with a coworker right around the time my mom got pregnant with me. Obviously, that woman was Paige's mom. I don't really know all the details that went down after my mom found out. All I know is that Paige was a part of our lives pretty regularly when we were little kids. We'd go to each other's birthday parties. We'd get together and play. She'd even come stay at our house on some weekends. But whenever she went back to her mom's house, the fighting started at mine. I'd hear Mom and Dad arguing in their room. Mom was always really mad." He shrugged. "I could never make out the words they yelled, but my mom just seemed to hate Paige. There were fewer and fewer hangouts with her. Eventually, I never saw her again. Until tonight."

"Why?"

Jake let out a long sigh. "I asked Dad about it a lot, especially when I realized she wasn't at my birthday parties and we didn't go to hers. He would never give me a good answer and told me she moved out of state. I tried to get him to talk about it more when I was like fifteen or something, but he just said he did what was best for the family."

"How'd you know it was her when you saw her tonight?"

He scratched at his temple with his free hand. "I've searched for her on social media every once in a while. So I've seen recent pictures of her. And did you notice that small scar on her right eyebrow?" Zoe nodded. "I gave that to her," he said with a small chuckle. "We were playing basketball in my driveway since we had a hoop attached to the garage. She was trying to steal the ball and I accidentally elbowed her. I don't think I've ever been so scared. There was blood dripping down her face and onto her shirt. I screamed and ran into the house to get Dad. She needed four stitches."

"Why didn't you reach out to her at some point?" Zoe asked.

"I don't know. At first I thought I'd get in trouble with my folks since they wouldn't talk about her. Every family has their secrets, right? Just always knew not to bring it up. Then as time went on and I got busy with school and baseball..." He shrugged. "I just didn't know what to say to her. If she'd even really remember me."

Zoe tried to process everything. Parents could really fuck their kids up. From everything Jake had told her and everything she'd witnessed over the years, his family seemed happy. His parents never fought or even quibbled much in front of her. Was that all a facade? She felt sorry for Jake and Paige, but especially Paige. Did she know Jake's mom hated her? How much did she remember of their childhood? What was she told growing up about where her dad was? Zoe had issues with her own parents but she knew they loved her.

"I'm sorry. That was a shitty situation to be in as a kid."

"Yeah, I guess it was." He yawned and covered his mouth with the back of his hand. "I'm sure you have a lot of questions and are still mad at me about all of it, but can we talk about it more tomorrow? I'm fucking exhausted."

"Sure," she murmured.

Jake gave her a quick kiss before turning around and shutting off the lamp. They slid down under the covers. Zoe turned on her side with her back to Jake, removing her glasses to her nightstand. As he slipped an arm around her waist, she fought against the urge to pull away from him. Sure, it was probably hard to talk about, but didn't three years together mean anything to him? She had shared so much with him yet he had held back with her. Why? Taking in a quiet breath, she knew she wouldn't get answers tonight or maybe even soon. So she closed her eyes and hoped that sleep would come.

* * *

Paige watched as Zoe retreated into her bedroom at the end of the hall. With a quiet sigh and slump of her shoulders, she walked into the guest bedroom and dropped her bags on the bed. She looked around, taking in the forest-green accent wall and modern dark-wood headboard. The comforter was a light gray and the dresser looked like it had seen better days with scratches on the front of one drawer and a chipped top corner.

The contrast between the newer furniture and the old reminded her of the apartment she shared with three roommates for her last year of college. The desire to feel like an adult and have adult things, but the reality of not being able to afford them.

She let out a breath through pursed lips and opened her duffel bag. Maybe it had been a mistake showing up here. Zoe obviously had never heard of her and was less than thrilled to have her stay. At least, her behavior after Jake got home made it feel that way. Zoe had spent the rest of the night sitting in a chair off to the side. Pouting? Fuming? Paige wasn't sure exactly what she'd been thinking. But she obviously wasn't happy about the situation.

Instead of emptying her bags and putting her clothes away in the dresser or closet like she'd do at any other place she was staying, she took out pajamas, her toiletry bag, and work clothes for the morning. Starting at six a.m. meant she liked to do as much as she could the night before so she didn't have to think that early in the morning.

Taking her toiletry bag into the bathroom, she set it on the counter and turned on the shower. As she brushed her teeth, she took in the teal towel with fraying edges and red washcloth on the counter. She quickly showered and went back into the bedroom. As she lifted a T-shirt over her head, she stopped as she heard Zoe's voice through the shared wall.

"Like that fucking matters!"

Paige's stomach dropped and she collapsed onto the bed. She pulled the shirt down and twisted the hem between her fingers. *Well I guess I know where I stand with Zoe.* She clearly didn't want Paige there.

Coming here was definitely a mistake. That was clear as day now. She didn't know what Zoe and Jake's relationship was like on a day-to-day basis, but she couldn't imagine it involved yelling like that. She'd known about Jake having a girlfriend from her dad and he'd made it sound like they were pretty happy together. Now it looked like Paige was messing with that happiness. She probably should've factored in that Jake had a girlfriend before showing up at their door with no warning. She had just been so defeated. She was all alone in a new city and the only other person she knew aside from Liz was her brother.

That thought made her pause. Could she even say she knew him anymore? She hadn't seen him since she was a little kid. She felt like such an asshole for barging into their lives. Jake didn't owe her anything. If he'd wanted to get to know her again, he could have regardless of where she was. Now that he knew she was in town, they could meet up whenever he wanted. After turning off the light and climbing into bed, she nodded to herself as she made her decision. She would stay here for tonight and be out of their hair once she left for work in the morning.

As she turned on her side and gripped the sheets up to her chin, she had another thought. Zoe hadn't even known she existed. Which meant Jake hadn't told her he had another sister. Did she mean that little to him? Would he even want to get to know her again? Tears pricked at her eyes and dropped onto the pillow as she tightly closed her eyes at the thought. A wet spot blossomed under her cheek as the realization set in. She didn't belong here. At all. Jake clearly didn't see her as family or even someone he wanted to know. If he did, he would have reached out at some point throughout all these years. Right? Or at least told his girlfriend about her.

But he didn't. And she had completely overstepped by showing up tonight. Tomorrow she'd tell them thank you for letting her crash. But then it was time to go.

CHAPTER FOUR

Groaning quietly, Paige rolled over, grabbing her phone from where she had tossed it onto the other pillow the night before. She checked the time—5:07 a.m. *Ugh.* Waking early for her job was a necessity that she was learning to live with, but waking up before her alarm was pure evil. *Guess that's what happens after tossing and turning all night.*

She let her head fall back onto the pillow as she rubbed at her eyes, which felt puffy and scratchy. Might as well get up since sleep wasn't happening. Kicking off the covers and swinging her legs over the side of the bed, she stretched her arms above her head but dropped them when she heard a door close. Someone was up. Hopefully it would be Jake so she could let him know she'd be leaving. Maybe she could make him and Zoe coffee as a way of saying thanks before she left.

After making the bed, she changed into the work clothes she had laid out last night. Shoving her pajamas into her duffel bag, she set both bags next to the door so she could easily grab them later. After a quick trip to the bathroom, she walked down the hallway to find an empty kitchen but with the light on. She noticed the small coffeemaker on the counter in the corner. Paige began rummaging through cabinets, trying to find everything she would need.

As she scooped coffee out of the container, she startled and gasped loudly when she heard Zoe say "Morning" behind her, spilling coffee grounds on the counter. "Crap." She poured the rest of the grounds into the filter basket before brushing the spilled grounds into her hand. "Sorry. Scared me a bit," she said as she turned toward Zoe. With a glance around the kitchen, she asked, "Um, garbage can?"

Zoe pointed behind Paige. "Under the sink."

"Ah, thanks." Paige had hoped she would have seen Jake first before Zoe. "And morning."

Zoe stood with her arms tightly folded across her chest, her wavy, chin-length dark brown hair tousled, and with black-framed glasses that she hadn't been wearing the night before. She wore loose, blue plaid pajama pants and the same sweatshirt from last night. "How'd you sleep?" she asked.

Paige's stomach tightened involuntarily at the roughness in Zoe's voice—the kind that a lot of folks have when first waking up. The kind that when coming from an attractive woman like Zoe, made her pulse quicken. Wow. Totally not the right moment to think that. And Zoe was totally not a person to think that about. She shook her head to get rid of the inappropriate thought. "Fine," she lied. "What about you?"

"Also fine," Zoe replied as she moved to grab two coffee mugs from a cabinet.

Paige let out a quiet snort. "Why do I get the feeling that neither of us slept 'fine'?" she asked, lifting her hands in an air quote on that last word.

Zoe's posture relaxed and she chuckled. "You caught me. It was anything but fine."

"I'm sor—"

Paige was interrupted as Jake rushed into the room as he was tying his tie. "Shit. I'm running late. Ian texted me that I need to pick up his dry cleaning before I go in. Gotta go." He quickly kissed Zoe's cheek. Zoe looked as if it took a bit of control not to pull away. "Love you." Jake nodded at Paige and said, "See ya."

After watching him hurry out the door, Paige busied herself with pouring coffee into the mugs Zoe had placed on the counter. "Ian?" she asked.

"Um, Jake's boss." She paused as if deciding on whether to say anything more. After a beat, she added, "He's an asshole. Makes Jake work all hours of the day. Usually without any heads-up. Treats him like shit."

"Yikes. That sucks. Sounds like it would be hard on you too." Zoe shrugged but stayed silent and Paige figured she didn't want to talk about Jake's boss anymore. Paige slid over the mug and asked, "How do you take it?"

"There's some creamer in the fridge," she replied as she went to move across the kitchen.

Paige held up her hand. "I got it." She grabbed the caramel creamer out of the fridge and started to pour it into Zoe's mug. "Tell me when."

After a second or two, Zoe said, "That's good. Thanks."

Paige then poured a splash into her mug. She normally didn't add flavored creamers into her coffee, instead preferring to just use a little half-and-half. But maybe Zoe would be more at ease if she took her coffee the same way. She hoped anything would help her case at this point.

They sipped their coffees in silence for several moments, avoiding eye contact. Paige leaned back against the counter with her legs crossed at the ankle while Zoe had moved to the other side of the counter and sat on a stool, holding the mug tightly in her hands.

Paige held back a sigh at the awkwardness heavy in the air. With each sip of her coffee, her stomach churned knowing that she was the cause. It was her fault Zoe seemed to balk at Jake's kiss goodbye and her silence now. "Thanks again for letting me stay."

"Mmm," Zoe muttered, staring at her mug in her hands.

Okay, not the warmest of replies but it was to be expected. Paige sighed and poured the rest of her coffee in the sink, losing any taste she had for it. "I'm sorry. I completely barged in on you guys. I appreciate you letting me stay the night, but I can find somewhere else. If you guys want to see me, you can just let me know." She put her mug in the dishwasher and turned to walk toward the guest bedroom.

"Wait," Zoe called out, stopping Paige in her tracks. "I'm sorry too."

Paige faced Zoe, her eyebrows drawn down in confusion. "Why are you sorry?"

Zoe licked her lips and rested her hands on the counter with one thumb quickly tapping on her opposite hand. "I feel like I haven't been the nicest person since you got here."

"That's not true," Paige replied, her voice firm as she moved back to the counter to face Zoe. "You fed me and let me watch *Station 19.* I'd say you're the nicest girl around."

Zoe rolled her eyes and ran a hand through her hair. "I don't know if I'd go that far," she said with a small laugh.

Paige smiled as Zoe relaxed a bit. When she caught Zoe's eye, she took in a deep breath. "You didn't know about me, did you?"

"Nope. Not a thing."

"Oh." Paige didn't know what to make of that. She could understand Jake not telling Zoe much about her. Shit, he didn't know much about her anyway so there wasn't much to tell Zoe. But to not tell her at all? Did he never think about her? Never wonder how she was or what she was doing with her life? She knew they hadn't seen each other in almost seventeen years. But did she mean that little to him to not even warrant a mention to his girlfriend?

Maybe he was ashamed. Ashamed that her whore of a mother ruined their family. Those were the words she'd heard Jake's mom scream at their dad one summer when she had spent the day playing in Jake's pool. She had needed to go to the bathroom and snuck inside, scared that they'd get mad that she was dripping water on the floor. She heard loud voices, hid behind a wall and listened because she'd heard her own name. Jake's mom yelled and yelled. Her five-year-old self didn't understand it back then, but now she understood. She was the daughter born out of an affair. And while Jake's dad continued living his happy life with his family, Paige's mom was left to pick up the pieces and care for Paige basically all on her own.

Paige closed her eyes tightly, trying to banish the thoughts of the not-so-fun years that followed after that day—the last day she had seen Jake. She opened her eyes when Zoe spoke.

"I should be the one apologizing."

"For what?" Paige asked.

Zoe cleared her throat. "For anything you heard last night. I know the walls are pretty thin. I'm sorry, I'm not mad at you."

The obvious "but" hung in the air. Paige bit at her thumbnail. "But you're mad at Jake?" After hearing them argue last night, it wasn't really a question. She was pretty sure it was the truth.

Zoe pushed her mug aside and folded her arms against her body as she sat back against the stool. "I...I don't know what I am."

Paige nodded and waited for Zoe to expand on it, but it seemed she didn't want to. "Fair enough. I'm going to look at a few more apartments this afternoon once my shift is over. As long as I can afford one, I'll take it no matter what."

Zoe's lips formed a thin line but she didn't seem to have an opinion one way or another. "Where do you work?"

"At Craft Café. When I moved here, I needed a quick job. It's a couple of blocks down from where I was staying, and thankfully they were hiring. Eventually I'll find a more permanent job or apply to grad school. I studied exercise science with the hopes of continuing on to get my doctorate in physical therapy. But then when I made the rash decision to reconnect with Jake and move here, making money became the top priority." She glanced at her watch and sighed. "Speaking of, I need to head to work. I'll, um, see you tonight and get my stuff then." She grabbed her phone and wallet from the bedroom before making her way past the kitchen and into the living room, getting her coat out of the closet.

Just as she buttoned it up, Zoe stepped behind her and said, "Stay."

Paige turned to find Zoe wide-eyed and pulling at the hem of her sweatshirt. "Huh?" She couldn't stay, she needed to get to work. If Zoe was trying to get to know her, her timing was really really bad.

"Stay with us. We have the space. You can stay in the guest room as long as you need. You're still free to look for places if you want, but you can live with us."

Paige's mouth dropped open. That was so not what she was expecting Zoe to say. Zoe—the girl who seemed to hate her wanted her to stay with them? No way. Although she also didn't seem particularly confident in her delivery. Not that Paige could blame her. "No. I couldn't. I've obviously caused enough problems. You don't need me around."

Zoe reached for her arm and held it firmly. At any other time, Paige would probably pull away from someone holding on to her like this, especially someone she didn't really know. But she didn't. She let the warmth of Zoe's touch spread through and Paige felt an inexplainable sense of calm.

"You're Jake's sister. It'll be good for you guys to get to know each other again. It wouldn't hurt for us to know each other too."

Well, not a ringing endorsement for Zoe genuinely wanting her to stay, but she didn't have the energy to fight. Or the time. She really needed to get moving so she wasn't late for work. "Wow. Um, thanks. I appreciate that."

"What time do you think you'll be back?"

"I get off work at four thirty."

Zoe stepped around her and snatched her keys off the small table just inside the door. She took a key off the ring and held it out to Paige. "Here. You'd get home before me or Jake. Take my key and you can let yourself in. I can get another copy made this week."

"But what about you?"

"Just make sure you're here around six, okay?"

Paige nodded dumbly. "Yeah, sure. Thank you, Zoe."

Zoe gave her a small and somewhat forced smile. "Mmhmm."

With a quick glance to her watch, Paige widened her eyes. "Shit. I gotta go. See ya." She rushed out the door and down the stairs, excited about the quick change in her circumstances. Maybe showing up on their doorstep had been a good decision after all.

CHAPTER FIVE

911 - lunch?

Zoe sent the text to Mia as soon as she got into work and sat down at her desk. She worked as an admin and social media manager for an accounting firm and so far had enjoyed it. It paid the bills. She still had yet to decide what to do with her life. Maybe grad school? She'd received a bachelor's degree in business administration from Ball State, but she had no real idea of how to make the best use of it. Jake had been the one to get a job in the city first so she applied to anything and everything that she felt she could tolerate. This job had been the first of an eventual three offers and she jumped at the chance so she wouldn't be moving to a new city without having work.

Within seconds, Mia replied, *Yep! Silo at 12:30?*

Zoe liked the message and set her phone on the charging stand, ready to try and distract herself with work. The morning dragged on as Zoe busied herself with scheduling future social media posts and responding to recent interactions. She still couldn't grasp that she had just blurted out for Paige to stay.

She'd done the same thing Jake had the night before—made a pretty big decision without any input from him. Although, she knew he'd probably be happy as it'd give them time to get to know each other again.

And that was what made Zoe irritated with herself. He would be happy and that was probably the driving force to tell Paige impulsively she could stay. Making him happy, or anyone in her life really, was what she did. No matter the cost to her feelings. She was trying to work on that and put herself first sometimes. But today was obviously not that day.

She grabbed her phone again and opened the message thread with Jake. She texted, *Told Paige she could stay with us.*

Really??? That's awesome! He followed up his reply with two kissy face emojis but nothing more.

The obvious joy in his texts brought a small smile to Zoe's face and it pushed down her unease about the whole situation. Well, a little bit at least. It would take a while for the hurt to go away completely.

Finally, the clock hit 12:15 and Zoe put on her coat and slung her purse over her head. The Silo was one of Zoe's favorite restaurants in the city. It was known for its farm-to-table dishes and a wide selection of beers on tap. The latter was something in which she wished she could partake, but unfortunately not in the middle of a workday.

She rounded the corner and spotted Mia crossing the street in front of the restaurant. "Hey!" Zoe called out.

Mia stepped onto the sidewalk and stopped just outside the front doors, bouncing from foot to foot with her hands stuffed into the pockets of her coat. "Hurry your ass up. It's freezing!"

Zoe rolled her eyes at her best friend's dramatics. It was actually a relatively warm day for the beginning of December. The sun was shining and Zoe felt its warmth seep through her coat. Mia had moved to Evansville from Florida just before their sophomore year of high school and she still wasn't used to the freezing temps. "It's like fifty out. Stop being a baby."

Mia stuck out her tongue and opened the door, holding it for Zoe. They quickly snagged an empty high-top table in the bar area, putting their coats on the extra stools at the table. Before either of them could say anything, a bartender placed a couple of glasses of water on the table and told them he'd be back to take their order in a few minutes.

As soon as he walked away, Mia reached for her water. "Okay, spill," she said as she took a sip.

Not wanting to sugarcoat anything, Zoe simply stated, "So Jake has a sister I never knew about."

Mia gasped which resulted in her choking and almost spitting out her water. She reached for a napkin and held it to her mouth as she coughed and sputtered out, "Excuse me? What the fuck?"

"Exactly my thoughts. And she's his half-sister."

"That doesn't fucking matter. She's still his sister!"

"Right? Exactly what I said." And this was why she loved Mia so much—they always seemed to be on the same wavelength. Zoe sighed as she continued, "She showed up at our door last night."

"With no warning?" Mia asked, eyes wide.

"Yep." After the bartender returned for their order, Zoe filled Mia in on the night before. Everything from Paige at their door to Jake's excitement when he saw her and ending with the fight she'd had with Jake.

"Wow," Mia replied, taking a fry off the plate the bartender had just set in front of her. "What's she like? Tell me everything."

Zoe shrugged. "She seems nice, I guess. We didn't talk that much." She took a bite of her burger and slowly chewed, letting out a sigh after she swallowed. "It was all just so fucking awkward. Awkward on top of weird on top of more awkward. Like seriously. How did I not know about her? I get that he hasn't seen her since they were kids, but she was a part of his life up until then. And we've been together for three years and he didn't think it was important to mention even once? Like does he not trust me?" She sat back in her seat, spinning her water glass on the table.

Mia sighed, pushing her plate forward so she could rest her arms on the table. She waited a beat as if gathering the words to say. "I'm going to try and be neutral and look at this from both angles. Don't hate me," she said as she held up her hands in surrender.

Zoe chuckled and waved her hand. "I won't hate you."

"Okay. Does it suck and is it absolutely shitty that he didn't say anything? Yes. I would maybe forgive him if you guys had only been dating for a few months and not a few years. But if he's really had no contact with her since they were kids? Maybe it's a bit of an out of sight, out of mind thing," she said with a shrug. "Or maybe it was such a super painful and confusing thing for him to go through, especially at that age, that he kinda blocked it out of his mind."

"But he said he's looked her up online over the years."

Mia shook her head from side to side. "Okay, so maybe it's not totally that second one. But it sounds like the whole situation was all kinds of fucked up. Even though it's probably not how you're feeling right now, I say go easy on him. Talk to him. Ask him why he never said anything. You do have a right to that answer."

Zoe threw her head back and groaned. "Ugh. You and talking. Why does your answer to everything have to be talking it out?"

"Hello? Therapist in training here," Mia replied as she pointed at herself. "If this was a less serious situation, I would say you could solve it by fucking, but I don't *quite* think that'll work here."

"Oh my god. Are you going to tell your future patients that?" Zoe adopted a professional tone and sat straight in her chair as she imitated Mia, "Well, I see that you're having a difficult time, but I think the tension between you two could easily be solved by a good fuck session."

Mia rolled her eyes. "Maybe not in those words. But am I wrong in saying that some good, hot sex doesn't make things a little better sometimes?"

Zoe sighed. "I hate to admit it, but you're not wrong. Maybe I'll do that after I talk to him."

"That's my girl," Mia said with a wink.

They finished their meals in relative silence. When the bartender brought the bill, Mia snatched it up before Zoe could and gave her a look that said "don't argue with me" and handed her credit card over to the bartender. Mia had been lucky that her parents were paying for school, along with giving her a generous allowance; a perk from having a wealthy family.

As they waited for Mia's credit card to be returned, Zoe took a breath and said, "I told her she could stay with us."

Mia stopped wrapping her scarf around her neck and stared. "You what?"

Zoe held her hands up. "What was I supposed to do? She told Jake last night that she got kicked out of her friend's apartment because the boyfriend was moving in. And she tried to find a place, but she either couldn't afford one or there were waitlists."

"For how long?"

"What do you mean?" Zoe asked.

"How long is she staying?"

"Oh. I don't know," Zoe murmured. "For however long she needs. She doesn't have anywhere to go."

Mia licked her lips and frowned. "You didn't ask her to stay in hopes that it would make Jake come home more, did you?"

"No," Zoe firmly said as she straightened in her chair before deflating and looking down at her hands. "But I'd be lying if I said it didn't cross my mind today." Her biggest issue with Jake at the moment was that he wasn't home enough. She knew having his sister there would make him want to spend time with her, which most likely meant he'd be home more. Zoe just didn't want to admit that she'd thought that. It made her feel selfish.

Mia sighed. "I just don't want you to get your hopes up."

"I know. I didn't do it for me. I did it for her. And for them."

"Like always," Mia mumbled.

"Huh?" Zoe asked, her eyebrows drawn down.

"You've always put everyone else in your life before yourself. Even if it makes you miserable."

Zoe stood and roughly put her arms through her coat as Mia signed the bill. "What's wrong with that?" she asked, her tone firm. "What's wrong with wanting to make people happy?"

Mia opened her mouth but closed it quickly before saying in a measured tone, "Nothing. As long as you're taking care of yourself in the process."

"I'm fine." Zoe could tell Mia wanted to say more but she forced an end to the conversation as she weaved through the restaurant and out the front door.

Mia caught up to her and gripped Zoe's elbow. "Keep me updated on everything. And if you need a break now that you have a new roomie, let me know. You're always welcome to crash at my place for a night or two or twenty," she said with a grin.

Zoe chuckled softly and nodded. "Thanks. And thanks for lunch."

"Anytime."

Zoe turned and walked toward her office. She repeated Mia's words in her head. "Even if it makes you miserable." She furrowed her brow as she thought about it. It didn't seem like a completely fair statement. *What was wrong with wanting the people in your life to be happy?*

CHAPTER SIX

"Vanessa!" Paige called, holding up a large vanilla latte.

A cute twenty-something with a fantastic undercut walked up to the counter and gave Paige a smile and a wink. Her straight, obviously dyed blond hair was parted on the left side and fell just below her ears. She wore bright red lipstick which contrasted with her fair skin. "Thanks," the woman said as she dropped a dollar in the tip jar before walking back to her table that was covered by a laptop and a couple of textbooks.

Paige looked around the coffee shop. The middle of the afternoon was always pretty slow. A handful of students were studying. A man and woman had a table in the corner and seemed to be having some sort of business meeting. And a couple of high schoolers had just stopped in and were talking loudly about last weekend's state championship football game. The shop catered to many diverse groups and that was what she loved about it.

She glanced at the clock. 4:23 p.m. Her shift was almost over and she was kind of dreading it. She was still amazed that Zoe had offered to let her stay but going to the apartment without

Jake or even Zoe there was weird. She felt like an intruder in their space even though she had a key. She was tempted to ask her boss if she could stay and work the next shift. After four, the shop started serving beer and wine, and Tuesdays were poetry nights. But she was tired. So so tired. A night of tossing and turning would do that to a person. Maybe she could take a nap before Zoe got home and she had to be social with basically strangers-turned-roommates.

Because even though Jake was her brother, he still felt like a stranger. Last night's talk with him was almost comfortable but Paige knew they needed to get to know each other all over again. Eighteen years was a long time to be apart from someone. People changed. Her shoulders deflated as that thought sunk in. He'd been her closest friend when she was five. She had loved going to his house and playing with him on the weekends. His house always had the best toys and games and he had a pool and a basketball hoop. But she couldn't base who he was now on those idealistic childhood memories.

She exhaled slowly as the clock hit four thirty p.m. and her coworker Tom came through from the back hallway and finished tying his apron around his waist.

"Hey. How's it going, Paige? Been quiet?" he asked.

"Yep. Only six or seven orders in the last half hour. I'm sure it'll pick up soon."

"Hope so. Daddy needs a new…"

"Ugh. Please don't finish that sentence. I don't need to know the details of what you and your boyfriend get up to."

"Okay, Miss Dirty Mind. That is so not where I was going, but I'm sure I could think of a few things that would spice things up," Tom replied as he waggled his eyebrows.

Paige laughed. "On that note, I'm outta here. See you tomorrow."

He smiled as he filled an order for a double shot of espresso and an IPA. Thankfully not together. She made her way into the back, grabbing her wallet and keys from her locker while hanging up her apron on the hook inside. Paige sent a small wave to Rebecca as she walked past her office door.

"Paige. Wait up," Rebecca called out.

Paige turned and stepped just inside the office, holding on to the doorframe. "Need something?" Paige asked quietly, a little afraid of what Rebecca had to say, especially after being such a disaster the week before. Rebecca hadn't said much to her since, but Paige had felt Rebecca's eyes on her during every shift. But she couldn't be in trouble. She hadn't messed up a single order today. And she didn't spill a drop of coffee, milk, tea, anything.

Rebecca stood and walked around the front of her desk, resting back against it as she held her hands loosely in front of herself. "I just wanted to say that you've really gotten your head in the game these past few days. I've noticed that your focus has improved and you're not making as many mistakes. Keep it up, okay? You're doing a good job."

Paige leaned into the doorframe as the tension and nerves left her body. Phew. Okay, not in trouble. *I can keep my job for another day.* "Thanks, Rebecca. I've really been trying." Even though it's been really really hard, she added in her mind.

"Well, it shows and I wanted you to know that. I'll see you tomorrow."

Paige nodded and gave her a small smile, feeling a bit lighter than she had in weeks.

That feeling lasted until she stood on the welcome mat outside Jake and Zoe's apartment. She held the key in her hand and stared at it for several minutes as if it was a difficult problem to figure out. Awkwardness lingered in the pit of her stomach. She tried to pump herself up as if it was no big deal. That she'd have the place to herself for a couple of hours until Zoe got home. She could unpack her bags, maybe take a shower and a nap. She'd be able to chill and calm her mind.

She took a deep breath as she unlocked the door and stepped inside. "Hello?" she called out. Rolling her eyes, she groaned. "No one's here, dork. Hence the reason Zoe gave you a key," she muttered to herself.

After taking a quick shower and getting into sweats and a T-shirt, Paige settled on the couch instead of trying for a nap. Her mind was too busy to relax enough for sleep. She figured zoning out to some random TV show would be as much as her mind could take at the moment.

The sound of a key in the door made her jump and she sat up, glancing at her watch—5:28 p.m. *Must've fallen asleep after all.* Her eyes widened and she relaxed a bit as Jake, rather than Zoe, walked through the door. Even though Zoe had asked her to stay, Paige still didn't think she was Zoe's favorite person.

"Hey," Jake said with a smile.

"Hey. I wasn't expecting you. Zoe said she'd be home first."

Jake shrugged. "Faked being sick to get out early. My boss is a big germophobe so I told him I was starting to feel nauseous and he made me leave."

"Won't that get you in trouble? Zoe said he's an asshole." Paige cringed and followed up with, "Maybe I wasn't supposed to say that. Don't tell her I told you she said that."

"No worries," he replied with a chuckle. "He *is* an asshole. But Zoe told me you're staying with us, which is awesome by the way, and I figured I'd get home early to celebrate." He pointed over his shoulder. "Let me go change real quick."

Warmth spread through her as she repeated his words in her head—he wanted to celebrate. He was happy that she was staying with them. Maybe her rash decision to move to Indy was going to work out after all.

Jake walked into the kitchen, opening the fridge and calling out to her, "Want a beer?"

"Nah. I'm good," she replied.

He sat on the couch, twisting off the top of a Bud Light and taking a swig. After a few moments of silence, he perked up and turned to her. "Remember how we used to play Dad's Super Nintendo all the time?"

She smiled as she recalled those days of playing *Super Mario Kart.* "Yes! I always beat you."

Jake stood and set his beer down on the side table. He opened up the door on the TV stand and took out what looked like a smaller version of the original Super Nintendo. "Not always," he replied as he stuck out his tongue. "I got this a few years ago when it came out. It's got like twenty of the classic games on it. Wanna play?"

"Oh, hell yes. Ready to lose?"

"Whatever." Jake rolled his eyes and unwound the cord from around the controller and held it up. "We'll need to sit on the floor as the cords are stupidly short." Jake pushed the coffee table back and grabbed the back cushions off the couch and propped them against the table. "*Mario Kart?*" he asked.

"I'm Yoshi!"

"Ugh. You always get to be Yoshi."

"You snooze, you lose."

He gave her a warm smile as they sat on the floor. "No new lines, huh?"

She smiled in return. It was the same thing she had always said to him after her mom had taught her the phrase when she was little. "Why change things?"

Jake laughed as he nudged her shoulder with his. "Well let's see what you got after all these years."

Her smile dimmed a bit at that reminder of how long it had been since she'd seen him. But as soon as they started playing, she was transported back to when she was five. Only now her hands held the controller better, which obviously meant she was going to have an even better chance at kicking his ass.

CHAPTER SEVEN

As Zoe walked through her apartment door, she found Paige and Jake sitting on the floor, pushing against each other as they played a video game. *Wow, he really did get home early.* She smiled at that thought and the scene in front of her. He and Paige looked like they were having a good time, so much so that they hadn't noticed her.

"Hey," she said as she kicked off her shoes and hung her coat up in the closet.

"Oh, hey," Jake said as he briefly looked in her direction before returning his focus to the TV. "Give me just a sec. This race is almost over."

Zoe sat on the armrest of the couch as she watched Paige and Jake play. As Mario crossed the finish line, Jake threw up his hands.

"Yes! Finally!" He pointed his finger at Paige and smiled widely. "I told you I'd beat you."

"Yeah, yeah," Paige replied, setting the controller on the floor and wrapping her arms around her legs as she brought them toward her chest.

Jake stood and gave Zoe a quick kiss. "How was work?" he asked.

"Fine. You're home early," she stated, her eyebrows lifted as if waiting for an explanation.

"Oh, yeah. Figured why not since Paige was here."

Right. Because of course he would make it a point to be home early to hang out with his long-lost sister, but not his girlfriend. She pulled back to put some extra distance between them. "I'm gonna go get comfy."

"Awesome. Thought I'd order us a pizza. That okay?"

"Sure," Zoe replied.

"Great." He sat back on the floor, grabbing his controller. "Then you can join us and we can do a mini tournament."

"Mmm." Zoe made her way into the bedroom and dropped onto the bed. She sighed as she ran her hand through her hair. It seemed that asking Paige to stay *had* made Jake come home earlier than normal. But why did that feel kind of shitty? Was Paige more important to him? Did he really not like spending time with Zoe anymore and work was just an excuse to avoid her?

She groaned as she stood back up to change. It was way too early to see if this was really going to change things for Jake and her. It wouldn't do any good to jump to conclusions. Not that her brain would behave and stop doing that very thing. Just once, Zoe would love for her brain to not overthink every little thing.

When she made it back out to the living room, Jake patted the floor next to him. "Come play. Pizza will be here in twenty minutes."

"Nah. That's okay," Zoe replied as she moved to sit on the armchair.

"Aww. Come on, Zo. It'll be fun." He gave her a puppy-dog pleading look.

Paige piped up behind him, "Yeah, come on. I'm sure you can beat Jake too."

Zoe caught her gaze and she smiled at the glint in Paige's soft blue eyes. "Well, in that case, how can I say no?" She sat next to Jake and Paige reached across him and handed Zoe her controller. "Thanks. All right. Who am I?"

"Yoshi, of course." Paige looked at her as if it would be ridiculous to be anyone else.

"Right. Of course."

They played until a knock sounded. Jake stood and headed for the door.

"Wait. Let me pay," Paige said.

Jake waved her off. "Don't worry about it. I already paid online." He put the pizza on the kitchen counter and grabbed plates from the cabinet. After piling a few slices on his plate, he went into the living room and moved the coffee table back to its original position.

Zoe snagged two pieces of the pepperoni pizza and sat next to him on the couch and Paige took a seat in the armchair. Jake had shut off the game and turned the TV to ESPN. They all ate in silence as they watched recaps from last night's NBA games.

"Favorite team?" Paige asked, taking a sip of her water.

"Chicago Bulls," Zoe and Jake answered in unison, giving each other a grin.

"Haven't converted to Pacers fans now that you've moved to Indianapolis?"

"Gross. No way," Jake replied, a sour expression on his face. "I feel like Mom would disown me if that happened. Her company had a box and I got to go to like ten Bulls games a season."

A hint of pain flashed across Paige's face and Jake seemed to pick up on it.

"Ah shit. I'm sorry. I didn't mean to bring her up. I'm sure she's not your favorite subject."

Paige wiped at her mouth with a napkin. "It's okay. She's your mom. Not really someone we could avoid talking about." She started picking at her pizza crust, breaking off tiny pieces and dropping them on the plate.

Jake scratched at his temple and cleared his throat. "Who's your team?"

"Well, we moved in with my aunt when I was seven. So—"

"Wait. Oh no. The aunt in Detroit?" Jake asked.

"That's the one," Paige replied, holding back what seemed to be a grin. Or maybe a cringe.

Zoe scrunched up her nose. "Please don't say the Pistons."

This time, Paige did cringe. "Sorry." She held up her hands as if to say she had no control in who she cheered for.

"Ouch. I almost want to take back my invite for you to stay," Zoe replied with a grin. "Can't believe we let a Pistons fan in here."

Paige laughed. "Maybe you guys could convert me back."

"Challenge accepted," Zoe said with a smile.

"You'll be converted in a week." He shook his head as if he couldn't believe it and murmured under his breath, "Pistons. Ugh."

Paige put her empty plate onto the coffee table. She sat back in the chair, lifting her legs onto it and wrapping her arms around her legs. "Thanks for the pizza. Um, we should probably talk about how much you want me to pay to stay here. And how we should split the bills. And all that."

Oh, right, Zoe thought. Rent and bills hadn't even crossed her mind. They hadn't *needed* to get a roommate before this because she and Jake had been able to manage just fine. But it would be nice to have help. More money to go to student loans. She shrugged as she replied, "Well Jake and I split everything evenly right now. Guess it would make sense to just split it three ways?" Zoe looked at Jake, wanting confirmation.

He spoke around a mouthful of pizza. "That would work with me."

"How much is rent?" Paige asked.

"Eighteen hundred."

"That should be doable." Paige looked down at her hands and picked at her thumbnail. "When would you need it by?"

Paige seemed a little hesitant. Did she not have the money? Obviously things were tight if she was limited in her apartment search. "We already paid today for December so let's just start after the new year. That okay?" she asked, looking at Jake.

"That works," Jake replied.

Paige let out a breath. "Sounds good to me. Thanks."

"Speaking of December," Jake started. "Any holiday plans? Where, um, does your mom live now?"

"She just moved to Tennessee a couple of months ago with her husband. Just outside of Nashville. His company is opening a new location and they asked him to head it up."

Jake nodded his head from side to side. "Not too far from here then. Are you going there for Christmas?"

"I think so. I didn't bring much when I moved here. It'll give me an opportunity to go get some of my stuff." She paused before her eyes widened a hint. "That's okay, right? I mean you guys obviously have everything for the apartment. I just thought I'd get some more clothes. Maybe some books."

"Of course," Jake replied. "Our place is your place now. I want this to feel like home for you. For as long as you need it to be."

"Might take some getting used to," Paige muttered.

"I get it," Jake replied softly. "But now that we've reconnected, there's no way am I letting us lose touch again."

Paige smiled. "What are you guys doing for Christmas?"

Ah crap, thought Zoe. How sensitive was the topic of Jake's parents? There was some obvious hurt related to Jake's mom if Paige's expression earlier was anything to go by. She didn't want to upset Paige or have her feel more excluded from his family than she probably did already. Zoe exchanged a nervous look with Jake. "My parents are going on a cruise with my oldest sister's family. And my other siblings are going to their in-laws' sides, so we're, um, going to Jake's parents for the weekend."

"Right. That makes sense. When are you guys going?"

"We'll head out after I get home from work on the twenty-third," Jake said. "My parents still live in the same house, so it'll only be a couple of hours. Then we'll be back late Christmas night. What about you?"

"Same actually. I only have Saturday and Sunday off since my boss is only closing the shop those days."

"Ugh. Stupid work. It's why our trip is so short too. One day we'll all be the bosses, right? Then we can make the rules," Jake replied with a laugh before stretching his arms above his head. "I'm fucking exhausted so I'm gonna head to bed. You coming, Zoe?"

"I'll be there in a minute."

Jake nodded. "Night, Paige."

"Night."

Zoe stood and stacked Jake's empty plate on top of hers and held out her hand toward Paige. "Here, hand me yours."

"I've got it," Paige replied as she grabbed her plate along with Jake's empty beer bottles. "My brother can't clean up after himself?" She wiggled the bottles in her hand before emptying the last remaining drops in the sink and letting the bottles clink to the bottom of the small recycling can.

Zoe rolled her eyes. "Not one of his strong suits, no." She rinsed the plates and put them in the dishwasher.

"Typical."

With a laugh, Zoe combined the leftover pizzas into one box and tossed it in the fridge. "I'll take the other boxes down to the trash in the morning. I guess I'll see you tomorrow."

"That you will, roomie," Paige replied with a wink.

Zoe's stomach did a weird little flip at the gesture. *Hmm, odd.*

CHAPTER EIGHT

Zoe opened the apartment door, expecting to see Paige chilling on the couch. It had become a familiar sight in the days Paige had been there. But today, the couch was empty. The living room lamp was on though so she must have come home. Zoe shrugged off her jacket and hung it up in the closet. She began unbuttoning her shirt as she walked down the hallway, pulling shirttails out of her pants. Paige's bedroom door was open but as Zoe peeked inside, the small amount of light coming through the window showed she wasn't in there either.

Shrugging, Zoe continued into her bedroom and changed into leggings and a long-sleeve T-shirt. She exchanged her contacts for glasses and released the clips that had held her hair back all day. She let out a slow breath and rolled her head from side to side as the day's stress started to drain away.

She rolled up her sleeves as she made her way into the kitchen, opening the fridge to pull out a package of chicken wings. Just as she bent down to grab a cutting board from a lower cabinet, the front door opened and closed. She stood to find Paige walking toward the kitchen, pulling earbuds out of her ears. Her face was red and tendrils of her dark blond hair that escaped from under her beanie stuck to her sweaty cheeks. Paige's chest heaved as she took several deep breaths. Zoe unconsciously licked her lips as she set the cutting board on the counter.

"Hey," Paige said with a smile.

"Hey," Zoe replied, giving Paige a once-over. "Went for a run?"

"Yeah. Figured why not since it was nice out."

"Nice?" Zoe asked, her eyes narrowing at Paige. "You do know it's only twenty degrees, right?"

Paige laughed. "I do. Better than the single digits we've had."

"True," Zoe said with a nod.

"Plus, it was sunny. Couldn't waste a good day like that," Paige replied as she took off her sweatshirt which caused the T-shirt underneath to ride up and reveal the flat plane of her abdomen.

Holy abs, Zoe thought, heat rising to her cheeks. "I'll just take your word for it," she murmured. How in the world did she have abs like that? No matter what Zoe tried, she always had a layer of stubborn fat on her stomach, and it was something she'd learned to embrace over the years. But that didn't mean she didn't appreciate a nice set of abs. She certainly did appreciate those on Paige.

Tossing the sweatshirt over one shoulder, Paige snagged a couple grapes from the colander on the counter. "Not a fan of winter?" she asked around the grapes in her mouth.

"I can take it in doses around this time of year, but once Christmas is done, it can go away. I might be able to tolerate it until after the new year, but I am so over it after that."

"So is summer your season then?"

"Ehhh." Zoe wiggled her hand in the air. "I don't like it too hot. Humidity is the worst. The summer storms are nice though. I just don't want it to be too hot or too cold."

"Okay, Goldilocks," Paige replied, grinning widely, to which Zoe stuck out her tongue. "Whatcha making?"

Zoe pointed to the package on the counter. "Some chicken wings and butter pasta. And either some broccoli or a salad. Any preference?"

"Hmm. Let's go with salad." Paige popped another grape in her mouth. "Let me go shower really quick and I'll help."

"You don't have to. It won't take much."

"But I'd like to." Paige looked at Zoe, a hint of wariness in her eyes. "If that's okay with you."

"Sure, I'd like that."

"Great. Be right back."

Paige walked away and Zoe snuck a glance as Paige made her way down the hallway. *Running tights sure were tight.* She shook her head at the thought and pulled a knife from the block. She broke down the wings into drumettes and flats, discarding the tips. She focused on not cutting her fingers instead of the weird feeling that had come over her the instant Paige had walked in the door all sweaty and out of breath. She didn't understand it at all. Zoe had a boyfriend and here she was a little hot and bothered by someone else. And by his *sister* for fuck's sake. She let out a groan. She could admit that Paige was rather attractive, but it didn't mean she needed to react to it.

Just as Zoe placed the last chicken wing on the cutting board, Paige came into the kitchen and stood next to her. Her hair was wet, making it look darker than normal, and she was dressed similarly to Zoe in leggings and a loose sweatshirt.

"What can I help with?" Paige asked.

"Grab two sticks of butter and melt them in a pan. Then we'll add some minced garlic."

"Is that already cut up?"

Zoe scoffed. "Oh, I use the pre-minced bottled garlic. So much easier."

"Got it. How much garlic should I put in?"

"As much as you want," Zoe replied with a shrug. "My mom always said to measure it with your heart. Truer words have never been spoken."

"I like her," Paige replied with a laugh.

Zoe tossed the chicken remnants into the trash and washed her hands. While Paige finished up with the butter and garlic, Zoe grabbed the ingredients for the coating.

"What are you doing next?"

"Mixing up parmesan cheese, parsley, oregano, paprika, salt, and pepper. We'll dip it in the garlic butter and then in this. Fucking delicious."

"Sounds like it."

Paige poured the melted butter into a shallow dish Zoe had set on the counter and they went to work putting the wings together. After Paige dipped them in the butter, Zoe rolled the wings around in the coating before lining them up on a baking sheet. They worked in silence and it felt like the most natural thing in the world. Like Paige was meant to be there.

"Where's Jake?" Paige asked.

"At some fundraiser with his boss. He probably won't get home 'til around ten. I did promise to save him some wings so we can't eat them all."

"Party pooper," Paige replied, a mock pout on her face as she bumped Zoe's hip with hers. "How long have you guys been together?"

"A little over three years. We met in an econ class and got put in the same group for a project."

"Love at first sight?" Paige asked, teasingly batting her eyelashes.

Zoe scoffed. "Hardly. I actually couldn't stand him. He kept picking fights with another girl in the group. Which to be fair, she was an ass and kept trying to take control of everything. But it was all just so annoying. I couldn't wait for it to be over."

"How'd you guys start dating then?"

"A month later we bumped into each other at a party. Literally." Zoe paused and let out a laugh, shaking her head at the memory. "He made me spill my beer plus half of his all over myself. My shirt was soaked to the skin. He was so apologetic and pulled me into the kitchen and ripped like ten sheets of paper towel off the roll and tried to pat me down. Until he realized what he was doing. Then his face got bright red and he just handed it all to me and turned away. Then he took off his flannel and told me I could wear it. After I went to the bathroom to change, he met me at the door with a fresh beer. We went out onto the back porch and spent the next hour just talking. Nothing else happened that night, but when I went to return his shirt the week after, he asked me out. Basically been together ever since."

Zoe coated the last chicken wing and put them in the oven, setting the timer for an hour. She rinsed off the dishes and washed her hands, leaning back against the counter as she dried her hands on a towel.

"That sounds like him," Paige said.

"What does?"

"Him being annoying. Pushing buttons. You see this?" Paige pointed at a small scar at the edge of her right eyebrow.

"Yeah. He said that's one of the reasons he knew it was you."

"Did he also tell you how it happened?"

Zoe shrugged. "He said he accidentally elbowed you playing basketball."

Paige snorted and held up her hands. "Maybe it was technically an accident because I'm sure he didn't mean to hurt me. But that entire day, he'd been pushing me around and I got tired of it so I shoved him back even harder. Then wham! Elbow to the face. Four stitches later and good as new."

"Kids," Zoe replied with a grin. She pushed her hair back, revealing a scar in the middle of her forehead that went into her hairline. "My brother was chasing one of my sisters around the house. I was going into the basement to put some toys away and they pushed open the door right into my forehead. Had to get seven stitches and I had a bald spot for weeks since they shaved the hair around the cut. My mom had to get very creative to try and cover it up."

Paige reached up and traced the scar with her thumb and Zoe sucked in a quiet breath. Her touch was so light and so tender. Paige met her gaze and smiled. "I wouldn't have noticed if you hadn't said anything." As if realizing where her hand was, she dropped it and put some distance between her and Zoe. "Sorry. I can be a bit too touchy-feely sometimes."

"It's okay," Zoe replied, wrapping her arms around her torso.

Paige cleared her throat. "So what's next?"

"I'll put on a pot of water for the pasta. Then we can make the salads." Zoe took care of the pasta pot while Paige took lettuce and cucumbers out of the fridge. "Is there anything you don't eat? Or can't eat? I typically like to make a meal plan for the week. Makes things a little simpler and cheaper."

"Nope. I'll pretty much eat anything. I've never been picky. Do you like to cook?" Paige asked.

Zoe shrugged. "It's a necessary evil. I'm not great at it and almost always rely on recipes aside from a few staples. Cheaper than getting takeout all the time though."

"Does Jake help?"

"Not really," Zoe murmured.

"Does that bother you?"

Zoe paused stirring the pasta. What could she say? This wasn't like complaining about Jake to Mia. If she told the truth, it would basically be bad-mouthing Paige's brother. But she also didn't want to lie to her. So she went with more of a diplomatic answer. "It's not ideal, no."

"Do you tell him that?"

Zoe sighed as she drained the pasta into the colander in the sink. Returning the empty pot to the stove, she tossed a stick of butter in the pot. "He works hard at this job which is really stressful for him. So if I can do some things for him that take any added pressure off him, it works for me."

"But you clearly don't like doing it. Shouldn't that also be taken into consideration? Why make yourself unhappy doing something every night and having all the responsibility on you?"

Anger bubbled up inside Zoe. What right did Paige have butting into things like this? She'd been here for five days and already thought she was some sort of expert on her relationship with Jake. "Look, can you just drop it? I really don't want to talk about this right now." Paige had definitely hit a nerve. Zoe hated that everything around the apartment fell on her shoulders. She liked doing things for Jake, but sometimes it just got fucking tiring.

Paige held up her hands. "You're right. I'm sorry. I don't know you. And I don't know what your relationship is like with him. I overstepped big time and I'm sorry." She turned away from Zoe and tossed the salad into two separate bowls.

Zoe took in a deep breath and let it out slowly. She didn't want to be mad at Paige when it was her inability to let Jake know how she was feeling that was really the issue. Why was Paige already able to see things that were wrong in their relationship when Zoe had been trying to voice her frustrations for months?

She reached into an upper cabinet for a bottle of garlic powder and shook it into the pot with the butter.

"Measure with your heart?" Paige asked with a soft smile, standing a bit closer to Zoe.

"Exactly. You're learning," Zoe replied as she stirred.

"Why'd you use that instead of the bottled stuff?"

Zoe shrugged. "Tradition, I guess. It's how my mom always made it."

"I could get on board with that tradition." Paige gently squeezed Zoe's forearm. "I am sorry, Zoe. I really didn't mean to upset you. Forgive me?"

Zoe chuckled at Paige's pouty lip and puppy-dog eyes, so reminiscent of Jake's. "I guess."

"Phew. It'd be pretty bad if I got myself kicked out of here after not even a week."

"Yeah, wouldn't be a good look. Let's eat. Table or couch?"

"Are you caught up on *Station 19* or are there still more episodes?"

"Not caught up. Still have a few on the DVR," Zoe replied. "Then definitely the couch."

Zoe dished up some wings and a serving of pasta on each plate as Paige put dressing on the salads. They settled on the couch and Zoe started the next episode on the DVR.

"Thanks for helping," Zoe said as she gestured to her plate.

"Anytime." Paige smiled and took a bite of a wing. "Oh shit, that is delicious. Are you sure we have to save some for Jake?"

"Sorry, I promised."

Paige sighed. "And again I say, party pooper."

With a laugh, Zoe settled into the couch and dug into her dinner. It had been nice to have some help in the kitchen and it almost felt natural with Paige. Maybe it would start to be a regular thing with them. An added perk to having her as a roommate.

CHAPTER NINE

Paige jolted awake when she heard the apartment door open. Looking at her watch, she groaned at the 5:37 p.m. staring back at her. She had meant to only rest her eyes after work. Famous last words. With Christmas at the end of the week, the coffee shop had been the busiest since she had started. She had wanted to get in a run before it got too cold and dark. Maybe she could still sneak in a small one before dinner.

Zoe's small frown met Paige's eyes. "Damn. Did I wake you?"

Pushing herself into a sitting position, Paige rubbed at her eyes. "No. It's okay. I wasn't supposed to be sleeping anyway." She opened her phone to check the weather app, hoping to see a decent enough temperature outside. Thirty-six degrees. Not too bad. She had a reflective vest so darkness wouldn't be a big issue. She stood and addressed Zoe, "I was actually going to go for a run. Wanna come with me?"

Zoe lifted an eyebrow. "You do remember my hatred for cold, right?"

"Right. Silly me," Paige said with a laugh. "I'm just gonna go get changed then." She started down the hall when Zoe called out to her.

"Wait." Zoe bit her lower lip. "Any chance you'd want to go to a spin class with me instead? My gym is just down the street."

"But I don't have a membership."

"That's okay. I can get a guest pass for you."

"Is it expensive?" Paige asked hesitantly. She had been trying to cut down unnecessary costs to save as much as she could.

"Free actually. But only once. After that, it's seven bucks, I think. Maybe if you like it, you could join too. It'd be nice to have someone to go with," Zoe replied, smiling.

Not something she would probably be able to afford, but Zoe didn't need to know that. "Sure. I'll have to see how it goes."

Zoe's smile dimmed a bit and she gestured toward her room. "I'm just gonna go change. We'll walk so you'll still need to dress warm. We can stuff our outer layers into a locker when we get there."

Paige held her hand to her chest and let out a small gasp. "You're going to go outside? In the winter?"

Zoe shoved her playfully down the hallway. "Shut up, smartass, and get dressed."

"Yes, ma'am," Paige said with a laugh.

They walked the four blocks to the gym. Zoe scanned her card at the front desk and asked for a guest pass. Paige quickly filled out the form and then they stopped by the locker room.

As Zoe pulled out a pair of spin shoes from her bag, Paige deflated a bit. "Should I have those too?" She'd never done a spin class before, so now that they were in the gym and ready to go, she was already feeling a little out of her depth.

"Oh, no. It's okay. The bikes also have toe clips. You'll be fine."

"Okay, great. One less thing to worry about," she replied as she shoved her sweats and hoodie into the locker on top of Zoe's extra clothes.

Zoe reached for her and lightly gripped her forearm. "Wait. Worried? Is this your first spin class?"

"Yeah."

"Don't worry about anything. I'll help you get set up. Plus, the instructor will be there to help too. I got you," Zoe said with a smile.

Her tension melted away and Paige smiled back. "Thanks."

Zoe led her into the studio to the second of the four rows of bikes. Each row had eight bikes and Zoe pointed to two empty ones just left of center. "We can take these." She put her water bottle in the holder below the handlebars and moved to Paige's side. "Okay. First we'll get the saddle height just right."

Paige's core tightened as Zoe held her hips and gently moved her into position next to the bike. It felt like Zoe's fingers were burning into her skin even through her leggings.

"All right. Hop on and then I'll see if we need to adjust."

Paige did as Zoe asked and slipped her feet into the toe clips on the pedals. She reached out and lightly rested her hands on the handlebars. "How's it look?"

"Good. Pedal a bit."

After that, Paige didn't really comprehend a single word Zoe said. Sure, she followed her directions but Paige's focus was on Zoe's hands. Specifically on every spot Zoe touched with those hands. Those beautiful hands. With a gentle touch to Paige's knee, Zoe stopped her from pedaling as she checked the alignment of who knows what. Paige didn't give a damn about what she was doing. She just didn't want Zoe to stop touching her. Every brush of her fingers sent a fresh round of tingles up Paige's spine. Her breathing quickened as Zoe lightly placed her hand on Paige's lower back. She closed her eyes as she tried to control her body's reactions. It had been a while since she'd been so quickly turned on by another woman. But Zoe was definitely not a woman to be turned on by. She was her brother's girlfriend. *So inappropriate, Paige. Get your shit together.*

"Go ahead and pedal again," Zoe said. She tapped the handlebars. "And put your hands here."

When Paige rested her hands on the handlebars, Zoe adjusted them until they were on the outside. Goose bumps erupted along the entire length of her arms.

"Cold?" Zoe asked.

Paige shook her head but didn't speak. Zoe stepped away and got onto her own bike, clipping her shoes into the pedals. Now that there was a bit of distance between them, Paige let out a slow breath. *My heart rate is up and class hasn't even started.*

"Are you nervous?"

"No. I'm ready to go."

Zoe gave her a soft smile. "You'll do fine. Just go at your own pace if you need to. No matter what the instructor is calling out, okay? Don't push yourself too hard."

"Got it."

A moment later, loud pop music erupted from the speakers. The instructor's voice blared out. "All right, everybody. Let's start at fifteen to twenty resistance and try to get your cadence between seventy and eighty."

Paige's brows furrowed as she looked over to Zoe. "What?"

Zoe pointed at the red knob between her legs. "Turn this to the right for resistance. The number is on the screen. Then start pedaling and you'll also be able to see your cadence there at the top of the screen. Remember. Your own pace, yeah?"

"Yeah, I got it," Paige replied with a nod.

As class continued, Paige found herself really enjoying it. The instructor had picked some great songs and she found herself bobbing her head to each one as she pedaled. But with just under ten minutes left, the instructor called out that they were going to do the biggest climb of the class. Paige adjusted her resistance to his cues and her legs began to burn within seconds. Fuck, this sure was different from running. She tried to keep up but had to lower the resistance to a more tolerable number.

She snuck a glance at Zoe who was still standing out of the saddle and powering through. Strands of hair stuck to her sweaty face and her breathing was quick but controlled. She certainly didn't look like she was struggling at all. Paige's gaze drifted downward to Zoe's legs. Her calf muscles popped each time she pushed down on the pedals and the sharp lines of her quads could be seen just past the hem of her shorts. Paige licked her lips, wanting to know what it would feel like to trace those lines of muscles with her fingertips.

Her foot slipped from the pedal and she winced as the pedal scraped her leg. "Ow. Shit." She quickly got herself under control and her wayward foot back on the pedal, sneaking a glance around to see if anyone noticed. Thankfully everyone else was focused on themselves. Glad I'm wearing leggings, she thought. She hoped it didn't draw blood.

Zoe stopped pedaling and asked in worried tone, "Are you okay? Did you hurt yourself?"

Heat rushed to Paige's cheeks. Guess not everyone was focused on themself. Paige waved her off. "I'm good. Lost my concentration for a sec." She turned her gaze back to the data on her screen, hoping Zoe wouldn't make too big a deal about it. *That's what I get for ogling someone I definitely shouldn't be ogling.*

Paige turned all her attention to the instructor for the last few minutes of the cooldown. Every so often she felt Zoe's gaze on her, but she wouldn't let herself turn and meet it. She was so embarrassed and angry at herself. She needed to get this little crush under control before it caused any issues. Paige didn't want to mess anything up with Jake. And crushing on his girlfriend would definitely mess things up.

Class over, Paige followed Zoe into the locker room. Zoe handed her a towel from her bag. As Paige wiped her face, she sat down on the wooden bench that ran almost the entire length of the room. But she let out a hiss as her butt met the bench, before standing back up. "Ouch. My ass is so sore from that damn bike."

Zoe chuckled knowingly. "You get used to it. So what'd you think?"

"I liked it." Paige pulled sweats over her leggings and put on her hoodie. She was a little too hot for the layers but knew she needed them for the walk home. "I just need to focus a bit more next time," she replied with a self-deprecating laugh.

"So there'll be a next time?" Zoe asked, her voice hopeful.

"I'll have to see if I can afford a full membership or just pay for a guest pass every now and then. But yeah, I wouldn't mind joining you again if that's okay."

"Totally," Zoe replied with a smile. "Now let's get home. You should probably put some ice on that leg."

Paige's cheeks warmed again at the reminder that Zoe saw her slip. She was glad Zoe had no clue of why and she was going to make sure to keep it that way.

When they got home and shed their outer layers, Zoe pointed to the couch. "Have a seat and pull your pant leg up. I want to take a look."

Paige followed her orders and sat on the couch. When she pulled her leggings up, she found a red scrape on her shin and a bruise forming underneath it. No blood thankfully.

Zoe sat on the coffee table and brought Paige's foot into her lap. She lightly traced the wound with her fingertips. Paige sucked in a breath and fought against the urge to pull away.

"Does that hurt?" Zoe asked, eyes wide.

"No. It's okay."

Zoe gently massaged Paige's calf, seemingly without thought as she continued examining her shin. She seemed unaffected by the touch and said, "I was thinking of making a chicken stir-fry for dinner. That work?"

"Y-yeah. Sounds good to me," Paige replied. She swallowed thickly. Why did Zoe's touch have to do such delicious things to her? She closed her eyes, trying to control her wayward thoughts.

"You okay?" Zoe asked softly.

Paige opened her eyes and met Zoe's gaze, her eyes warm but worried. "Yeah," Paige whispered. "Tired, I guess."

Zoe held her gaze for a moment. Until they heard a key in the lock.

Jake walked in the front door and Paige immediately pulled her leg out of Zoe's grasp. "Hey, Jake," she said, her voice pitched a bit higher than normal.

"Hey. What are you guys up to?" he asked, tossing his coat over the armrest of the chair and loosening his tie.

"We just got back from spin class. Paige bruised her leg when her foot slipped off the pedal."

Jake winced as if he felt her pain. "Ouch. You okay?"

"Yep. Never better." Paige stood quickly, ignoring the confused look on Zoe's face. "I think I'm just gonna go shower and head to bed." She walked around the coffee table and started toward the bathroom.

"But what about dinner? You haven't eaten anything," Zoe said.

"I'm not that hungry. Just tired. See you guys tomorrow."

With that, Paige shut herself in the bathroom. She leaned back against the door and closed her eyes. Could she eat? Sure. Should she? Definitely. But what she desperately needed was a shower. A cold one. One to hopefully wash away the lingering heat that had settled low in her belly.

The physical reaction she'd had to Zoe all night was messing with Paige's mind. It wasn't normal for her to be a raging hornball but that was how she'd felt ever since Zoe had helped her adjust the bike. Why couldn't her brain take over and tell her body that Zoe was so not a person she should be attracted to? Paige would have to start watching how much she was around Zoe, at least until her little crush was under control. She had no fucking idea when that would be.

CHAPTER TEN

Christmas had come and gone and Paige was happy the holiday season was almost over. The time she'd spent at her mom and stepdad's new place was nice and relaxing, but it was back to the grind as soon as she'd returned to Indy.

On New Year's Eve, Paige finished work at three and was excited to have the following day off so she could relax at home. She still had a few boxes to unpack that she'd brought back from Tennessee. Work had just kept her so busy ever since that she would get home and barely have enough energy to eat dinner and converse briefly with Jake and Zoe. But now she was ready to have her room feel a bit more like home.

Jake and Zoe had plans to go to some masquerade New Year's Eve bash so she would have the apartment to herself for the night. They had invited Paige to join them, but she didn't want to feel like the third wheel and she had no idea where she'd find a date. Plus, she didn't have the hundred and fifty bucks for a ticket. Instead, she figured she'd spend her night relaxing, maybe with some hot chocolate and a good book. She might even throw in some ice cream. Talk about a wild night.

Just as she settled on the couch and wrapped a blanket around her legs, Jake walked in, straightening his tie underneath his navy vest. "Are you sure you don't want to come with us? They're still selling tickets at the door."

She looked down at herself and laughed. "No thanks. I think I'm a little underdressed."

Jake rolled his eyes. "I'd give you time to change, dork. It'll be fun."

"Nah, that's okay. I'm just gonna stay home and probably go to bed early. Work really kicked my ass this week."

Disappointment flashed across his face before he recovered and smiled widely. "Okay, old lady. If you do change your mind, we'll be there all night."

"Thanks," Paige replied. She was a bit tempted to go. It was New Year's Eve after all. But being around mostly drunk people all night didn't sound like much fun. She'd much rather have a quiet night in.

"Zo, you ready?" Jake called out, shrugging into his suit jacket.

"Yeah, yeah," she muttered as she walked up behind him while putting in an earring.

For a moment, Paige couldn't breathe. Zoe wore a deep red, long-sleeve wrap dress that stopped a few inches above her knees. The off-center slit gave a delicious peek of her thigh. Her wavy brown hair was pulled up on one side, showing off the small diamond drop earring. Fuck, she looked good. Paige had to remind herself not to stare. And to take a breath. Because breathing was good. Necessary even.

"Hot damn! You look amazing, babe," Jake said as he kissed Zoe's cheek.

"He's right. You look great," Paige choked out. She cleared her throat. "You both do."

"Thanks, sis. Can you take our picture?" he asked, holding out his phone to Paige.

Paige tossed aside the blanket as she stood and reached for the phone. "Sure," she said, hoping her voice didn't sound as strained as it did in her head.

Jake wrapped his arm around Zoe's waist and pulled her closer. She rested her hand on his stomach as she turned into him. They both smiled widely as Paige took several pictures. Paige held back a sigh as she continued snapping. They were a good-looking couple.

"Now, our masks," Jake said as he grabbed the two masks off the kitchen counter.

As Zoe carefully pulled hers over her head, Paige was struck by how perfectly the black and silver mask framed her brown eyes. The ornate design and rhinestone embellishments only added to Zoe's beauty. Paige knew she could lose herself in those eyes and she reluctantly switched her focus and watched as Jake put on a dark gray, more masculine-looking mask.

After Paige took a few more pictures, Jake motioned for Paige as he slipped off his mask. "Get in here with us."

Paige shook her head. "Oh no. Not when I look like this compared to you guys."

"Aww. Come on. You look fine. Right, babe?"

Zoe lifted her mask and bit her lower lip, meeting Paige's gaze. "Yep, perfect," she replied with a soft smile. Then she laughed. "And you're definitely more comfortable than me. I guarantee it." She looked down at her heels. "Not sure I'll be able to walk tomorrow. Good thing I plan on just chilling on the couch all day."

Jake pulled away from Zoe, leaving space for Paige. "Get in here," he said.

When she took her spot between the two of them, Jake wrapped his arm around her shoulders and Zoe lightly rested her hand against Paige's lower back. Tingles shot up her spine and she fought against the shiver coursing through her body. How could one touch set off so many feelings? As Jake held the phone out in front of them, Paige tried her best to look nonchalant when she was feeling anything but. She worried that her smile would look more like a cringe.

Jake brought the phone down and scrolled through the pictures. "Perfect. All right. We should head out." He held out Zoe's coat as she slipped her arms through it. "Remember, if you get bored, come join us."

Paige just nodded. "Have a good time."

Zoe followed Jake but met Paige's gaze as she reached to close the door. "Good night," she said softly.

"Night," Paige replied.

Paige collapsed onto the couch. Wrapping the blanket around herself again, she reached for the TV remote on the coffee table. She needed to find something to distract herself from the mental images of Zoe in that dress. Scrolling through the guide, she stopped at the movie, *Hereditary. What better distraction than to watch something that will probably freak me the fuck out?*

By the end of the movie, she was definitely distracted. And definitely freaked out. She shook her whole body out as she stood, stretching her arms above her head. She was about to grab the Super Nintendo but a huge yawn stopped her in her tracks. She checked her watch—10:12 p.m. *Maybe going to bed is the better option, she thought.* So instead of gaming she got ready for bed. As she pulled up the covers, she hoped for no nightmares from that damn movie.

A thud sounded somewhere in the apartment and Paige popped her head off her pillow. She reached for her phone and lit up the screen, squinting at the brightness. It was a little after one in the morning. Jake and Zoe must be home. She quietly groaned and rolled onto her side. She had just started to fall back to sleep when she heard another noise but couldn't really make it out. But the next noise she definitely knew what it was—a low groan coming from Jake.

Paige took hold of her pillow and pressed it hard against her head. *Dear god, please tell me they're not having sex. Please make me go back to sleep. Please. Please.* Her silent prayers had obviously been ignored as she now heard a higher-pitched moan from Zoe.

At the uncontrollable jolt to her core, she threw back the covers and grabbed a pair of jeans from her drawer. "Oh hell no," she muttered. She put the jeans on and left her room as quickly and quietly as she could, shutting the door behind her. She needed to get out of there and she needed to do it now. She shoved her feet into her shoes by the front door and shrugged into her coat, buttoning it as she walked out the door and rushed down the stairs. She hadn't even wanted to bother with the elevator.

The cold night air blasted her face. She took in a deep breath until her lungs burned. Anything to shift her focus from what she'd just heard. She turned right and started walking, ignoring the rowdy and probably drunk people she passed along the way. Maybe their loud voices could replace what was replaying on repeat in her head—Zoe's moan. *If only Paige had been the one to make her... No! Stop it!*

She groaned. It wasn't like this was never going to happen. She was living with a couple and lots of couples had sex. It was just pretty awful to hear her current crush doing it. And with her brother. *Eww.* She shuddered. As she made a second lap around the block, she pulled out her phone and started searching for noise-canceling headphones. She sighed at the high prices, but she still had a bit of money left over that her mom had given her for Christmas. *Guess it's worth it if it'll save my sanity.* She found a pair that were reasonably priced and had good reviews. She clicked "buy now" and the site gave her an estimated delivery date of January fifth. She only hoped she wouldn't need them before then. If she did, then she figured she'd be going on another walk.

As she approached the entrance of the apartment building, she took a deep breath and sent another prayer to the universe that they were finished, hoping it would be answered this time. She skipped the elevator again and took her time walking up the stairs and quietly opening the front door. Soft light poured into the living room from the kitchen, signaling that just the small light above the sink was on.

She stopped dead in her tracks and held back an expletive. There was Zoe, standing on her tiptoes and reaching into a cabinet. She was wearing a T-shirt and seemingly nothing else if the expanse of skin on display was anything to go by. Her mind immediately conjured up a scenario where Paige stepped up behind her and trailed her fingers along the back of Zoe's thigh, teasing just as... Stop, stop stop, she screamed inside her head as she covered her eyes with her hand. She shook her head, trying to dispel the image from her brain. This was so not what Paige needed to see right now.

And she didn't know what to do. Did she just stand still, hoping Zoe wouldn't see her? Did she quietly back into a dark corner? Or did she just walk past her as if nothing was amiss? The decision was made for her when Zoe turned toward the sink, but instead of filling her cup she threw it at Paige with a gasp. Thankfully, it was only plastic and made a dull thunk as it hit the floor.

"Holy shit," Zoe whispered. "You scared me. What are you doing?"

Paige picked up the cup and handed it back to Zoe. "I, um, went for a walk."

Zoe's cheeks immediately turned bright red and she pulled down on the hem of her T-shirt, seeming to understand the implication of why Paige had gone on said walk. She cringed as she said, "Sorry. I thought you were sleeping. We were probably a little loud, huh?" Zoe avoided her gaze as she asked the question by filling up her cup with water.

"No worries. It's your place and you guys can do whatever you want." Paige gestured down the hallway. "I'm just gonna head to bed. Good night." She heard Zoe mumble a "Night" reply as she walked away.

Once in her room, Paige stripped off her jeans and climbed under the covers. She took a deep breath as she curled onto her side. She just didn't understand why she was having such a strong attraction to Zoe. She'd only had one serious relationship in college as well as a couple of quick flings. None of those compared to how her body and brain reacted here. Maybe it was the whole idea of wanting what you can't have. Her chest tightened as she remembered why she couldn't have Zoe. Her brother. She'd come to Indy to reconnect with Jake, not to develop a huge crush on his girlfriend.

She could be better. She needed to be. Moving here was supposed to be a fresh start for her. And a fresh start for her and Jake. Fitting that the new year just started.

Guess it was time to make her one and only New Year's resolution—stop lusting after her brother's girlfriend.

CHAPTER ELEVEN

Zoe cracked open one eye, pushing her face into the pillow at the bright light peeking through a gap in the curtains. She gave herself a moment before rolling onto her back and stretching her arms above her head. Looking at the clock, she saw it was just after eight in the morning—later than her normal wake-up time for work but still too early. Last night had been a late one and she was tired.

Last night. She groaned at the memory of her encounter with Paige in the kitchen. How embarrassing that she'd heard them. She knew it was within the realm of possibility since the walls were pretty thin, but she'd thought Paige would've been sleeping. And she didn't think they'd been *that* loud. Although she'd also had several drinks throughout the night so she probably hadn't been in the right frame of mind to control her volume.

Though Paige had been right. It was her place and she had a right to do what she wanted. But she still had a niggling disquiet. Maybe it was because Paige was Jake's sister? But it felt like more than that. It was just that Zoe couldn't quite put her finger on the reason.

Jake was lightly snoring next to her so she quietly pushed back the covers, sat up and swung her legs over the side. Her head pounded and she had to brace herself with her hands on the side of the bed. She needed water and she needed coffee. Maybe then she'd be able to put into words why she was feeling so disturbed.

As she padded into the kitchen, she found Paige eating a bowl of cereal and scrolling through her phone. She looked up mid-chew and quickly averted her gaze. "Morning," she mumbled.

Heat rushed up Zoe's neck and into her cheeks. "Morning."

"There's more coffee in the pot," Paige said, pointing to the coffeemaker.

Zoe's shoulders sagged in relief. "Oh thank god. I need it."

"I'm sure you do." The corner of Paige's mouth turned upward in a smirk.

If possible, Zoe's cheeks felt even warmer, but she let out a chuckle. Maybe laughing about it would be the best way to get past it. "Again, I really am sorry."

Paige waved her off before moving to put her bowl in the dishwasher. "Like I said, no big deal. But I ordered some noise-canceling headphones for next time."

It was Paige's turn to chuckle, but Zoe could tell her energy wasn't fully behind the laugh. But why, she wondered. Maybe they'd made Paige more uncomfortable than she was admitting. Before Zoe had a chance to ask, Paige started putting on her running shoes.

"I'm gonna head out for a run. Be back in about an hour."

"Okay, see ya," Zoe replied and Paige threw a wave over her shoulder.

She didn't even let her cereal digest before leaving, Zoe thought as she poured herself a coffee. Did she want to get away from the embarrassing situation that badly? If anyone should be embarrassed, it should be Zoe, not Paige. Now Zoe was questioning every reaction or remark Paige had said to her last night and this morning. Sure, it had been awkward, but she thought it could be something they could easily brush off.

Her thoughts were interrupted as Jake snuck up behind her and wrapped his arms around her waist, nuzzling and placing soft kisses just below her ear. "Morning, babe," he rasped.

Zoe tilted her head and reached up to hold on to the back of his neck, brushing her fingers through his hair. His kisses almost lulled her into a complete state of relaxation until she remembered how her morning had started. She bumped him back with her butt before turning in his arms and leaning back against the counter. He was shirtless and she rested her hand on his chest. "Paige heard us last night."

"Well, you weren't exactly quiet," he replied, grinning as if proud that he'd done that to her.

"Shut up," she said, pushing him away. "We need to be more careful next time."

He pulled on his shirt over his head and then poured himself some coffee. "She's an adult, Zoe. She knows we're going to be having sex."

Zoe sighed. "I know that. But this is her space too now and we need to respect that. If it means being quieter or making it a point to do that when she's not here, then we should."

"Okay. I get it," he replied huffily as he took his coffee into the living room.

"We still need to talk about her and why you never told me about her." She followed him and sat on the opposite end of the couch.

"Jesus, Zoe. Now?" he asked, scrubbing his hands over his face. "I just woke up and I'm fucking hungover. Can't we do this another time?"

"When, Jake? I didn't make you talk about it that first night and then you kept putting it off because of work or the holidays or simply because you didn't feel like it. But we can't keep avoiding it."

He sighed and took a long sip of coffee. "What do you want to know?"

"Why didn't you tell me about her? She's your family."

"I...honestly, I don't know," he said as he sat back on the couch and cradled his cup in his lap. "The whole thing was just so fucked up from the beginning. I mean, my dad cheated on my mom. That's not exactly something I want to talk about. Or deal with. Who knows if he's done it again? I didn't really understand the situation when Paige was around back then. So I grew up thinking we were a relatively happy family. Yeah, they fought but that was usually about Paige. Then once she was gone, they seemed fine. At least that's what they always tried to portray to me, Sarah, and Derek. I told you I tried asking about her, especially in the first couple of years after she left. I guess I got shot down so many times about it that I tried to put it out of my mind."

"But you still have looked her up over the years. Why didn't you ever reach out to her?" Zoe asked, raising an eyebrow.

"I don't know," Jake replied, setting his mug on the coffee table and crossing his arms over his chest.

"Yeah you do. Come on," Zoe said softly.

He shrugged. "I...I was scared I guess."

"Of what?"

"That she wouldn't remember me. Or worse, that she would remember me but hated me. That she hated me for what my mom and dad did to her."

"I can understand that," she said as she scooted closer to him and rested her hand on his knee. "Still doesn't really explain why I never heard about her until now."

"I'm sorry. At first, it just seemed too heavy to bring up. We were in college and having fun. Hearing about my dysfunctional family wouldn't have been a good time."

"But once we got serious? Why not then?"

"Eventually it just felt like the longer I waited to tell you, the worse it would be when I did so I just kept putting it off. Lot of good that did, huh?" He rolled his eyes and reached for her hand to intertwine their fingers.

"Mmhmm," Zoe muttered.

"I didn't think she would ever be the one to reach out. Not with what happened. I mean, why would she want anything to do with my family anymore? And since I was too scared to reach out, I figured you'd never meet her."

Zoe pressed her lips in a thin line and didn't reply. It did not seem like a really good reason to her. She still felt something that big and that important should have been mentioned at some point. At least if they were going to make their relationship work.

"I know, I know. It was dumb."

"I was just thinking that. How'd you know?"

"Because I kinda know you," he said with a wink.

Did he though? If he really knew her, he'd know that she was also struggling with his work schedule and how work always seemed more important than her and their life. She knew he couldn't always control how much he worked, but he could control how much he contributed around the apartment. She just wanted him to show her that she was a priority to him. That their life and their future were things he wanted.

As she stared at their entwined fingers, she tried gathering the courage to talk to him about this. To let him know that she was finding it all very hard. But instead, she chickened out and kept the conversation about Paige.

"So, how do you feel now that she's here?"

He smiled widely. "Well she clearly doesn't hate me so that's fucking fantastic." His expression sobered and he squeezed her hand. "I know we still have a lot to learn about each other and how we're going to fit into each other's lives. But I think we'll be okay. I don't think either of us is going to let the other disappear again. We are now the ones that have a say in how things go between us, not our parents. I guess I just have to wait and see."

"I am happy that you guys are reconnecting again. That was never the issue. I was just upset with how I found out."

"I know. And I will apologize over and over for that. I should've told you a long time ago. I'm sorry," he replied, giving her a light kiss.

"It's okay. I get it."

Now that they'd talked, she thought maybe they could put it behind them. Which meant she could start to address her other issues. But before she had a chance to, the front door opened and Paige walked in.

"Hey, guys," she said as she pulled out her earbuds.

"Hey. How was your run?"

"Good," Paige replied, taking a deep breath. "Cold though."

"See. And that's why winter is awful," Zoe said, giving Paige an "I told you so" look.

Paige rolled her eyes and let out a small laugh. "I'm gonna go shower."

Jake stood and rested his hands on Paige's shoulders, giving them a little shake. "Hurry up. I'm gonna make pancakes."

"Will they be edible?" Paige asked skeptically.

"He hasn't poisoned me yet," Zoe replied with a chuckle.

"Give me fifteen," Paige said before heading down the hallway.

Zoe watched as Jake started pulling the ingredients. She should be happy they had at least one serious conversation, right? That was plenty of talking for one day. Mia might not agree, but it had definitely been enough for Zoe. The rest could wait for another time. A time when she found a bit more courage.

CHAPTER TWELVE

Zoe dropped her towel on her bedroom floor and sat on her bed, lifting a leg to pull on her underwear. Spin class earlier had been particularly brutal and her legs still felt wobbly so she needed the assistance of her bed as she got dressed. It was the first trivia night after the holidays and Zoe was looking forward to a date night with Jake.

Just as she pulled a sweater over her head, her phone chimed with an incoming text.

Not gonna make it. Sorry.

Zoe let out a groan and unlocked her phone. "For fuck's sake," she muttered. Instead of replying with a text, she called him and he picked up after two rings.

"Sorry. I really can't talk right now," Jake said.

"Jake, come on. What happened to making it home early and us actually having date night again? Things were better once Paige showed up but not anymore. What's wrong? Has the shine of her being around worn off?"

"Hey. That's unfair. You know I am busting my ass at this job. And that eventually it will pay off. We just need to make it through at least these next seven months."

"At least?" she asked, her voice rising. "You said it would be no more than a year of this crap. And you're telling me it could be even longer than that?"

Jake sighed. "Can we just talk about this later? I really need to go. Why don't you take Paige to trivia? She's new to the city and doesn't really know anyone but us. It'll be good for her to get out." Zoe heard voices in the background and before she could reply, Jake said, "I gotta go. See you tonight. Love you."

He'd hung up without giving her a chance to say it back. Not that she really wanted to in that moment. She clutched the phone until her knuckles turned white and made herself take a few slow, deep breaths. Disappointment settled in her at the thought of not having an end in sight to Jake's long hours.

Zoe glanced down at herself, dressed and ready to go out. Might as well ask Paige if she wanted to go as Jake suggested. She took another calming breath, not wanting to seem upset or frustrated when she spoke with Paige.

Paige was curled up into a corner of the couch with her purple blanket wrapped around her legs. The TV quietly played in the background while she read a book.

Zoe cleared her throat. "Hey, um, would you want to go to trivia with me? It's usually my date night with Jake but he just called to bail." Zoe wrung her hands together and then widened her eyes as she mentally replayed what she'd just said. "Not that that's the only reason I'm asking you to go. I mean, I don't want you to think you're just a last resort or anything. It's just that since he *did* cancel and I was already dressed, it'd make sense to still go and he suggested I take you. It's not that I wouldn't have thought to ask you myself anyway. I just…" She sighed as she scrubbed her hands over her face. "I'll just stop talking now," she mumbled.

Paige chuckled and stood, slipping a piece of paper inside her book and tossing it onto the coffee table. "I'd love to. Let me go change."

Zoe trailed her eyes up and down Paige's body. She was wearing black leggings and a long-sleeved maroon shirt. Her feet were bare so she'd need shoes, but she didn't see anything wrong with her outfit. "What you're wearing is fine. Trivia is just at a laid-back bar. It's not fancy or anything."

"Well I should probably put on a bra at least," Paige replied with a small laugh.

Unthinkingly, Zoe's eyes traveled to Paige's chest. Oh, yep. No bra. Not super obvious since the shirt wasn't too tight. And Paige's breasts were a nice size. Not too small and not too big. They'd be a perfect handful. *Wait. Perfect handful? Not my handful.* Zoe swallowed at her very, very inappropriate thoughts.

Paige cleared her throat, startling Zoe to look up. Paige's lips turned up in a grin and she looked as if she was two seconds away from laughing. Yep, definitely caught staring, Zoe thought. "R-right. Sure. I'll just wait here," she muttered as she sat on the couch, forcing her eyes to look anywhere but at Paige.

Without a word, Paige went to her bedroom and with a soft *click* shut her door.

"Oh my god," Zoe whispered, standing to pace around the living room. "What the hell was that? Why the fuck were you staring? You can't do that. It's wrong. And rude. And... and...you're taken." She stopped abruptly as she finished the thought—by her brother! She groaned and sat back on the couch, bouncing her leg up and down. She shouldn't be ogling someone that wasn't her boyfriend, especially when that someone was her boyfriend's sister. That was fucked-up on so many levels.

A moment later Paige came out of her room. She had changed into dark-blue jeans and put on some brown ankle boots. *Don't look at her boobs. Don't look at her boobs.* Thankfully her eyes didn't betray her as they continued up to meet Paige's gaze. "Ready to go?"

"Yep. Still okay?" Paige asked. She gestured at herself with a challenging glint in her eyes.

Zoe refused to give Paige another once-over. "Yep. You look great. I'll drive," she replied, grabbing her keys and opening the door.

Behind her, Paige chuckled softly.

The drive to the bar was quick and quiet and they got there with a few minutes to spare before the first round of trivia was scheduled to begin. Zoe led Paige through the bar and toward the back where they were able to snag one of the last tables.

As Paige took a seat, Zoe unbuttoned her coat and hung it on the back of the chair. "Be right back. I'm gonna go get answer sheets and a pen. I'll explain everything in a sec."

Zoe walked up to the table where the trivia host, Ryan, sat and took the items he held out to her—score sheet, answer slips, and a pen. "Thanks."

"New teammate?" he asked.

Zoe and Jake had been playing at least twice a month since they had moved to the city so Ryan was very familiar with them. "Yep."

"Awesome. Good luck."

When Zoe got back to the table, a waiter was taking Paige's drink order. "I'll just have a water."

"And for you?" he asked.

"I'll have a Gumballhead," Zoe replied, taking her seat and setting the papers on the table.

"Great. I'll get those in and be back to take your food order."

"You have to try their cheese skewers. They are so good."

Paige gave her a skeptical look. "Cheese skewers?"

"Fried cheese on a stick. Like two-inch square pieces of cheese. Need I say more?"

Paige laughed. "Definitely not. I'm in."

After ordering with the waiter, Zoe grabbed the answer sheet and turned it so Paige could read it. "Okay, so here are the rules. There are five rounds and each round has four questions. He'll give us the category for each question and we'll have to wager two, four, six, or eight. So we need to be strategic with our points," Zoe said, giving Paige a serious look.

Paige bit her lower lip as if to stop herself from laughing. "Yes, ma'am," she replied with a mock salute.

Zoe laughed and rolled her eyes. "Hey, we can win a gift certificate. I wouldn't mind getting our night paid for, would you?"

Paige adopted a serious face at that. "Wouldn't mind that at all."

"Then there will be a question after the third round that's worth sixteen points. And then a final question where we can wager any or all of our points. Or anything in between, of course. He'll give us the category for it and we have to turn in our wager before we hear the question. Got it?"

"Pretty straightforward. I think I can handle it. Anything else?"

"No phones, obviously. And just have fun. Though winning is really great too."

Paige laughed. "Do we have a team name?"

"We do. And I will preface it by saying I didn't pick it."

"Okay," Paige said, dragging the word out.

"It's Sasquatch Spidermonkeys."

"What the hell is that?" Paige asked.

"Honestly, I have no idea. I just know it was like the mascot of Jake's cabin one year at summer camp," Zoe replied, shrugging. "It's been our team name since we started playing trivia together in college."

Ryan announced the first round's categories of TV, literature, science, and sports. Just as he finished, their waiter delivered the cheese skewers to the table.

Paige's eyes widened. "Damn. Those are huge." She reached for a skewer and tried to grab a piece of cheese with her fingers but winced as she dropped it and pulled her hand away. "And fucking hot. Ouch."

"A little impatient?" Zoe asked with a smile.

"I'm hungry," Paige replied. "I got three miles in after work and never had anything after that."

"It was twenty degrees!" Zoe gave an exaggerated shiver. "You should have come to spin class with me again. Have you thought any more about joining up?"

Paige seemed a little hesitant. "I think I need to hold off for now. Maybe do the guest pass once in a while. If that's okay? I just can't really afford it right now."

Zoe shrugged. "It's okay. Totally understand. If it wasn't my way of keeping sane, I wouldn't be doing it either. I have spin and you have your crazy run at god-awful temperatures. We all have our thing," she said with a grin.

Their attention was pulled away by Ryan. "Question one. In *Ted Lasso*, where is Ted from?"

"Kansas," Paige said loudly enough that the two surrounding tables heard her and looked over at them.

Zoe covered Paige's mouth with her hand. "No shouting." She met the narrowed gaze of a woman at the next table. "Newbie," she said with a shrug.

When Zoe pulled her hand away, Paige slightly cringed. "Oops. Sorry. Got a little excited," she said, chuckling. "You didn't tell me I couldn't say the answer out loud."

"I didn't think I had to," Zoe said, throwing her hands in the air. "Good with the rules now?" She raised her eyebrows and gave Paige a pointed look.

With a sheepish smile, Paige said, "I'm good now."

"Okay. Are you sure of your answer?" Zoe asked.

"Definitely," Paige replied with a nod before taking a sip of water. Then she almost-slammed down the glass and looked at Zoe with wide eyes. "Wait, you haven't seen *Ted Lasso*?"

"I have not. It's on my never-ending list of shows to catch up on."

Paige gripped her forearm and practically begged, "Please please please tell me we can binge that soon. You totally need to see it."

A warm feeling spread through Zoe's chest at Paige's eagerness to spend time with her. "We can indeed."

"Yes," Paige said with a smile. "You're gonna love it."

Zoe returned her smile. "Eight points?" Zoe asked and Paige nodded in agreement. "I'll just go take this up."

When Zoe returned, she grabbed a piece of cheese, taking a moment to herself to think about why bingeing a TV show with Paige sounded so great. She bobbed her head to the song the trivia host played as if she was just enjoying the music, when she really was trying to hide the confusion she was feeling. She thought having Paige live with them would be a pretty uncomfortable situation. But aside from a few bumps, she'd found herself enjoying her company. Sometimes more so than Jake's. A feeling she'd have to unpack later as her thoughts were interrupted by Paige.

"So you and Jake have been playing trivia since college?"

"Yeah. I actually started playing with a girlfriend before him."

Paige spluttered as she took a sip of her water. She patted her chest as she cleared her throat and coughed into her napkin. "Sorry, wrong pipe," she choked out. She took another small sip and was able to speak clearly again. "So friend that's a girl or girlfriend girlfriend?"

"Girlfriend girlfriend. We dated almost my entire freshman year."

Paige nodded, a far-off look in her eyes. "Right. Got it."

"I'm bi, Paige. Is that a problem?"

Paige shook her head and quietly chuckled. "I'd be a bit of a hypocrite if it was."

Zoe furrowed her brow. "Huh?"

"I'm a lesbian."

Oh. Oh did not see that coming. Zoe's stomach flipped at the new information but again tried to ignore it. "Nice." Zoe held up her hand and Paige high-fived her with a strange look—perplexed yet amused. Zoe then covered her face with her hands. "Sorry, that was weird. I didn't know what to say. Clearly I never learned how to talk to pretty girls," she mumbled.

"You think I'm pretty?" Paige asked, the corner of her mouth turned up in a sly grin.

Zoe's face felt hotter. She wanted to facepalm herself in the worst way. *Did you really have to admit that,* she thought to herself. "You're all right," Zoe said, shrugging.

"Gee, thanks," Paige replied good-humoredly.

Zoe breathed a sigh of relief as Ryan turned down the music and said, "Okay. The answer to question number one—Kansas." Paige nudged Zoe with her elbow and smiled. "Knew it."

"Now, question two—literature. In what year was the first book in *The Hunger Games* series published?"

Paige scooted her chair closer and her arm brushed against Zoe's, and she leaned into her warmth. As she thought of an answer, she could smell the floral hints of Paige's shampoo and could see the faint line between her eyebrows.

"Okay, what do you think?" Paige asked. "I read it maybe when I was eleven or twelve but it had been out by then. But I'm not really sure for how long."

"Yeah, I think I was about the same age."

"When were you born? 2000 like me and Jake?"

"Yep. So maybe 2009? 2010?" Zoe asked.

Paige tapped her finger against her lips. "Let's go with 2009. Four points or two?"

"Maybe four? I'm not great with science so might want to keep two for that."

"Sounds good," Paige replied. She filled out the answer slip and stood. "I'll take it up this time."

A couple of minutes later when Ryan gave the correct answer of 2008, Zoe groaned. "We were off by one damn year."

"Good thing we didn't put it down for six," Paige said.

"That's true."

The rest of the rounds went by in a flash. If neither of them knew the answer, they listened to each other as they tried to think, all while still sitting close together. Zoe loved that they were getting more answers right than not and she thought they'd have a pretty good chance of coming in the top three at least, which would mean winning a gift certificate of either ten, fifteen, or twenty-five dollars.

After Ryan gave the answer to the final question in the fifth round, he started listing team scores in order from lowest to highest. Zoe sat in anticipation as each team was called out and she still hadn't heard their name.

When Ryan announced the team in third place, Paige turned to Zoe with an excited glint in her eyes. "Oh my god, we might come in first," she said, holding up her hands with her fingers crossed.

Zoe smiled and leaned forward as Ryan continue with the scores. "Sasquatch Spidermonkeys in second with eighty-eight. And in first place, we have team No Name with ninety-two. Category for the final question is movies. You have sixty seconds to make your wagers."

"How much do you think we should wager?" Paige asked. Her excitement had turned to seriousness. "Do you know how this other team typically bets?"

"They're tough to read. Sometimes they bet it all. Sometimes just enough to win."

"Then let's bet it all."

"Are you sure? You feeling confident with movies?"

Paige shrugged and smiled. "Eh. Who knows? Might as well risk it."

"All right. If we lose it all, you're cooking next week," Zoe said with a wink as she stood to turn in their wager.

Ryan took the mic again. "Here we go with our final question of the night. Category is movies. In *Back to the Future*, what kind of car does Doc Brown use to build his time machine?"

Paige cringed. "Shit. I have no idea. I haven't seen it."

"Really? It's my dad's favorite movie. We watched it all the time growing up. Oh, and it's the DeLorean." Zoe wrote down the answer but stopped herself before she got up. "Any issue with my answer?"

Paige shrugged. "I trust you."

An instant smile lit up Zoe's face and warmth spread through her entire body. She didn't know why Paige's trust meant so much to her but it did.

When Zoe sat back down, she said, "Now we wait."

The wait wasn't too long as all the teams turned their answers in within a minute, and Ryan's voice came back over the speakers again. "And the answer to the final question—it was the DeLorean." He started rattling off the list of names again and Zoe and Paige waited and waited to hear whether the team ahead of them bet it all or not. "Coming in second place with a score of one hundred and seventy-six is Sasquatch Spidermonkeys."

"We got second," Paige said, pumping her fist. "Does this mean I'm out of cooking next week?"

Zoe sighed dramatically. "I guess so."

Paige bumped Zoe's shoulder with hers. "If you're nice to me, maybe I'll pitch in my oh-so-awesome kitchen skills."

"Now I have to be nice to you? Ugh, sounds awful," she said sarcastically.

"So what don't you like about cooking?" Paige asked before finishing her water.

Zoe sat back and shrugged. "Sometimes it just feels like mentally exhausting. I miss being in college and on a meal plan where I don't have to think about what to make each day and then make a grocery list on top of it. Plus you need to think about it being healthy and edible and not too expensive. There's days where I'll cook just because I need to make something for Jake and I won't even want to eat it once I'm done."

"I get that. I promise to help where I can. Make myself useful since you guys have been so great about letting me stay."

Zoe didn't have to answer because Ryan came up to their table. "Congratulations." He handed them their gift certificate and retrieved the pen and leftover answer slips. "See you next week?"

Zoe looked to Paige for confirmation. Smiling, Paige turned to Ryan and said, "Definitely."

A quick flutter went through Zoe's chest and she accepted the bill from the waiter. "So you had fun?"

"Yeah. They certainly ask some tough questions." Paige pulled out her wallet and held out some cash.

Zoe waved her away. "Don't worry about it. Not much is left after the gift certificate. Come with all those right answers next time and you can get the bill."

"Deal," Paige replied with a wide smile.

They put on their jackets and made their way to the parking lot. But just as Zoe reached out for the handle of her car door, Paige quietly asked, "Do you mind if I drive?"

"Huh? Why?"

"I know you only had one beer and I'm sure you're fine, but it's kinda my thing to not get in cars with anyone who's been drinking."

Zoe's brow furrowed. It wasn't like she was drunk. She'd had one beer and that was finished over an hour ago. She was absolutely fine to drive and she was just about to tell Paige that until she met her worried, determined eyes. Clearly something in her past had been the reason for this rule of hers. Zoe had no desire to make Paige uncomfortable so with a simple, "Okay" she handed over her keys.

The drive home wasn't exactly tense, but it wasn't exactly comfortable either. There was a sense of anticipation in the air. Zoe quietly hummed along to a song on the radio while tapping her fingers against her thigh.

Paige pulled into a parking space and shut off the car, silently handing the keys back to Zoe without looking at her. She stared ahead and spoke in a quiet voice. "My mom used to drink. After Jake's...my dad cut off contact with us, my mom had it tough. Got depressed and all that. Started drinking." She took a deep breath and wiped her palms on her jeans. "We were on our way to the store one day and, um, she'd been drinking. I didn't really understand it then, but I do now. Back then, I just thought she was tired. Anyway. We lived in a quiet area and just outside our neighborhood was this windy road. Well, she took the turn wrong and we spun out, scraping the back end of the car against a tree."

"Oh my god," Zoe whispered.

"We didn't get hurt. And the car was still drivable. So she drove us home and just started bawling in the driveway. I was so scared and I didn't know what was happening. We went inside and she went around the house finding all of her bottles and emptying them in the sink, crying the entire time. After she was done, she called her sister and she made sure my mom got help. And I swore to myself that I would never get in a car with someone who'd been drinking. No matter how little it was or how long it had been since they'd had a drink."

"And is that also why you don't drink?"

"Yeah. For the most part at least. I tried once or twice in college. To be honest, I don't like the taste either so figured I'm not missing much," she said with a small chuckle.

"So her sister is the aunt you moved in with in Detroit?"

"Yeah. I stayed with her while my mom went to rehab. Then we lived together for a few years 'til mom felt she was ready for us to move out." Paige shrugged and her expression closed slightly. Maybe not noticeable to most people, but Zoe saw the change—her lips thinned and her eyes seemed distant.

Zoe felt the shift and figured Paige was having a hard time talking about this. Or maybe she just didn't want to share it with someone she didn't know all that well yet. Maybe it'd be a deeper conversation for another time. So Zoe decided to change the focus.

"And also the reason you became a Pistons fan huh? Still can't believe that one," Zoe said with a shake of her head.

Paige chuckled and let out a slow breath. "Yeah. It was something she got us to bond over when we first got there."

Zoe reached over and squeezed her hand. "Then I guess I can't blame you for that. Let's head in. It's getting cold in here."

Paige got out of the car and looked over the roof of it at Zoe and said, "Of course you're cold."

"Hey. I'm delicate," Zoe said, clutching her chest before holding open the lobby door.

Paige met her gaze and her eyes held an intensity Zoe hadn't seen before. "I don't believe you're delicate for a second."

Heat rushed to Zoe's cheeks and she didn't know what to say so she just smiled and pressed the button for the elevator.

As the elevator rose, Paige gently grasped Zoe's wrist. "Thanks for not thinking I was some overbearing weirdo about the driving thing."

"Well, thank you for trusting me to tell me. You can always tell me if something I'm doing makes you uncomfortable. Okay?"

"Same goes for you," Paige said.

Zoe unlocked the front door and called out, "Jake? We're home."

"Doesn't look like he's up," Paige said as she followed Zoe inside.

"Guess not." Zoe found a bowl with leftover milk on the coffee table. "Guess he couldn't clean up again either," she mumbled. She reached for the bowl and emptied it in the kitchen sink. Paige had turned off the living room light and was standing at the entrance to the hallway as if waiting for her. Zoe set the bowl and spoon in the dishwasher and followed Paige down the hallway until they stopped in front of Paige's bedroom door.

"I had a really nice time tonight. Even if I wasn't your first date choice," Paige said with a wink.

Zoe quietly chuckled. "I had a good time too." For some strange reason, she didn't want to be the one to walk away first, but she knew she needed to. She needed to get to bed. To the bed she shared with her boyfriend.

Paige also seemed hesitant as she bit her lip and played with her shirt sleeve. A hint of pain flashed across her eyes before she straightened her shoulders and stepped into her room, leaning into the edge of the door. "Good night," Paige murmured and then softly shut the door.

"Good night," Zoe whispered to the closed door.

She opened the door to her own bedroom and found Jake asleep as expected. She quickly got ready for bed and changed into pajamas. As she got under the covers, she took a moment to look at Jake. He was sleeping on his stomach with his arms up and wrapped against his pillow.

She sighed softly. He must be so exhausted if he was already passed out by nine thirty p.m. A wave of guilt washed over her as she thought about how hard he was working. And while he was working, she was out having a good time and not thinking about him once. What did that say about their relationship? Were they in that bad a place where his absences weren't missed anymore? If only they could spend some time together and not worry about work or what needed doing around the apartment, then maybe they could get back to how they were. Zoe wondered when they'd started to lose it and if only his job was to blame. Or was it something more?

As she lay down next to him, she lightly traced her fingers down his bare back. He stirred and rolled over, wrapping his arm around her waist and mumbling, "Love you."

Her first instinct was to smile at his adorable sleepiness, but as she tried to sleep, she felt weighed down by his arm. She used to love when he reached for her in the middle of the night. Now she felt trapped. She closed her eyes and wondered when that had started to change.

CHAPTER THIRTEEN

"Yes!" Paige cheered quietly to herself as she finished making a customer's latte.

Rebecca had taught her how to make designs with the milk foam and until now it had been a disaster. But in front of her was her first successful heart. Well, mostly successful as she looked a little closer. If you squinted just right it *was* a heart. But improvement was still improvement. She'd keep telling herself that.

With a smile, she turned and handed the drink over to the middle-aged woman at the counter. "Thanks," the customer responded as she took the mug back to her table by the front window.

As Paige cleaned up her station, she thought about how work had improved over the past couple of weeks. She no longer had to ask Rebecca, Tom, or other coworkers for drink recipes. Rebecca had been giving her more responsibility and even was having her be the primary opener one day a week. Paige finally felt like she was finding her groove and she was starting to enjoy work.

It probably helped that things were also going well with Jake and Zoe. Although things seemed to be going a little too well with Zoe. Paige knew she had a big crush on her and it was growing stronger every day. Didn't help that she now knew Zoe was queer. Paige just had to keep reminding herself that Zoe was completely off-limits.

As Paige finished wiping the counter, Tom came up behind her and elbowed her as he took inventory of supplies. "Hey. How was your night?" he asked.

"It was really good. Zoe and I went out and played trivia at a bar."

Paige had quickly bonded with Tom once they started working together more frequently. He was easy to talk to and made work fun. She had confided in him a couple of weeks ago about why she had moved to Indy and wanting to know her brother. Paige had also confided in him with her huge crush on Zoe.

"With Zoe, huh?" he asked, eyebrows lifting. "And where was your brother?"

"Working. He bailed on their date night. And that wasn't the first time."

"And what? You were her savior and took her out instead?"

"She asked me," Paige replied, putting her hands on her hips.

"Oh really?" he said in a singsong voice.

"It wasn't like that." *Unfortunately*, she silently finished.

Their conversation was interrupted as Paige took the order for an Americano and a hot chocolate for a mom and her young daughter. Beaming and showing a missing front tooth, the little girl took hold of the whipped-cream-topped drink. "Enjoy, kiddo." She turned back to Tom and leaned back against the counter, crossing her arms over her chest. "I was just a last resort for her."

"But you wouldn't have turned her down, no matter what she asked. Would you?"

"Probably not," she muttered. Paige didn't think she ever could turn Zoe down. She scrubbed her hands over her face.

"I don't normally out people, but I really need to tell someone. Last night, Zoe told me she's bi. Why? Why does she have to be queer?"

"How'd that come up?" Tom asked.

"She mentioned an ex-girlfriend." Paige sighed. "It was so much easier when I thought she was straight, knowing I never had a chance."

Tom turned and rested his hip against the counter, and gently said, "But you still don't have a chance. Because she's taken. By your brother."

Paige deflated and felt like the biggest asshole on the planet. The entire fucking universe even. "I know, I know. But my heart did this like lurch when she told me. Like jump out of my chest lurch. I keep telling my brain that she's off-limits but my fucking heart isn't listening."

"I'm sure it's not only your heart that isn't listening," he said, giving her a pointed look.

Paige held up her hands in surrender. "Okay, there may be other body parts that still aren't getting the memo either."

"Maybe you need a distraction."

"What kind of distraction?" she asked.

"Maybe you need someone to quiet those certain body parts. Go on a date. Get laid. Find someone to help you forget about your unfortunate crush."

"Like who?"

"Don't think I haven't noticed the extra attention you get from certain customers." He looked past her and nodded toward the front door. "Speaking of. Here's that cute blonde who comes in almost every day and will only order from you."

"She does not," she mumbled, knowing very well that he was right. Vanessa had come in almost every day she'd worked so far and always seemed to wait until Paige could take her order.

Vanessa stepped up to the counter, clutching her backpack strap to her right shoulder. "Hey. Can I get a medium caramel macchiato?"

"Sure thing. That'll be four dollars," Paige said. Tom took Vanessa's money while Paige made the coffee.

"Slow day?" Vanessa asked.

"Not too bad. It's been pretty steady. How's your day going?"

"Better now that you're making my coffee. You always seem to have that special *touch* to make them oh-so delicious," she replied with a sly grin.

Laying it on a little thick, Paige thought. But she couldn't deny that it still made her feel good. "Just doing my job," Paige mumbled. She handed the coffee over to Vanessa. "Enjoy."

"I'm sure I will," Vanessa said. She winked and headed to her usual table.

Tom grinned widely. "See. It seems someone has a crush of their own. You should ask her out."

Paige picked up a towel from the counter and played with a loose strand. "I don't know."

"Just think about it."

Paige nodded as she moved to take another order. Maybe Tom was right. Maybe she should find someone to take her mind off Zoe, whether that was Vanessa or someone else. She needed to find a way to stop torturing herself from wanting someone she couldn't have.

CHAPTER FOURTEEN

Zoe walked out of her office building to a rather balmy sixty-five degrees, at least balmy for the end of February. Quickly checking her weather app, she saw that it was supposed to stay that mild even into the late evening. Knowing the ups and downs of weather in the Midwest, she knew the warmth could be gone in an instant and they could even have a blizzard. She pulled out her phone and texted Jake, wanting to take advantage of the nice weather. *Mini golf?*

She hadn't received a reply by the time she made the four-block walk to her parking garage. She'd hoped he'd agree soon so she could just meet him there instead of heading home first, but it didn't look like that was going to happen. She didn't actually receive a reply until she was just about to make it into the apartment building.

Can't. Ask Paige.

Zoe rolled her eyes at the reply. No apology. No *I love you*. She was no longer disappointed. It was just something she came to expect. The idea of asking Paige brought a smile to her face though. She'd probably have a better time with her anyway.

Over the last month, Zoe had found that she'd gotten into a pretty good routine with Paige. Things had definitely become so much more comfortable with her. Most nights, they cooked together and then watched a show or played video games. Jake had been better about getting home at a decent hour a few nights a week. Guess not tonight though, she thought to herself.

Any awkwardness had basically gone now. Zoe had found that she felt totally at ease around Paige and looked forward to spending time with her. It helped that Paige was a genuinely nice person and fun to be around. Zoe also loved that Paige was a good listener and actually cared about what she had to say. Who knew that when Jake's long-lost sister showed up on their doorstep that she would become a pretty important person to Zoe in such a short time?

When she walked in the apartment door, Paige was sitting on the couch with her laptop. "Hey," Zoe said. "Wanna go play some mini golf? I really want to take advantage of the nice weather."

Paige shut her laptop and tossed it onto the couch cushion next to her. "Yes please. Much better than what I was doing."

"And that was?" Zoe asked.

"Paying bills. My least favorite thing in the world," Paige grumbled.

Zoe groaned. "Ugh. Tell me about it. I feel like I cry a little inside every time I pay my student loans. If only I'd thought about that when I chose to go to college. Maybe I wouldn't have had loans." She shrugged before gesturing over her shoulder with her thumb. "I'm gonna go change out of these work clothes and then we can head out."

"Sounds good."

After quickly slipping into jeans and a hoodie, Zoe drove to the north side of the city. The mini-golf course was pirate-themed and she and Jake had come here once not long after moving here. In the early weeks, they had spent a lot of their weekends exploring things to do in their new city. It also helped that mini golf was pretty cheap.

They stepped up to the counter to pay. Zoe chose a red ball while Paige asked for a purple one. They tested out putters from the rack until they each found one that was comfortable. Then they made their way outside to start the eighteen-hole course.

"I hope you know you're gonna lose," Paige said as she playfully elbowed Zoe in her side.

"Oh really? What makes you so confident?"

"Because I was mini-golf champion at my elementary school in 2010."

Zoe searched Paige's face to see if she was telling the truth. She had a pretty serious expression, but Zoe was still skeptical. "Wait. Really?"

Paige chuckled. "Oh hell no. Actually I think I've only played a couple of times over the years. Who knows? I might even need a little assistance with how to hold the putter," she said with a wink.

Zoe stopped at that. Was Paige flirting? No way. Why would she? But Zoe recognized the tightening of her stomach at the thought of wrapping her arms around Paige from behind. She shook her head to get rid of the image despite how much she kind of liked it.

Paige took her shot. It bounced off the bricks lining the hole and her ball stopped a few inches away from the hole. "Dang. I almost thought I was gonna get a hole in one. Your turn."

Zoe set her ball down and lined up for her shot, feeling Paige's eyes on her from behind. She took a deep breath and hit the ball. It rolled over the small hill, gaining too much momentum, and it hit the bricks and popped into the air before landing in the mulch just outside of the designated area. Her cheeks warmed and she winced. "Oops."

Paige laughed as Zoe retrieved her ball. "Maybe I will win after all."

Zoe stuck out her tongue and dropped the ball back at the start. "I just need to warm up. Let me redo that." She rolled her shoulders and lined up for the shot again. This time she hit it with a bit more finesse and it slowly went over the hill and barely missed the hole by about an inch. "See. Just needed to warm up."

"Mmhmm," Paige said, shaking her head. "That first shot still counted. There's no cheating in mini golf." She gently tapped her ball into the hole.

"Yes, ma'am," Zoe replied with a salute. She got her ball in the hole with one more shot.

They played the next few holes and Zoe was happy to see she didn't launch the ball out of play again. While Paige took her next shot, Zoe took in a deep breath, enjoying the lingering warmth in the air even though the sun was mostly gone and they had to rely on the course lights.

"Can I ask you about something you said earlier?" Paige stepped to the side after taking her shot and rested her hands on top of her putter.

Zoe shrugged as she lined up her shot. "Go ahead."

"What did you mean when you said you maybe wouldn't have had loans? Would you have done something else?"

"Yeah, probably," Zoe replied with a sigh. "I just didn't think about what happens after college, ya know? I mean, I knew college was expensive and knew I was taking out loans. But at that point, you don't really think about what that means. At least I didn't."

Zoe quickly sunk her next shot, an easy one since the ball was only a couple of inches from the hole. As she waited for Paige to take her turn, she took a moment to process her thoughts. She'd never really explained to anyone how jumbled her thoughts and feelings were surrounding college and everything that came with it.

Paige hadn't said anything or really acknowledged what Zoe had said so far. But she had an openness in her eyes as if she knew Zoe had more to say and was just waiting for her to continue.

"When I was choosing a college, I always figured I'd find a good enough job out of college and that I wouldn't have that hard a time paying for my loans. Like I was gonna be making six figures right after graduation or something. So stupid and naive," Zoe said, shaking her head. "If I could have a do-over, I would've just stayed in Evansville and gone to Southern Indiana and lived at home. With what my parents were paying and my scholarship, I probably would've only had eight thousand in loans instead of what I do now."

"How much do you have?"

"Forty."

Paige whistled. "Shit. And I thought my twenty thousand was bad. Why didn't you do that?"

"I didn't want to go where my brother and sisters went. And I just wanted to get away from home. Kicking myself now about that." She took a deep breath and let it out slowly. "Plus...I don't know. Not sure if I would've even gone to college if I'd thought about what I really wanted. Or if I'd known then what I do now about life and adulting," she said with a humorless chuckle.

"What would you have done?"

"Maybe have gone to a trade school. I have this weird fascination with woodworking and carpentry. I think I would've enjoyed it."

"Why didn't you?" Paige asked.

Zoe stared at the ground, twisting the end of her putter into the mulch of the flower bed. "Growing up, we're told constantly about how important college is and that we *had* to go. I mean my high school always bragged about their hundred percent college acceptance rate in all their newsletters and whatever. We were never even really told about alternatives to college. Then I got there and slowly realized that it wasn't really what I wanted to do."

"Why didn't you make some sort of change then? Or drop out?" Paige paused before gently gripping Zoe's forearm. "And I'm not judging. I hope it's not coming across that way. I was just curious."

"I know you're not." Zoe smiled and then shrugged. "I don't know. Scared I guess."

"Of what?" Paige asked.

"Disappointing people—my parents. They spent so much money on school for me, I didn't want them to think I was taking anything for granted. Or taking advantage of them in any way. And I had a cousin who switched majors a couple times and even switched schools after sophomore year. His parents were supportive but when my mom would tell me about it, I guess I could hear in her tone that she didn't approve. I didn't want to hear that. I'm the youngest and while it was pretty great at times, and yes I was spoiled, I also got to see what happened when my brother and sisters got in trouble or failed. I don't like getting yelled at or any type of confrontation so I just do whatever I can to avoid it."

"Even if it makes you unhappy?" Paige asked quietly.

"I'm not unhappy. I don't mind what I'm doing and I've got a pretty good life."

Paige nodded like she understood, but the wariness in her eyes said something different.

But I do want more, she thought. Zoe felt a little unsettled by the conversation. Not because of the topic but because Paige was able to get her to talk so openly about how she felt her life was going up until this point. She liked to keep her innermost thoughts close to her. Letting Paige in felt good though. Different. Like she was meant to. But Zoe couldn't explain why and trying to figure that out was probably for another time. Definitely not while she was playing mini golf.

Zoe met Paige's gaze and found Paige giving her an almost thoughtful expression. Like she was trying to figure her out but wasn't sure if she should or not. But Zoe was ready to change the subject and get back to something a little less serious. So she pulled out the scorecard and showed it to Paige.

"One hole left and you're losing by two. Looks like it's time for you to step up your game a bit."

Paige smiled. "Oh, so you want me to play for real? I hope you know I've been taking it easy on you this whole time."

"Oh, please," Zoe said. "Let's see what you got."

Paige set her ball on the ground and lined up her putter. Right before she hit it, Paige turned her head toward Zoe and winked. "Watch this."

Zoe's stomach did a little flip. She watched as Paige hit her ball. It bounced off the side bricks, over a bump, and around a circular obstacle before hitting the back bricks and coming back toward the hole. Zoe held her breath as it rolled. And rolled right into the hole.

Paige dropped her putter and threw up her hands. "Oh my god. I can't believe I did that. Did you see that?"

"How in the hell did that happen?" Zoe said as she gaped at what had just happened. She groaned as she stepped up to take her turn.

As she visualized where she wanted to hit it, Paige stepped up behind her and whispered in her ear. "Gotta get it in two to win, Zo. No pressure."

A shiver raced down Zoe's spine and she almost dropped the putter. She tightened her grip when Paige stepped out of her space. Concentrate. On the ball. Not on how good it felt to have Paige so close. She closed her eyes as another thought slammed into her consciousness—she was supposed to react this way to Jake, not Paige. But she couldn't even remember the last time her body had such an instantaneous reaction to being near Jake. Even though he'd been a bit better about being home, they hadn't had much time to just themselves since Paige was always at the apartment too. Maybe she needed to force him to take some time so they could have a date night. *But why should I have to force him?* He should want to be with me, spend time with me, engage in our relationship instead of treating me like his housekeeper.

She shook her head to try and get rid of the intrusive thoughts. This wasn't the time to try and dissect her relationship issues with Jake. She needed to focus on making this shot and winning. Not that she was that invested in winning tonight. She'd just been happy to get out of the house for some fun.

Zoe hit her ball and groaned as it made it over the bump but bounced off the back bricks and stopped just behind an obstacle. She'd have to hit it off the bricks in two spots just to get it around and into the hole. Unfortunately for her, the attempt was an utter failure and the ball stopped about six inches from the hole.

"Oh, darn," Paige said, giving her an exaggerated snap of her fingers.

Zoe grimaced before tapping her ball in. "Looks like it's a tie."

Paige slipped her arm through Zoe's as they started walking back to the main building to turn in their golf balls and putters. "Aww. Cheer up. At least you didn't lose."

"Yeah, yeah. Good game," Zoe replied, rolling her eyes. She handed her putter to the worker behind the counter and turned to Paige with a mischievous grin. "Ice cream for dinner?" she asked, raising her eyebrows.

Paige laughed. "Count me in."

As they pulled up to the ice cream place, Zoe saw that others had the same idea as there was a line of about ten people at the window. They quietly took their place and Zoe studied the menu. She had a handful of favorites that she typically rotated through and tonight she was feeling a butterscotch sundae. Once she ordered and Paige ordered her peanut butter cup mixer, they snagged one of the picnic tables on the side of the building.

Zoe began her ritual of eating the whipped cream first before starting on the actual ice cream, something she'd done ever since she was a kid. "How's yours?"

"Delicious," Paige replied around a mouthful of ice cream. "This was a great idea."

"I'm glad you approve. So how are you feeling?" At Paige's raised eyebrows, she added, "About being here. Getting to know Jake all over again."

Paige blew out a breath. "I'm feeling...relieved I guess. I'm not really an impulsive person so moving here was really scary. Then with the whole fucked-up housing situation, I didn't know if he would tell me to fuck off or welcome me. I am so so happy it was the latter." She reached across the table and covered Zoe's hand with her own. "I need to thank you for that too. I know it all was kinda thrown at you unexpectedly. Getting to know you has been quite the added bonus."

When Paige withdrew her hand, Zoe immediately missed her warmth. She smiled and gave Paige a small shrug. "I like that I've been able to get to know you too." She held Paige's gaze and it felt as if Paige was trying to read her deepest thoughts. And that was thrilling and disconcerting all at once so she broke the eye contact by taking the last few bites of her sundae. She set the empty cup to the side and crossed her forearms on top of the table. "What was Jake like as a kid?"

Paige smiled. "Loud, messy, thought he knew everything."

"So things haven't changed then I see," Zoe replied with a laugh.

"Doesn't seem that way, does it?" Paige joined in with a laugh but then her expression turned softer and almost wistful. "But he was sweet and kind too. He would share all his toys with me, made sure his neighborhood friends would let me play with them. That time he elbowed me, he wouldn't let me out of his sight. Threw a tantrum until Dad agreed that he could go with us to the hospital. Held my hand the entire time."

"Yeah, he can be really sweet," Zoe said, looking off into the distance.

"When he's around?" Paige asked quietly.

Zoe turned and looked at Paige in surprise. It was like she'd been reading her mind because that was exactly how she'd finished the sentence in her head. Was she that easy to read? Or was it something only Paige could see? Jake clearly didn't see how much she'd been struggling with his absence, and the feeling of not being enough. Sure it didn't help that she wasn't voicing it as much as she should but she didn't want to nag.

Zoe just shrugged and gave a noncommittal, "Mmm."

"Have you ever said anything to him?" Paige then straightened and held up her hands. "Not that it's any of my business. You don't have to say anything if you don't want to."

"No, it's okay. I don't mind that you ask." Zoe bit her lip. "And yeah, I have."

"But it doesn't change anything?" Paige asked, even softer this time.

"Maybe for a little while. But what can I do? I can't tell his boss to stop being an asshole. I know Jake would be here if he could."

Paige's silence said more than her words ever could. She didn't seem to believe Zoe's last statement either. Zoe didn't feel like dwelling on the fact that her boyfriend was never around. Although ignoring it didn't solve anything either.

Her thoughts were interrupted when Paige asked, "Ready to head out?"

"Yeah, let's go."

When they got back to the apartment, Zoe felt like she needed some time to herself. While she liked being around Paige, she also made her feel a little out of sorts and she wasn't ready analyze why.

"Thanks again for coming with me tonight. Sorry if I keep monopolizing your time," Zoe said.

"Like I said, I'm glad I'm getting to know you. You're fun to hang out with," Paige replied with a smile.

Zoe's eyes were drawn to Paige's lips. She really had a great smile. So genuine and like it was meant for only her. But that was ridiculous. Paige was just a nice and friendly person. She would give that smile to anyone.

"You too," Zoe whispered. "I'm just gonna head to bed. See you tomorrow."

"Night," Paige said.

Zoe closed her bedroom door and leaned against it. She just needed a good night's sleep. Then maybe these confusing feelings would go away.

CHAPTER FIFTEEN

"You were right."

Tom stopped tying the apron around his waist and stared back at Paige. "Well, hello to you too. And I usually am, but what am I right about?"

"I need something…or I guess someone to help me forget about my crush on Zoe," Paige said.

"Oh no. What happened?"

"Jake missed another date last night." She paused and then held up her hand. "Okay, I guess they really didn't have a date planned, but Zoe wanted to go mini golfing with him since it was so nice out. He couldn't so she asked me."

"He's certainly not going to win any boyfriend-of-the-year awards," he muttered.

"Doesn't seem that way." She shook her head. They didn't need to get off topic and start bashing Jake. Because even though he was kind of being an ass to Zoe, he was still her brother and it didn't feel right to bad-mouth him. "But that's not the point."

"So what *is* the point?" he asked over his shoulder as he filled an order.

"I'm starting to feel out of control with my feelings for Zoe. We're together almost all the time when we're not at work. I find myself flirting even when I don't mean to. And she does it back! Though I don't think she realizes."

"What are you going to do about it?"

"I think I'm gonna ask Vanessa out. If she comes in today."

"You know she will," he said, tossing his hand towel over his shoulder.

"We'll see."

But Tom was right again a few hours later when Vanessa stopped in during a small afternoon rush. Paige didn't get to talk to her much when Vanessa ordered but she had taken a seat at her usual table and was working on her laptop.

When the steady flow of customers came to an end, Tom gave Paige a pointed look and nodded his head toward Vanessa's table.

Paige held up her hands and mouthed, "Okay." She smoothed down the front of her apron and walked around the counter and up to Vanessa's table.

She cleared her throat and Vanessa turned to her with a wide smile. "Hey, Paige."

"Hey. I, um, was just wondering if you'd like to go out sometime."

Vanessa's smile grew even wider and Paige's eyes dropped to her lips painted with her signature bright red lipstick. "I thought you'd never ask. What's your number?" she asked as she reached for her phone.

Paige rattled it off and a minute later she felt a buzz in her back pocket, but didn't pull her phone out.

"Just texted you my address. Why don't you pick me up on Friday and we can go out for drinks?"

Oh here it goes, Paige thought. She'd have to explain that she didn't drink, but unlike with Zoe she didn't have the natural urge to make Vanessa understand the reason behind that decision. With a slight frown, Paige replied, "I don't drink."

Vanessa shrugged. "No biggie. How about sushi instead?"

"That works," Paige said, blowing out a quiet breath.

"Great. Pick me up at six."

Well, that was easy, Paige thought as Vanessa turned back to her laptop. Paige went back around the counter and started cleaning the blender Tom had just finished using. She blew out a breath to try and relax. She wasn't used to asking women out. The girlfriend she'd had in college had asked her out so this was new territory and she felt a little uneasy. There was a lingering feeling in the back of her mind that she was using Vanessa. She knew there was no way of getting over her feelings for Zoe unless she tried to date other women, but she still felt a little icky.

"How'd it go?" Tom whispered, his eyes wide with curiosity.

"We're going out for dinner on Friday."

Tom whistled. "You did it! Way to go."

"Thanks," she muttered. Paige twirled the stack of paper cups on the counter. "I think I also might need to start looking for my own place again. I think I might need that extra distance."

"But what about getting to know Jake again?"

"It's not like I won't ever see or talk to him if I move out. This way, I'll be able to make plans with him and not necessarily have Zoe there. Now I just need to save up enough money to find a place."

"Ask Rebecca if you could pick up some extra shifts. Or you can start working later with me," he said with a big smile. "I get more tips from the beer drinkers than the coffee drinkers. And since you're such a nice person, I'm willing to share those with you."

"So generous," she said as she rolled her eyes. "But that's a good idea. I'll go talk to her now. You good up here?"

"Yeah, yeah," he replied, waving her away. "I've got this."

Paige found Rebecca doing an inventory check in the back storeroom. "Hey, Rebecca. Could I talk to you?"

"Yep. Give me just a sec." She counted the boxes of napkins and made a note on her clipboard before setting it on the shelf. "Let's go."

Paige followed her into the office and sat in one of the chairs in front of Rebecca's desk while Rebecca turned the other chair toward Paige and sat down. "What's up?"

"I like to think that I've been doing a good job. I'm on time, friendly to customers, and I'm getting quicker every day." Paige wanted to make sure to highlight her positive traits so maybe Rebecca would more easily say yes to her request. "I was wondering if I could pick up some extra shifts. Maybe stay longer than I usually do or I could even come back in the evenings and work the closing shift."

"You're already working at least forty hours a week. I don't want you to get overworked."

"I know and I appreciate that. But it wouldn't be forever. I'm just trying to save up a bit of money to get my own apartment."

"If you think you can handle it, I don't see why not. I like your dedication and your positive attitude. I hope you know that I value your work ethic. I'll start adding you to evening shifts next week."

"Thanks, Rebecca. I really appreciate it." Paige stood and shook Rebecca's hand before resuming her position behind the counter.

First, she was able to score a date. And now she had more work on her hands. That would certainly help take her mind off of Zoe, right?

CHAPTER SIXTEEN

By the time Wednesday rolled around, Zoe was ready for a break. All week, she'd had to sit in on meeting after meeting and they were always followed by an unending string of phone calls. She was looking forward to her lunch break and it wasn't getting here fast enough. She'd made plans to meet up with Mia at a deli down the street and she couldn't wait. Zoe was in desperate need of some best-friend time. It had been way too long since they'd hung out together. They needed to catch up properly on what had been going on in each other's lives.

As she stepped through the front door of the deli, she caught sight of Mia already in line and giving her order to a young guy behind the counter. Zoe took her place in line and browsed the menu on the large chalkboards as she waited. Her stomach growled at the thought of getting her go-to turkey sandwich with lettuce, bacon, and mayo plus a bag of barbeque chips and a water.

She took her goodies to Mia's table in the corner and sat down. "Oh my god. I'm starving. I was running late this morning and didn't get to eat breakfast. All I've had so far is a granola bar I found in my desk and I don't even want to think about how old it was."

Mia chuckled. "I hear you. I feel like today is the first day I've come up for air since the semester started. So *thank you* for the invite," she replied as she took a bite of her salad.

"It's what I'm here for, my friend." Zoe held out her bottle of water and tapped it to Mia's cup. "Cheers."

"So tell me what's new in your world. I feel like I haven't seen you in forever," Mia said.

"I went mini golfing with Paige on Monday. God it was so nice out. And a couple weeks ago, we played trivia and came in second."

Mia gave her a confused look. "You and Paige?"

"Yeah," Zoe replied excitedly. "She was so good. Came in clutch like four times with her answers. Wouldn't have won without her."

"Was Jake there too?"

Zoe rolled her eyes. "Of course not. He bailed as usual. But I still had fun. Probably more so," she said, shrugging nonchalantly before taking a bite of her sandwich. "Oh, and she made me dinner the other night because I was too tired to cook. It was called Tuscan chicken mac and cheese. It had spinach and sun-dried tomatoes and so much ooey gooey cheese. Might be my new favorite food."

"Sounds tasty," Mia murmured. She tossed her fork into the salad and pushed the bowl to the side. Resting her forearms on the table, she raised her eyebrows as she said, "Also sounds like you've been spending a lot of time with Paige."

Zoe shrugged and smiled. "Yeah, it's been great. She's really chill and so easy to get along with."

"Do you have a crush on her?"

Zoe choked on the sip of water she had just taken. "What?" she asked in a strangled voice. "Why would you ask that?"

"Oh, I don't know. All I've been hearing is Paige and I did this or Paige and I did that and how you've been having so much fun with her. But yet, no real mention of Jake except when

I asked about him. Kinda makes a girl wonder," Mia replied, giving Zoe a pointed look.

"No. No way. I'm with Jake." But was she really? It didn't feel like it. Jake had basically pushed her aside for work time and time again. She understood the desire for advancement, but at what cost to personal relationships?

"Just because we're with someone doesn't mean crushes can't happen." Mia paused, taking in a quiet breath. "Or feelings for that matter."

Zoe wanted to say something. Wanted to defend herself, set the record straight. But could she? Hanging out with Paige was great. It felt nice. It felt natural, and she found herself wanting to spend more time with her with each passing day. But that didn't mean she had feelings for her or even a crush. They got along. They liked the same shows and movies. Paige listened to her and picked up on things that Zoe never told her. That's what happened when you became friends with someone, right?

"I know," Zoe said quietly, not meeting Mia's gaze. She didn't want her to see her conflict. Her confusion.

"Zoe. Look at me," Mia said, her tone soft as if trying not to spook Zoe.

Zoe hesitantly raised her head to meet Mia's gaze.

"Do you have a crush on Paige?"

"I...maybe?"

"Do you have feelings for her?"

Zoe tried to speak but she couldn't form the words. She didn't want to admit something that was becoming glaringly obvious. Zoe couldn't deny that she looked forward to spending time with Paige and she certainly couldn't deny that Paige was attractive. But did that mean she had feelings for Paige? Maybe they were just spending too much time together. Time that Zoe was supposed to be spending with Jake. Maybe Paige was just filling the void of Jake's absence. That was what was happening. All she needed to do to fix it was to spend more time with Jake. Not Paige.

"Look. I'm not going to tell you how you feel or what to do about it. Only you can figure out what you're feeling. But I know how it feels to be cheated on. If you think you might have feelings for Paige, you need to figure that out and not string Jake along. It's not right, Zo."

Zoe averted her gaze at Mia's rebuke. Mia's college girlfriend had cheated on her in their junior year. Mia had walked in on her fucking another girl and a guy in their bed. She hadn't really been able to date much since then. She couldn't trust anyone. So hearing those words from Mia put things into perspective. Zoe needed to get her shit together and figure out what was going on in her brain. And her heart.

Mia looked at her watch before gathering her things and standing. "Sorry. We can talk more about this later but I need to head out. I have class in fifteen minutes."

Zoe shook herself from her thoughts and stood along with her, grabbing her half-eaten sandwich. She thought about taking it with her back to work but her stomach was feeling a bit off. Getting a dose of reality shoved in your face can really bring on the nausea, Zoe thought. "Right. I should head back too."

After tossing away their trash, Mia stood on the sidewalk with her hands in her coat pockets. "Be careful, Zo," she said, her tone serious. "Don't cross the line. You're not that person."

"I know. But it's nothing. We get along, that's all," Zoe replied. But that wasn't the full truth and the lie felt sour to the taste.

Mia's lips formed a thin line and she nodded once. "If you say so. I'll catch you later," she said before turning around and walking away.

Zoe waved at her back. "See ya." She took a deep breath as she watched Mia turn the corner out of sight.

Turning in the opposite direction, Zoe walked back to work, plopping down onto her desk chair. She still had a few minutes until her lunch break was technically over so she avoided looking at her emails. She leaned her head back and stared at the ceiling, gently using her foot to turn her chair back and forth.

Her stomach still felt off. It was a weird sense of dread and excitement. If she was being honest with herself, Mia might be right. So what if she'd developed a little crush on Paige? She wasn't acting on it and she didn't have any plans to. She was in love with Jake. Simple as that.

But, it wasn't as simple as it used to be. They were fighting more often and she didn't feel like she was important to him anymore. He didn't ask about her day, unlike Paige. He would just go on and on about his own work. Not a great example of partnership, she thought. But just because they were having some sort of rough patch, didn't mean she should give up on them. Jake said himself that his crazy hours at work would only last a year. And that year would be up in just a few more months. She could deal with the late hours and lack of attention.

Maybe she just needed to make more of an effort herself when Jake was around. She hadn't exactly been super touchy-feely with him lately and they hadn't had sex since New Year's. They just needed some time to reconnect as a couple. Although why did it always feel like everything fell on her shoulders? Jake was the other half of their relationship and he needed to act like it too.

Paige was a friend, nothing more. But why did excitement shoot through her when she thought about the idea of something more?

CHAPTER SEVENTEEN

Paige's shift on Friday was coming to an end, but she couldn't help looking at the clock every few minutes. She'd agreed to stay a little longer when someone on the night shift called out sick. Thankfully Tom had been able to come in on his day off and was covering the rest for the night.

"What's the rush?" he asked as he served his first beer of the night.

"I've got my date with Vanessa and I don't want to be late. I still have to go home and change. Maybe shower if I have time."

Tom grinned. "Right," he said. "The big date. You nervous?"

"A little," Paige murmured. "Who isn't on a first date, ya know?"

"True," Tom replied with a knowing nod.

"I'm heading out. You working tomorrow?"

"I'll be here."

"See you tomorrow then," Paige said.

She hurried home and rushed through the front door. She really hated being late but she had about twenty minutes before she absolutely had to leave so she at least had time for a shower.

And okay, maybe a quick shave. Be prepared and all that in case it turned into something more than just dinner.

Just as she walked into her bedroom, Zoe came out of her own and leaned in Paige's doorway. "Hey. You're home late. How was your day?"

Paige shrugged as she toed off her shoes into her closet. "I stayed because someone called out."

"Gotcha. Wanna get pizza tonight? Then I thought maybe we could finally start watching *Ted Lasso*. What do you think?" Zoe asked, her smile wide.

"I can't," Paige replied as she avoided Zoe's gaze. "I've got a date."

Zoe's voice lost its excitement and became quiet, almost defeated. "A date? With who?"

As Paige scanned her shirt options, she hesitated at hearing Zoe's letdown. Was it her mention of a date that made her lose her animated tone? Or was it just that she wouldn't have anyone to hang out with tonight, especially if Jake was going to be late again? Without much thought, she quickly grabbed a light-gray button-up out of the closet and tossed it on her bed, followed by a clean pair of jeans from her dresser drawer. Paige wouldn't let herself dwell on why Zoe might be disappointed, and frankly she didn't have the time.

"Her name's Vanessa. I met her at Craft. We're going out to dinner. I need to go shower."

Paige went across the hall and closed the bathroom door. She hadn't looked at Zoe once. Paige couldn't let her read on her face that this was a date for the sole purpose of trying to get over her. Or at least figure out that there was a sliver of hope that she could.

Once she was finished, Paige took a quick breath, hoping that Zoe hadn't been lingering in her room or in the hallway wanting to know more about her date. A quick peek around the door as she opened it found both her room and the hallway clear so she made her way into her room and got dressed. She used her hair dryer just enough so that her hair had a bit of wave and it didn't look as if she'd just gotten out of the shower.

Paige tightened her watch as she walked into the living room. Zoe was sitting on the couch with her legs curled to her side and she was leaning on the armrest with her head in her hand. Paige finally met Zoe's gaze and it immediately made her want to look away again, but she held firm. "I've got to get going. Um...have a good night."

"You too," Zoe said in that same odd tone. Then she reached for the remote on the coffee table and turned on the TV without giving Paige another look.

After shutting the door to the apartment, Paige had to take a moment. She closed her eyes, trying to chase away the look on Zoe's face. It had been brief, but Paige had seen it. Zoe had been hurt. Maybe she had gotten so used to hanging out with Paige that she was upset that they couldn't do that tonight. It couldn't be because Paige was going on a date. Why would Zoe care? They would just have to start *Ted Lasso* another time.

Paige found a parking space on the street a block away from Vanessa's building. She rode the elevator up to the seventh floor, all the while tapping a beat against her leg with her fingers. She was getting nervous. She'd never purposely asked someone out in the hope of getting over someone else. She would have to be up front with Vanessa and let her know that she didn't think she could do anything serious right now.

Paige took a deep breath as she raised her hand and gave two quick knocks on Vanessa's apartment door.

Within a minute, Vanessa opened the door with a grin. "You made it."

"That I did. Ready to go?" Paige asked as she gave Vanessa a quick once-over. She wore a white halter top, a bit out of place for a winter's night, but it showed off Vanessa's small yet toned arms. Her tight black pants stopped at the ankle, giving full view to yellow heels. Paige couldn't deny that she looked beautiful. Just not as beautiful as Zoe, she thought. Paige mentally slapped herself. She needed to focus on the present, on Vanessa. Not on Zoe and her disappointment that made Paige want to hurry back to the apartment so she could make it all better.

"Definitely," Vanessa replied, shrugging into a red trench coat. Paige admired Vanessa's bold choice of clothing. It wasn't particularly Paige's style, but Vanessa easily pulled it off.

They rode the elevator down in silence and stepped onto the busy sidewalk in front of Vanessa's apartment building. People were obviously heading home after work and a few couples that looked as if they were also on dates.

Vanessa linked her arm with Paige's. "The sushi place is just a few blocks away. You okay to walk?"

"I should be asking you that," Paige replied as she glanced down at Vanessa's three-inch heels.

Vanessa chuckled. "Don't worry about me. I'll be just fine."

Arm in arm, they made the short walk to the restaurant and were quickly seated at a small table tucked into the corner of the dining room. The sense of intimacy added to Paige's nerves and she discreetly wiped her palms on her jeans before taking hold of the menu the waiter held out to her.

"Do you come here a lot?" Paige asked.

"I've been here a few times. The food is so good and I could probably eat here every day, but my wallet disagrees. I try to only come on special occasions or when I'm celebrating something."

"So is this a special occasion or are you celebrating something?"

"A little bit of both," Vanessa said, giving Paige a wink. "A beautiful woman asked me out. That's certainly special and worth celebrating." Paige blushed but didn't reply. "Anything you don't eat? Any allergies?"

"Not really. And nope."

"Perfect." The waiter came up to the table and asked for their order. Vanessa rattled off four of their specialty rolls and an order of edamame. Paige was getting the hint that Vanessa liked to take charge and she didn't mind one bit. Once the waiter walked away, Vanessa reached across the table and lightly traced the back of Paige's hand with her finger. "I'm glad you asked me out. I just didn't think it would take so long."

Paige quietly chuckled. "I can be a little dense sometimes and I tend to let others do the asking out."

"Well, what made me so special that you went outside your norm?"

Shit. She couldn't just blurt out that she was falling for her half-brother's girlfriend and she needed to see if dating would make those feelings go away. That would easily be a mood-killer. Plus, while Vanessa seemed nice, Paige didn't feel the need to confess all of her secrets. "Just needed a change of pace," Paige finally said.

Vanessa nodded and squinted her eyes ever so slightly, as if she knew there was something more to that statement, but wasn't going to ask why. She raised her water glass to Paige. "Well cheers to switching things up," she said with a wink.

Paige clinked her glass to Vanessa's and took a sip. The waiter set their order on the table and checked if they needed anything else. As they ate, the conversation was superficial—hobbies, where they went to college, and where they grew up. There were no awkward moments of silence, but Paige wouldn't say things felt easy with Vanessa. It wasn't anything like how she was with Zoe.

After a brief argument over the bill, they agreed to split it and then began their walk back to Vanessa's apartment. Vanessa hadn't linked their arms together again but she had brushed her hand against Paige's a few times as they walked. Paige figured Vanessa wanted to hold her hand, but it felt wrong to initiate the contact.

"I had a good time," Vanessa said as they stopped in front of her apartment door. "Want to come in?"

Paige noticed the glint in Vanessa's eyes and figured Vanessa was hoping to go inside and make this date a little more physical. Vanessa was gorgeous and Paige was attracted to her but she hesitated. Tonight was just the first step into getting over Zoe. Sure, going inside and making out with Vanessa, or even more, could maybe speed that along, but it felt wrong. Paige didn't think she'd be able to force it. Falling out of love with Zoe would need to be a gradual process.

With an apologetic frown, Paige said, "I'm sorry, but I have an early shift in the morning so I should probably head home."

A hint of disappointment flashed across Vanessa's face before she grinned. "Maybe next time then." She said it as a statement, but Paige heard the hope behind it.

Next time, she thought. Maybe Paige could feel a bit more confident in her plan. The date had been nice enough and she wouldn't mind hanging out with Vanessa again. Even with the implied promise of more, Paige agreed, "I'd like that."

Vanessa leaned in and gave her a soft kiss. With a quiet "Good night," she disappeared into her apartment.

Paige let out a breath. The kiss had been…nice. Nothing earth-shattering but she also didn't dread that another one would probably happen on their second date. This whole getting over Zoe thing was going to be way harder than she ever imagined.

CHAPTER EIGHTEEN

When Paige walked out the door, Zoe was left with an odd feeling of emptiness. Like she wanted to throw open the door and tell Paige not to go. But why? She didn't have any say in whether Paige dated or not. It was probably good that Paige was getting out and meeting other people, especially since she'd be calling Indy her home for the foreseeable future. But why did Zoe feel such a sharp ache?

Before she could try and figure it out, the door opened and for the briefest moment, the weird pain lifted and she felt a bit lighter. *Maybe Paige decided not to go.*

But her mood crashed back down as Jake walked through the door, smiling as he saw her. "Hey, babe." He kicked off his shoes and tossed his jacket onto the chair. Walking up to her as he loosened his tie, he leaned down for a kiss. "Thank god it's Friday. Where's Paige?"

"She had a date," Zoe murmured.

"Really? That's great." He waggled his eyebrows. "Then we have the place to ourselves for a bit. How about our own date night in? Chinese and a movie?"

Zoe had to force enthusiasm into her tone as she replied with a thin smile, "Sure." As he kissed her again, a new scent hit her nose. It wasn't completely different but it wasn't completely Jake either. She gripped his tie when he started to straighten. "You smell different."

"Different? Different how?" he asked, lifting his arm and sniffing.

"I can't explain it. But it just doesn't seem like your usual cologne."

"I did stop at a bar for a quick drink with some guys from work. It was pretty crowded. Maybe it's from that," he said with a shrug.

Zoe met his eyes and tried to see if he was telling the truth and it seemed like he was. She wasn't getting the vibe that he was cheating on her or anything. Plus, it wasn't like he was smelling like women's perfume. "You could've let me know."

"I know. I'm sorry. It was a last-minute thing. Can you order while I go shower?"

Zoe nodded as Jake walked down the hallway to their bedroom. She collapsed back against the cushions and grabbed her phone, quickly ordering their usuals from their favorite Chinese takeout. She then tossed her phone back onto the side table and leaned her head back, staring up at the ceiling as her thoughts returned to Paige and the fact that she was on a date. *What is wrong with me?* Jake was home at a semi-normal hour and wanted to spend time with her. Was her chat with Mia earlier in the day getting to her that much? Did she have a crush on Paige? Or even worse, feelings?

She shook her head at the thought. It wasn't a crush and it definitely wasn't feelings. She had just liked the fact that someone had enjoyed spending time with her and wanted to get to know her. Zoe only found that comforting because of all the issues she'd had with Jake over the past few months. Maybe tonight was just what they needed—something to get them back on track as a couple.

Jake grabbed himself a beer from the fridge. "Want one?" he asked.

Zoe shook her head. "No thanks."

He sat on one end of the couch, extending one arm along the back and stretching out his legs onto the coffee table. "Come here," he said with a soft smile.

Zoe took up what had been her normal position when they'd had chill time on the couch together in the past. Before Paige, she thought. She closed her eyes as she cuddled up next to Jake, leaning into his side and resting her head on his shoulder. *Stop thinking about Paige. Tonight is about you and Jake. No one else. There is no one else that is part of this equation.* She tried to remind herself that she had decided she should make more of an effort, yet it felt wrong. Maybe that told her everything she needed to know about the state of their relationship.

He started flipping through their seemingly unending list of recorded movies, but had just never found time to watch. He stopped at one and asked, "This one okay?"

She nodded, but she hadn't even registered the title. "Yeah, that works."

Jake softly kissed the top of her head. As the opening sequence played, he let out a satisfied sigh. "This is nice. I've missed this."

You could have it if you came home more, Zoe immediately thought. She inhaled deeply and tried to erase the negativity in her mind. She needed to focus on the present. He was here with her now and seemed to be happy about it. Zoe needed to let that thought put her mind at ease. "Mmhmm," she mumbled.

Her thoughts stayed in the moment for a little while at least. Their food arrived and Jake quickly devoured his while Zoe took a few bites, but mostly just moved her fork around in her shrimp fried rice. Once they had finished and all the leftovers were stashed in the fridge, they resumed their previous position as the movie continued to play.

Jake started scratching up and down on her arm and it made her feel like she was crawling out of her skin. She didn't want his touch, but when had that changed? And why was her mind constantly straying to Paige and what she may or may not be doing on her date? Was she having a good time? Would she kiss the other woman? Or worse, have sex with her? Zoe was thankful that she hadn't eaten much as her stomach turned and she had to take slow, shallow breaths until the feeling passed.

Zoe kept trying to blame her fixation on Paige and her date on her chat with Mia. She'd also started making comparisons to how she was feeling right now versus how she was feeling when she went mini golfing with Paige. And those feelings were drastically different. Paige and her touch, heck even just her closeness, had given her butterflies in her stomach and tingles along her spine. Now, sitting here with Jake, all she felt was the need to get some space. But she couldn't do that. He'd ask what was wrong and she honestly didn't know what she could say. *I don't know if things will work with us. Oh and by the way, I just realized I might have a massive crush on your sister.*

Jake interrupted her thoughts as he tossed the remote onto the table. Zoe looked up to see that the TV was off and Jake had started to stroke his fingers long the length of her thigh.

"That movie was great, don't you think?" he asked.

"Oh yeah. Great," Zoe replied, nodding as if her attention hadn't been elsewhere for the entire movie.

Jake cupped her face in his hand and turned her toward him, capturing her mouth in a fierce kiss for which she hadn't been able to prepare. He used his strength to pull her onto his lap and she straddled his legs. He pulled away from the kiss and peppered soft kisses along her neck.

"We have the place to ourselves for the night it seems. I think we should celebrate."

Jake moved to kiss her again, but Zoe turned her head and slid off his lap. She ran her hand through her hair and sighed. "Not tonight, Jake. I'm tired."

"Then when? It's been weeks."

She turned to him with fire in her eyes. "And whose fault is that? You're never home."

He sighed as he stood, making his way into the kitchen and grabbing another beer. "I'm working my ass off. I think I deserve a little credit."

"And what? Credit means sex?"

Jake groaned. "That's not what I meant and you know it. I took this job because it could take me down a fucking awesome career path, and that could set us up really well in the future. I just don't think you appreciate how hard I'm working. It's for us."

"I never asked you to do that, Jake. Our lives are comfortable and we're getting by just fine. I would much rather have a partner that wanted to spend time with me and explore this new city we're in than spend every waking hour at work. I feel like I'm fucking alone in this relationship."

"Look. I'm sorry. I know this hasn't been easy on you. But Ian looks super highly on those that show dedication. Every time I tell him I'm good to stay late or do some stupid task for him, he sees me as someone he wants to keep around. And eventually promote."

It took a moment for Zoe to register what he'd just said. But when it did, she gripped the couch cushions instead of standing to pace around the room. "Wait. You've been *volunteering* for all of these late nights?" she asked in a low tone.

Jake's face paled a little and his mouth dropped open. "Well, no. Um, yes. Not every time," he muttered.

"Why do I get the sense that it's been more often than not?" Unable to sit any longer, Zoe stood, needing to release some of the angry energy that had started coursing through her body.

Jake sighed. "Zoe, I'm sorry. But this is the only way I am guaranteed any path I want in the company."

"You know what this all tells me?"

"What?" Jake asked, looking as tired as Zoe felt.

"That your career is your focus. Not me and not us. No matter how much you try to tell yourself that you're doing all this for us, you're not. If you were, you'd make an effort to find some sort of balance."

Jake downed the rest of the beer and rolled the bottle in his hands. "I don't know what to say, Zoe."

"If you want this to work, you need to show me that. I'm not gonna wait around forever. Because I have a feeling that this year will turn into two and then it will turn into five."

"I get it," he replied softly. "I'm sorry. I know I've been a little selfish. You're right that my career means a lot to me. And you do too." He sighed. "It's just hard to find a way to have it all, isn't it?"

"Yeah," Zoe whispered.

Jake opened his mouth but closed it just a second later. Whatever he'd been about to say wasn't going to be said tonight. Instead he said, "Look. Your birthday is coming up. How about I take you out for a nice dinner and we can find a way to...I don't know...reset? How's that sound?"

The hint of hope in his eyes softened Zoe a bit. "That sounds nice."

"Then it's a date," he said with a smile. "I'm gonna go to bed. You coming?"

"No. Not right now." Zoe folded her arms across her chest and looked away.

Jake sighed and stood, taking his beer bottle into the kitchen and dropping it into the recycling bin with a louder than normal *clank*. "Night, Zo," he called out. "I love you."

She looked up and met his seemingly helpless gaze. "I love you too."

As she watched him walk away, she had a feeling that things would be coming to an end for them soon. He would ultimately pick work over trying to fix their relationship. And even though that was how she thought things would play out, it felt like a punch to the gut.

* * *

Paige stopped in front of the apartment door and just stared. 508. The number that had meant she'd found a home for the past few months. But it seemed a home wasn't meant to last. With the extra money she'd be making as Rebecca put her on the schedule more, she'd soon be able to afford her own place. And for the sake of her heart, the sooner she found that place, the better.

Paige found Zoe curled up in the corner of the couch and when she met Paige's gaze, she wiped at her eyes with the back of her hand.

"Hey," Zoe rasped. "How was your date?"

Paige frowned, gently closing the door behind her before going to sit on the coffee table in front of Zoe. "It was fine. Are you okay? Have you been crying?"

"I'm okay," Zoe said with a sniffle. "Jake and I had a fight."

"Do you want to talk about it?" Paige asked, reaching out to touch Zoe's knee and stroking her thumb along the fabric of her leggings.

Zoe shook her head and gave her a sad smile. "Not really. But thank you though. Any chance you'd be up for starting *Ted Lasso* instead? I think I could use a distraction."

Paige hesitated. She was supposed to be finding distance, not spending more time with Zoe. But how could she ignore Zoe when she was hurting? Paige would just have to deal with being around Zoe for the night. "Sure. Let me go change."

This time Zoe gave her a wide and genuine smile. "Great. I'll get it pulled up."

As Paige changed into sweats and a T-shirt, her mind went back and forth between being angry at Jake for making Zoe upset and being unsure that watching a show on the couch with Zoe was a good idea. She already knew her feelings had ventured into the way-too-serious category and the only way to stop that was to avoid Zoe. But that wasn't an option tonight. She just had to remind herself that she was being what Zoe needed—a friend. And it would never be anything more.

Zoe had moved closer to the center of the couch and rested her feet on the coffee table with Paige's purple blanket covering her legs. Zoe lifted one end of the blanket and said, "Come on. Just need to press play."

Great. We'll be sitting so close, we'll practically be on top of each other. As she sat next to Zoe, Paige took in a deep breath and let it out slowly. She could do this. She could pretend that her heart wasn't feeling like it could beat out of her chest at any moment. Zoe covered Paige's legs with the blanket and then stuffed her hands underneath it, bringing it closer to her chest. Paige decided to make sure her hands were on top of the blanket. Much safer that way.

As the episode played, Zoe seemed to be enjoying herself, but Paige hadn't been able to pay attention to a single thing on the screen. It'd helped that she'd seen it before, especially whenever Zoe made a comment about it. Paige was able to "Mmhmm" or add in her own thoughts when necessary.

The credits rolled and Zoe looked over at Paige with a hopeful smile. "Another one?"

No, Paige's brain said. But what came out of her mouth was, "Sure."

The episode started but once again Paige wasn't comprehending any of it. She was making a mental list of where she would start looking for an apartment. She tried to remember how much she had in her bank account and how much she would still need to save to feel comfortable moving out on her own. If she moved out as early as tomorrow, she could swing it, but the deposit would probably wipe out most of her savings. Then she'd end up living paycheck to paycheck. Not ideal but doable. Paige had just hoped to get a little bit of a buffer before moving.

The anxious thoughts caused Paige to start biting her thumbnail, but within a second Zoe reached over and grabbed her hand, holding it between them on top of the blanket. "You're gonna make yourself bleed," Zoe said distractedly.

Paige glanced over at Zoe, whose attention was still taken by the show. The fact that she was still holding Paige's hand didn't even seem to register with Zoe. It just seemed like a natural reaction for her.

But for Paige, it made her chest tighten and a hint of tears pricked at the back of her eyes. She couldn't do this. She couldn't sit here and act as if Zoe's touch and even just her closeness had no effect on her. Paige needed space and she needed it now.

Paige pulled her hand away and shifted down the couch so they were no longer touching. "Can we finish this another time? I just got really tired and I have to work early in the morning."

Zoe frowned and her eyebrows scrunched down for a moment, but then she tried to smile. "Yeah. No problem. I should probably head to bed too."

Paige stood quickly and mumbled, "Good night," before hurrying to her room. She didn't even bother turning on the light, climbing under the covers, closing her eyes tightly.

Paige took several slow, deep breaths until her heart stopped racing. As she wished for sleep to come, she made a plan—pick up as many shifts as possible, find an apartment, and avoid Zoe. Her heart was already doomed, but that didn't mean she should make it worse by being around Zoe like usual. Soon she would move out and only be with Zoe if it was absolutely necessary. And Paige hoped that it really wouldn't be for a very long time.

CHAPTER NINETEEN

For the next week, Paige was able to avoid Zoe as much as possible. When she wasn't picking up extra shifts in the afternoons and evenings, she was looking for an apartment. Unfortunately the pickings were slim. She almost had enough saved for a deposit, but most places had monthly rents that were more than she wanted to spend or no available apartments for the next four months.

Friday night came around and Paige was looking forward to having the night off from apartment hunting. What she really wanted was to just go home and crash on the couch, even if Zoe was there, but Paige had already made different plans. Vanessa had texted her the night before asking if she wanted to come over for dinner and Paige had agreed since she still needed to work on the whole getting-over-Zoe thing. When Vanessa ended the text conversation with a smirking emoji, Paige knew she had other plans in mind aside from dinner.

Sex with Vanessa. It was definitely an appealing thought. Paige couldn't deny that. After their first date, she'd thought maybe it would be a good idea to take things slowly and gradually try to get rid of her feelings for Zoe. But maybe what she really needed was a swift kick in the butt via sex with Vanessa. Looked like she would know if that was the answer by the end of the night.

As she walked out of her bedroom buttoning up her shirt, Zoe exited her room. Paige stuttered to a stop, hand pressed to her chest at the surprise. "Oh, hey. What's up?"

"I'm heading out to meet Jake at his company party. I guess Ian and a couple others are getting promotions. The last thing I want to do is celebrate Ian," she said. "I was hoping we could watch some more *Ted Lasso*. It's been a while." Zoe's voice lowered and Paige saw the hint of sadness in her eyes.

It had been a while, but Paige needed to try and protect her heart. She was afraid of what would happen if she didn't. Paige cleared her throat as she noticed Zoe's low-cut black dress. *So beautiful.* Paige didn't acknowledge why she'd been so absent lately. "Sorry to say, even if you didn't have plans, I do. Um, I have another date with Vanessa."

"Oh." Zoe played with one of her earrings. "Um, what are you two doing?"

"I'm going to her place for dinner."

Zoe clenched her jaw and her expression seemed to completely shut down. "Well I hope you have a good time. I'll see you later."

She walked away before Paige could reply. Instead, Paige let out a breath and did a final check of herself in the bathroom mirror. She ran a hand over a few flyaway strands on the right side and then flattened her collar where it was bent up near the back before deeming herself presentable enough.

She quickly grabbed her keys and was on her way to Vanessa's apartment, focusing on her drive instead of the fact that Zoe was having her own date night with Jake. Well as much as going to a company party could be a date. Her stomach turned as her brain shifted to New Year's Eve and overhearing Zoe and Jake. She dreaded having a repeat of that night, but maybe things would go so well tonight with Vanessa that she'd stay the night and Paige wouldn't have to worry about that.

After three quick knocks, Vanessa opened her door and gestured inside with her arm. "Hey there. Let me take your coat."

Paige handed it over to Vanessa who then turned to hang it in the closet. Without trying to be a creep, Paige gave Vanessa a quick up and down look. She couldn't deny that Vanessa was incredibly cute. Tonight she wore a flowy black button-up and a short, red skirt. Her feet were bare, revealing red-painted toes and a floral tattoo covering the top of one foot.

"My roommate is out of town for the weekend so we have the place all to ourselves," Vanessa said as she slowly walked toward Paige and guided her backward until she was pressed against the door.

Then Vanessa's lips were on Paige's in an instant, and Paige let out a surprised yelp. Wow. This was so different than their first kiss. Vanessa's lips were soft and warm and moved with skill. But even with the amazing kisses, Paige's mind was still trying to catch up.

She rested her hands on Vanessa's hips and gently pushed her away. "Hold up. What's going on? I thought we were having dinner."

"You were looking pretty delectable so I thought, why not skip right to dessert?" Vanessa replied with a grin before kissing Paige just under her ear.

Paige's stomach tightened at the contact and she framed Vanessa's face with her hands and brought her up for another kiss. She could do this. She could lose herself in Vanessa's kiss and touch for a little while. Maybe it would be enough to dull the ache in her heart.

But that quick thought brought Zoe's face to the front of Paige's mind. It was almost enough for her to pull away from Vanessa again, but she mentally shook herself and focused on how Vanessa was lightly nipping at her bottom lip. Paige trailed a hand back down to Vanessa's waist and pulled her closer. She slipped her hand under Vanessa's shirt and lightly traced her thumb along the soft skin. Vanessa rolled her hips forward and she let out a soft moan.

The sound urged Paige on and she reached down to Vanessa's bare thigh and lifted it to wrap around her waist. She lightly traced her fingertips along the smooth skin beneath her fingertips and moaned as Vanessa pressed herself more tightly to Paige. But it wasn't Vanessa's touch that brought on the moan. It was the image that flashed through Paige's mind. The image of Zoe on New Year's Eve in their kitchen as her T-shirt rose up and almost gave Paige a glimpse at what she imagined was a glorious ass. Fuck, she thought as she quickly broke the kiss.

"Wait. Stop." Paige dropped Vanessa's leg and slipped away so she wasn't sandwiched between Vanessa and the door anymore. "I can't do this."

Vanessa looked confused but not hurt and her chest heaved with quick breaths. "Why not?"

What could Paige say? *I can't stop picturing my brother's girlfriend's face when you kiss me. Your moan sounded nothing like Zoe's.* She shook her head and started to pace in the small living room. As she gathered her thoughts, she took in more of Vanessa's apartment—the expensive-looking road bike in the corner, a couple of textbooks on the coffee table, and a half-eaten apple pie on the breakfast bar.

"I'm not being fair to you," Paige muttered as she stopped and looked at Vanessa with a frown. "Like at all."

Vanessa narrowed her eyes for a moment and then nodded, recognition seeming to set in. "There's someone else," she said matter-of-factly.

"No, not really. Well, yes." Paige dropped onto the couch and rubbed her face with her hands. "Not someone I can have though."

"Do you want to talk about it?" Vanessa asked, moving to sit on the armrest of the opposite side of the couch.

"That seems even less fair to you," Paige mumbled around her hands that still covered her face. She dropped them and, frowning, looked at Vanessa. Paige wondered if she looked as pathetic as she felt.

Vanessa chuckled. "Not ideal I guess. But I think you can tell I asked you here for some fun. I wasn't really expecting or wanting anything serious. So the fun isn't happening," she said with a shrug. "People tell me I'm a good listener. So if you'd like to share, I'm here to listen."

Paige hesitated, still unsure about the protocol in a situation like this. She shouldn't even have come here in the first place, knowing her heart wasn't in it, and she felt like a complete asshole. But Vanessa didn't seem bothered and had offered to listen. "If you're sure?" Paige asked.

"Of course," Vanessa replied, standing and gesturing toward the kitchen. "Want something to drink? Juice, iced tea, water?"

"Just water, please."

"Coming right up." Vanessa grabbed a beer from her fridge and handed a glass of water to Paige. "And I did get you here under the guise that you'd be getting dinner. Are you hungry? I could order a pizza."

Her stomach was in knots from the night so far but she didn't want to be rude. Even though Vanessa had pounced on her as soon as she had arrived, she probably hadn't eaten dinner, and Paige didn't want her to have to sit through her sob story without food. So she nodded and said, "Sure."

"Any preferences?" Vanessa asked as she pulled out her phone.

Paige shook her head. "No. Get whatever you'd like."

After a few minutes, Vanessa set her phone on the coffee table and took a seat in the chair, crossing one leg over the other. "Ordered. Now start talking. Who is it?"

"My brother's girlfriend. I think I'm falling in love with her."

Vanessa let out a whistle and then took a long gulp of her beer. "Wow. Wasn't expecting that. I think you better start from the beginning."

So Paige did, recounting every single detail. Everything from why she moved here to Jake bailing on dates and Paige going out with Zoe instead, finishing it up with her reactions tonight and why she had to stop things. Just saying it out loud made her feel like an even bigger asshole.

"I'm sorry," Paige said, biting her thumbnail. "I feel like I've used you."

Vanessa tilted her head from side to side then shrugged. "Yeah, you kinda did." Paige groaned and Vanessa held up her hand. "But I'm not mad. Like I said, I wasn't looking for something serious. Just needed a little fun and some stress relief."

"What's stressful for you? If you don't mind me asking."

Just then a knock sounded at the door. "Hold that thought," Vanessa said.

After taking delivery of the pizza, Vanessa grabbed a couple of plates, ripped off a few sheets of paper towel and set everything on the coffee table. Paige took a slice of pepperoni pizza, more to be polite than anything. The whole night had made her feel a little queasy.

Once Vanessa settled in her seat with a few pieces of pizza, Paige said, "Back to what I asked earlier. What's stressful?"

"Oh the usual—school, family, work, yada yada."

"Tell me about it," Paige said before taking a bite of her pizza.

As they ate, with Paige taking more pizza now that she felt more at ease, Vanessa told Paige about her family and how she was studying to get her master's in bioinformatics. Their conversation had much more substance than their first date, and even though the night didn't go as planned for either of them, Paige felt like she might be gaining a friend in Vanessa. And that was something she desperately needed. Her focus had been so set on work and then trying to get to know her brother while simultaneously crushing on Zoe that she hadn't let herself get close to anyone. At least outside of work. She considered Tom a friend, but they hadn't yet seen each other outside of Craft.

As their conversation came to a natural end, Paige checked the time on her phone. "I should head out. I'm opening tomorrow."

"No worries," Vanessa said as she stood.

Paige helped Vanessa clean up and then grabbed her coat from the closet. As she finished putting it on, Vanessa grabbed the lapels and gave Paige a kiss on her cheek. "I had a good time tonight."

"Yeah?" Paige asked, a hesitant smile on her face. "Even with the lack of sex?"

"Okay. So that would have made it a little better," Vanessa replied with a wink. "But I mean it. Tonight was fun."

"I had a good time too," Paige said, this time giving Vanessa a genuine smile. "How about we go out for dinner again sometime? As friends. I could use another friend in the city."

"Definitely."

"Great. I'm sure I'll see you at Craft," Paige said.

"Fuck yes. I don't just order from you because you're hot. You also make a damn good cup of coffee."

Paige blushed and looked away. "Thanks. Probably not when I first started though."

Vanessa laughed. "Yeah, not so much. Your sexy smile kept me around back then," she said.

Paige snorted. "Good to know."

With a wave, Paige was out the door and headed to her car. The night made one thing clear to her—if she was going to have a chance of getting over Zoe, she didn't need someone to distract her. She needed distance. Her apartment hunt was about to get slightly more desperate.

CHAPTER TWENTY

The Uber pulled up to the Conrad, a swanky hotel in the heart of downtown Indy. Zoe smiled as the door attendant opened her door. He gave her a slight nod and said, "Good evening, miss, and welcome to the Conrad."

"Thank you," she murmured and continued into the hotel. She found signs for Wexler Investments, Jake's firm, directing guests to the Artsgarden, a glassed dome above the intersection of Washington and Illinois streets. Had Jake mentioned that in his texts? He told her about the party at the very last minute. It had started at seven and he'd texted her at 6:45. She'd quickly had to shower and get into the first dress she found in her closet. Her initial reaction had been to tell him she wasn't coming, but then her brain reminded her of the fact that she was trying to make more of an effort. Plus, they hadn't had a date night out in ages. But how much of a date night could a company party be?

Walking out of her room and running into Paige hadn't helped her mood either. Once she learned Paige had a date of her own, jealousy had threatened to overwhelm her, especially when Paige had looked so fucking good in a pair of khaki chinos and a dark blue button-up with tiny white polka dots. Her collar had been folded up in the back and Zoe's hands had itched to reach out and fix it, but she somehow had restrained herself.

As she stepped into the Artsgarden, she let out a slow breath, wanting to get rid of the ill feelings swirling through her mind. Even though this was Jake's work party, maybe they'd actually be able to have a good time. Have some drinks, dance a little, finally spend some time together.

She scanned the already impressive crowd. High-top tables were spread through the large space and most were occupied by people with drinks and little plates of food. Wait staff walked around with trays of hors d'oeuvres, stopping to offer the tiny yet delicious-looking bites to guests. Zoe's stomach growled. Her lunch had consisted of a salad and bag of chips and she'd not had time to grab a snack in the afternoon.

A waving arm across the room stole her attention away from a tray of stuffed mushrooms. The arm belonged to Jake and even though she was still a little annoyed with him, she couldn't help but return his wide smile. She made her way across the room, slipping between groups until she stood in front of Jake.

"You made it!" He gave her a quick hug and a slow kiss. When he pulled back, his eyes clearly strayed to her chest. "And you look so damn good."

Zoe looked down at what she felt was just a simple black dress. It had a scalloped V-neckline that maybe went a little lower than appropriate for a company party and it hit a couple inches above her knees with a six-inch slit up the left thigh. If Jake's obvious appreciation was anything to go by, then simple seemed to work for her.

"Thanks," she replied, feeling a hint of warmth in her cheeks. "So when did you find out about this?" Her pointed look hopefully told him that she didn't necessarily appreciate something so last-minute.

Jake groaned. "Earlier this week." Zoe's eyebrows lifted even higher. "Ugh, I know. I'm sorry. It just completely slipped my mind." Jake gestured behind to a table. "Let me introduce you to some people."

With an arm around her waist, Jake steered her to the table a few feet away. The guy had on a fitted navy suit and a pompadour hairstyle heavy with product. Seriously, it looked like he could stand in a tornado and his hair would still be perfectly coiffed. He looked several years older than Jake, but the woman standing next to him looked to be their age.

"This is Mason and Cassie."

Zoe reached out her hand to Mason and he gave it a firm shake. She'd heard his name before as he had started working at Wexler a few months after Jake, but she'd never met him.

"He's Ian's first assistant," Jake continued.

"Was," Mason emphasized with a grin.

"Was?" Zoe asked as she quickly shook Cassie's hand.

Jake's smile got even wider. "Right. Still not used to it I guess." He fully turned to Zoe and reached for her hand. "As of today, I'm Ian's *first* assistant."

Zoe smiled and hugged him like a dutiful girlfriend should, but she didn't know how she truly felt about this news. She was so happy for him because she knew how hard he'd been working but she just didn't know what this would mean for them as a couple. Would he have even more work now and be absent even more? Or would it mean that he'd be home more because he wouldn't have to do all the bullshit tasks that he'd had to do as Ian's second assistant? Guess time would tell once he started his new role.

"Congratulations," Zoe said, giving Jake a tight squeeze around his waist. "I'm so proud of you." She kissed him lightly before gliding her thumb over his bottom lip, wiping off her lipstick.

"Thanks. But this means it's time to celebrate." He signaled to the waiter, holding up his empty glass and pointing to it and then holding up two fingers.

Within minutes, two glasses filled with amber liquid and garnished with an orange peel were set on their table. They all raised their glasses in cheers and Zoe took a sip, quickly recognizing it as an old-fashioned, Jake's favorite cocktail.

Over the next hour, Zoe chatted with Mason and Cassie and a few others who had come to join their table. Jake had introduced everyone, but their names didn't seem to stick in her brain. She tried to sound enthusiastic with each person Jake had introduced her to but her energy was waning fast.

Needing a break from mingling, she excused herself to go to the bathroom. When she was finished, she found Jake animatedly talking to the group still at their table. Instead of going back to join them, she walked to the opposite end of the room and stepped in front of the big windows that gave her a view south down Illinois Street. She lost herself in the headlights of cars heading north. That was until she saw a reflection of someone coming up behind her.

Ian.

Jake's boss came to stand next to her with a rocks glass of clear liquid in one hand, staring out the floor-to-ceiling windows overlooking the city. After taking a small sip, he turned to her. "It is so lovely to see you again, Zoe. You're even more beautiful than the first time I met you," he murmured as he reached out and stroked his fingers down her arm.

Zoe swallowed hard as she fought not to shudder. This guy was so gross. When she'd interacted with him briefly at the Labor Day picnic, she could tell immediately that he was a man who got whatever he wanted and he knew it. She looked around to see if anyone was paying them any attention. Zoe didn't necessarily think Ian would try anything more physically inappropriate than he already had, but she also didn't want to find out how reckless he could be.

He leaned forward, invading her personal space to the extent that she felt his breath on her cheek. "You know, Wexler booked rooms for all the employees and I have the biggest one of them all. What do you say we sneak away for a bit of fun? We can even grab Jake on the way. I'm quite certain he'd enjoy it."

When he reached out to push her hair behind her ear, Zoe stopped him with a hand on his wrist. *What the fuck?* Attempting to register his proposition, she felt nauseated and pissed off. She dropped his wrist and stepped back to get some space between them. The first thing her brain could make sense of was that she was utterly disgusted. The second thing was that this was Jake's boss. That fact made her rethink what her next move should be.

She wanted to say or do something, but she didn't want there to be any repercussions for Jake, especially now that he'd been promoted.

Did Jake know Ian was this much of a sleazy asshole? And if he did, why the hell would he still want to work for him?

As those questions rolled around in her head, Jake came up to them, eyes wide as they darted between Zoe and Ian. "I see you two have met again. Great party. Isn't it, Zoe?"

Sure, if you like being propositioned by a creep, Zoe thought. "Yeah, great," she replied, trying to plaster on a genuine smile. But if the wariness on Jake's face was anything to go by, she failed miserably.

"I was just telling your beautiful girlfriend that Wexler generously made room reservations for each employee," Ian said as he gave Zoe a quick smirk before turning a less creepy but still-not-innocent smile toward Jake. He took a sip of his drink before giving a small nod to someone or something behind them. "I need to go mingle a bit more. Do enjoy your night. If you need anything at all, I'll be available all night." He winked at Zoe before walking away.

Zoe folded her arms across her chest, trying not to snarl at Ian's retreating form. Jake's arms wrapped around her waist and he leaned down, his lips brushing against her ear.

"It is great, right? We can enjoy ourselves and then go up to our room and have some proper alone time."

"Alone or with your boss?"

Jake pulled away and met her gaze, though he still kept his arms tight around Zoe's waist. A deep V formed between his brows. "What the hell are you talking about?"

"Your boss just invited me up to his room. What a dick." She pushed out of his grasp and stepped back, wrapping her arms around her torso as if protecting herself.

"What? No way. He's not that kind of guy. It's loud in here. You must not have heard him correctly."

Zoe narrowed her eyes. "I know what I heard, Jake. You want to know what else I heard?"

Jake swallowed. Even in the dimmer light, Zoe could see his Adam's apple move up and down.

"He said we could grab you on the way. That you'd enjoy it. What the fuck does that even mean?" Zoe asked, her voice rising.

Jake stepped forward, lifting his hands and making shushing noises as if to placate her. "Can you keep your fucking voice down? These are my coworkers. I can't make a bad impression."

"All about work as always," Zoe replied, rolling her eyes. "Aren't you even going to confront him about it? Stand up for me?"

"Zoe. He's my boss, and I just got promoted. He did—"

Zoe didn't even care what Jake had to say so she just walked away. Like time and time again, his work was coming first. Not her. Not her feelings. Work. Did Jake not realize how gross she felt? How inappropriate Ian had been? She understood that he was Jake's boss but that didn't give him the right to be a fucking sleazy douche-canoe.

Jake gripped her arm and spun her around, fear and desperation swirling in his eyes. "Look. Whatever Ian said, I'm sure he didn't mean it and was just joking around. Let's go get our room key and head upstairs. We can talk this out. Get away from everybody."

Zoe wrenched her arm out of Jake's grasp. "Fuck that. I'm going home." She turned away from him again, spotting the nearest exit.

"Zoe, stay. We can talk about this," Jake pleaded as he fell into step behind her.

"I don't want to talk about this right now. And *don't* follow me."

Zoe rushed out of the room and into an elevator. She quickly pulled up her Uber app and requested a car which arrived within two minutes. Fuming, she ignored any attempts the driver made at small talk. She needed to get home, go to bed, and forget about this horrible fucking night.

Zoe pushed open the apartment door and found Paige sitting on the couch with a bowl of popcorn in her lap. Her hair was up in a high bun and she had her purple blanket wrapped around her legs which were pulled up onto the couch. And for the first time all night, Zoe felt at ease. She let out a slow breath and gave Paige a small smile.

Paige tilted her head and paused what she was watching. "No Jake?"

"God, no," Zoe murmured, clenching her keys in her hand. "He's still at the party."

Paige's eyebrows shot up and Zoe would have laughed if she'd had the energy to do so. "Everything okay?" she asked quietly.

"Not really. No," Zoe replied, letting out a humorless chuckle. She tossed her keys onto the side table and held on to the door handle as she took her heels off one at a time.

Paige set the bowl onto the coffee table and dropped her feet to the floor, leaning forward with her forearms on her thighs. "Do you want to talk about it?"

"Not really," Zoe said. She probably should talk about it, but she just felt tired. So tired. Between Jake's job taking over his life and then him not really doing anything about his boss's disgusting behavior, Zoe wondered if she and Jake would even make it until the end of his first year at Wexler. The openness and sincerity on Paige's face made her want to blurt out everything though. Just not tonight. "Maybe some other time?"

"Anytime," Paige said. She gestured to the TV screen that looked to be paused on Reese Witherspoon. The scene looked familiar but Zoe couldn't place it right away. "I just started *Legally Blonde*. Have you seen it?"

Zoe shook her head. "Only a couple scenes. We were pretty young when it came out."

Paige laughed. "True since it came out just after we were born. It was one of my aunt's favorites," she said with a slight shrug.

"Let me go change out of this dumb dress and then I'm all yours." Zoe quickly headed for her bedroom, but before she could make it down the hallway, Paige called out to her and Zoe turned at the sound of her name.

"Zoe. It's not a dumb dress. You look beautiful," Paige said, her voice holding a hint of huskiness.

Zoe's cheeks immediately warmed and she bit the corner of her bottom lip. "Thanks," she whispered. Zoe held Paige's gaze until that all too familiar flutter in her stomach took over. The flutter that made her curious and unsure all at the same time.

After she shut her bedroom door, Zoe leaned back against it and closed her eyes. It was just the events of the night that made her have such a strong reaction to being called beautiful. It had nothing to do with the fact that when she was around Paige, she felt safe. She felt loved. But it wasn't supposed to be Paige that made her feel that way. It was supposed to be Jake, but he hadn't made her feel that way once tonight.

Happy to get out of the dress and into sweats and a T-shirt, Zoe sat on the couch. Paige offered her the blanket and the popcorn. Both of which Zoe gladly shared with Paige.

"I'd only been watching for a few minutes so I just restarted it. Ready?"

"Yep," Zoe replied. But as Paige lifted the remote, Zoe stopped her with a hand on her forearm as she remembered that Paige had also had plans earlier. "Wait. How did your date go?" Zoe cringed as the question came out of her mouth. "Maybe not great if you're home this early?"

Paige waved her off. "We just decided we're better off as friends."

"Are you okay with that?" Zoe asked quietly.

"I am." Paige opened her mouth but quickly closed it before clearing her throat. "It was my doing so I'm fine with it."

A quick burst of excitement shot through Zoe before she regained control of her brain. Or really, her hormones. She didn't want to admit she really had to regain control of her heart. "I'm sorry."

Paige shrugged as she pressed play. "All a part of dating, right?"

"Right," Zoe replied.

They watched the movie in silence and the bowl of popcorn was quickly consumed. Once Paige set the bowl on the coffee table, Zoe shifted until she was lying down with her head resting against Paige's thigh. Immediately Paige's fingers started combing through Zoe's hair. It all felt like the most natural thing in the world. The comfort this simple act brought almost made her forget about everything that had happened earlier.

When the movie ended and Jake still hadn't come home, Zoe sat up and gave a quick glance to the door. A move that Paige must've noticed.

"Are you going to wait for him to come home?" Paige asked.

"No," Zoe replied with a shake of her head. "I'm gonna head to bed. I want to fall asleep before he gets home. I really don't want to deal with him again tonight."

Paige briefly bit at her thumbnail before dropping her hand to her lap and pressing it between her knees. "Um, do you want to sleep in my bed? I can take the couch."

No, I want to sleep in your bed with you, Zoe thought unhesitatingly. She swallowed as she tried to think of anything but that. The offer was so tempting but she knew she'd have a harder time sleeping because she would be in Paige's bed—feeling the softness of her sheets, smelling her shampoo on her pillow. That was not something she needed to pile onto her already shitty night. Well, shitty night until she got home and spent time with Paige. That would never make her night feel shitty.

Zoe squeezed Paige's hand. "I appreciate it, but I think I'll sleep in my own bed."

"Are you sure?" Paige asked.

Zoe's stomach clenched. Was that disappointment she heard in Paige's voice? She closed her eyes at the intense desire to say yes. But she couldn't. Not with her emotions so out of control from the night and the confusion of what was going on with her and Paige. And of course, she had a boyfriend, even if she was pissed off at him. "I'm sure." Paige nodded and took the bowl into the kitchen. Zoe made sure the front door was locked and begrudgingly left a light on for Jake even though the thought of him stubbing his toe in the dark brought her some satisfaction.

When she reached Paige's door, Zoe stopped and faced Paige. "Thank you for everything tonight. For not making me talk about everything. It...well, it was exactly what I needed." In her mind though, Zoe said, *You were exactly what I needed.*

Before she could second-guess herself, Zoe pulled Paige in for a hug, tightly wrapping her arms around Paige's waist. As Paige returned the hug, Zoe let out a slow breath and melted into the embrace. She never wanted to let go of this safety, but she knew she had to so after indulging a moment longer, she forced herself to step away.

With a quiet, "Thanks again," Zoe hurried to her bedroom and got under the covers. Sleep was desperately needed. Because lately it seemed that it was only in her dreams when she was truly happy.

CHAPTER TWENTY-ONE

Over the next week, Paige did everything she could to avoid spending a lot of one-on-one time with Zoe. When Zoe had come home after Jake's company party, she knew immediately that something was wrong. Zoe just didn't look like Zoe. There was no spark in her eyes and the slump of her shoulders and her frown had told Paige that Zoe had not had a good night.

Paige had accepted that Zoe hadn't wanted to talk that night, but over the following couple of days, Zoe had filled her in on exactly what had happened and what Ian had done. As well as what Jake hadn't done. God, Paige had been so fucking mad. She'd wanted to march right up to Jake and give him a piece of her mind, but Zoe had made her promise that she wouldn't say anything. That it had been between her and Jake and that Zoe didn't want anything to come between Paige and Jake.

So Paige had reluctantly agreed to keep her mouth shut and tried to avoid the apartment because of what she might have said. But also because it had been so tense and awkward to be around Zoe and Jake. The first couple of days they hardly said a word to each other, although Jake had tried his hardest. He had started coming home early and brought Zoe flowers and shrimp rolls. Zoe had grudgingly accepted the peace offerings and the iciness in the apartment had started to melt. Zoe and Jake weren't back to what Paige considered their normal, but they were close. Paige had picked up extra shifts as a way to stay away from the apartment but the increased hours at Craft were starting to wear on her.

Paige still hadn't found a place to stay, but she was on the waitlist at one apartment. The building manager told her that the next scheduled opening wasn't for a few months but if anything changed, the woman had promised to call Paige and let her know. So for now, Paige was stuck where she was. Stuck living with someone who held her heart but didn't even know it. The only positive aspect was being able to keep saving her money so she would feel more secure once she finally moved out.

As she walked into the kitchen after a twelve-hour shift, Paige's stomach grumbled. She took a spoon from a drawer and grabbed her jar of peanut butter. Paige had made sure to label her jars when she moved in because she had a habit of doing what she was about to do—crash on the couch to watch some TV and eat a couple of spoonsful of peanut butter straight out of the jar. At least until she could find the motivation to cook an actual meal.

She hadn't seen Zoe or Jake, but noticed that their bedroom door was closed. She figured one of them, or both, were in there since they usually kept it open when they weren't home. She wouldn't be upset if she didn't see either of them for the rest of the night. Especially Zoe. The week was only half over and she was already exhausted. She wouldn't mind a night where she didn't have to socialize or work on protecting her heart.

She collapsed onto the couch and put her feet up on the coffee table, crossing her legs at the ankle. Just as she dug a spoonful of peanut butter out, she heard the couple's bedroom door open.

When Zoe walked into the living room, Paige froze with the spoon halfway to her mouth. Zoe wore a navy, knee-length dress. It had long sleeves and a high neck, but as Zoe bent at the waist to adjust the strap of her heel, Paige saw that Zoe's entire back was exposed. Oh, how she wanted to reach out and stroke her fingers down the length of Zoe's spine. Her hair was loose and wavy, now almost hitting her shoulders. So much for protecting my heart, she thought as it skipped a beat at the sight.

Paige stuffed the spoon into the peanut butter and set the jar on the coffee table. Her mind was working overtime and she tried to find something to say, but what? She didn't think there were enough words in the world to do Zoe justice and Zoe had the uncanny ability to turn Paige's brain to mush whenever she walked into the room. "You...you look beautiful, Zoe," Paige finally was able to get out.

Zoe blushed and she averted her gaze, pressing down a nonexistent wrinkle in her dress. "Thank you," she said quietly.

Paige cleared her throat. "What's the occasion?"

"Oh, it's my birthday," she mumbled. "Jake's taking me out to dinner." She looked at the thin silver watch on her wrist. "He should be home any minute."

"What? Happy birthday! Why didn't you say anything before? I could've baked you a cake or cookies or something."

Zoe shrugged. "I don't really like to make a big deal about it. It's just another day really."

Paige's heart clenched. She loved celebrating people—their birthday, a job promotion, anything. People deserved to feel loved. "It is so not just another day. It's a day for it to be all about you. Or if you're anything like my aunt, it would be a full week. A month even, if she had her way," Paige said with a chuckle. "Where are you guys going?"

Zoe opened her mouth to answer but stopped and looked at the phone in her hand. Her face fell and Paige could see the whites of her knuckles as she clutched her phone. "Nowhere apparently. Jake's stuck at work." Zoe turned around and started down the hallway, tossing her phone carelessly on the kitchen counter as she passed.

Paige couldn't take it. Couldn't take the disappointment that Zoe was clearly feeling. She had looked as if she was a second away from crying. Something that was completely unacceptable to Paige. She couldn't let Zoe cry again because of Jake. Particularly on her birthday.

"Zoe, wait." Zoe stopped but didn't turn around so Paige stood and went to her. "I'll take you. Let me just go get changed and then we'll go."

"No, it's okay. You don't have to do that," Zoe muttered.

Paige reached out and gently gripped Zoe's wrist until Zoe looked up and met her gaze. "But I'd like to. Give me five minutes. Okay?"

Zoe still looked hesitant but silently nodded and walked back into the living room. Paige went into her bedroom and turned on the light. She'd never been more grateful that she had brought all her clothes from her mom's at Christmas. She grabbed the first dress in her closet. It was the dark green one she'd worn to Christmas Mass. After putting her hair up in a quick twist, she slipped on a pair of flats. She decided to skip the makeup to save time. She was afraid Zoe would change her mind and get changed into her pajamas.

Paige found Zoe sitting on the couch, one leg crossed over the other and staring off into space. "Hey," she said quietly, not wanting to spook her. "Ready to go?"

Zoe gave her an obviously forced smile. "Sure." She reached for her keys but Paige stopped her.

"You don't have to do anything tonight, okay? It's *your* night. I'll drive."

This time Zoe gave her a more genuine smile, but it still wasn't the usual bright one Paige had come to know and love. "Whatever you say."

Paige's heart broke that Zoe was so dejected on her birthday. God, she was so mad at Jake. How could he bail on Zoe today of all days? How did he not see how much his actions were hurting her? Did he not care? Was he really that absorbed in his damn job that everyone else didn't matter?

As they made their way down in the elevator, Paige forced herself to take a few deep breaths. It wouldn't help the situation if Zoe could sense Paige's anger. Although, Zoe was probably feeling the same so she'd understand. She wanted Zoe to feel like this was what was meant to happen all along. That nothing was ruined and she could still have fun on her birthday.

At Paige's car, Zoe reached for the door handle, but Paige stopped her with a gentle grip on her forearm. "I got it." She opened the door gallantly and gestured inside and, adding a bit of haughtiness to her voice, she said, "Your chariot awaits." Paige then shook her head from side to side. "You know, if a chariot was a ten-year-old Civic that used to be your mom's car."

Zoe blushed and then laughed. "Thanks," she replied as she slid in, gathering her dress skirt in her hands.

Paige closed the door and hurried around to the driver's side. She turned on the car, hoping it would warm up quickly. *Can't have Zoe being cold on her birthday.* "Where to?"

"Jake had reservations at Harry and Izzy's."

Paige had heard of the expensive downtown steakhouse. Not exactly what she could afford and it would put a rather large dent in her wallet, but if that's where Zoe wanted to go then that was where Paige would take her. "Is that what you want?" Paige tried to ask the question in as neutral a voice as possible. She didn't want Zoe to think she was trying to sway her decision in any way.

Zoe shrugged. "It's a nice place but pretty pricey. Not exactly where I would've chosen."

"Then where would you like to go? Your birthday, your choice."

"What about Athens?" Zoe asked hesitantly.

"Well, if you think going to Harry and Izzy's was pricey, I think going to Greece would cost a pretty penny itself. Plus, I don't know if I could get the time off," Paige replied, her tone deadpan.

Zoe playfully slapped at her arm. "The restaurant. It's on Eighty-Sixth."

"Oh," Paige said, dragging the word out. "Then yes. We can definitely go there."

"Goof," Zoe said with a smile.

After a twenty-minute drive, they arrived at the restaurant, one of several businesses in a strip mall. Paige loved the soft yellow lights strung up underneath part of the building that covered about five tables outside. Too bad it was the middle of March and close to freezing. Maybe she'd have to bring Zoe back here when it got warmer so they could enjoy a nice dinner under these lights.

That thought almost brought her to a halt but she had enough awareness to keep walking. She wouldn't be bringing Zoe back here. Not unless they were hanging out. As friends. This wasn't a date and there wouldn't be dates in the future. Her fucking brain, but especially her heart, needed to get their shit together.

Giving herself a mental shake, she led Zoe inside and requested a table for two. They were seated right away at a quiet table in the far corner of the front room. Long waits at restaurants could be so tedious and Paige was thankful that hadn't happened tonight. The host handed them menus and left them alone.

"This place seems great. Have you been here before?" Paige asked.

Zoe grinned and said, "Yeah. It's one of my favorites and I've come here with Mia a few times." Her smile dimmed and she continued, "But Jake isn't a huge fan of Greek food."

"Then tonight we will get whatever you want. I love Greek so I'm excited," Paige replied.

Zoe's smile returned. "Then you have to try the pastitsio. It's so good."

Paige browsed the menu. "What about appetizers? Wanna share some hummus and saganaki?"

"Yes, please," Zoe said.

Even though Paige should save as much money as possible, she was absolutely willing to give Zoe whatever she wanted tonight. Her smile alone could make Paige want to order everything on the menu for her. She closed her eyes and took a sip of her water. Now wasn't the time to think that either. She was here to make sure Zoe had a great birthday despite Jake being a massive dick and bailing on her. No one deserved that on their birthday.

After their waiter took their order, Paige raised her glass and said, "Cheers. To someone who is smart and kind and…" She wanted to add in beautiful or hot or sexy as hell but knew that would be inappropriate. "And to someone I am lucky to call a… friend. Happy birthday, Zoe."

Zoe raised her glass and touched it to Paige's. "Thank you," she replied quietly. "I think I'm the lucky one."

Zoe held Paige's gaze as she sipped and Paige's stomach tightened. The intensity in Zoe's eyes made Paige want to melt into a puddle right then and there. But it also made her feel extremely confused. Zoe's look didn't exactly scream, "We're just friends." Especially if Paige considered the two times so far tonight that Zoe's gaze drifted down to her chest. Had Zoe even known that she'd done it? Probably not, Paige thought.

Paige broke the eye contact and played with her fork, turning it over and over again. She was thankful as the waiter dropped off their appetizers, especially the plate of flaming cheese.

Zoe's eyes danced with excitement as the waiter extinguished the fire with juice squeezed from a lemon. She reached for a slice of pita bread. "I am starving and this looks so good."

Paige cut a slice of cheese and rolled it in her own piece of pita. "Mmm. So good," she said after taking a bite.

"Right? This saganaki alone makes this my favorite place," Zoe replied with a laugh.

They ate their appetizers with little conversation but plenty of murmured appreciation. Just as they were finishing, the waiter brought out their main courses.

As Zoe cut her lamb chop, she asked, "Have you talked to your dad since you moved here? I've wanted to ask but didn't want to be nosy."

Not exactly the question Paige expected, but it felt nice that she was curious and wanted to check in with her. "I did when I moved in with you guys but haven't since."

"Did you talk to him much before you moved here?"

"Not really," Paige said around a bite of rice. She took a sip of water and continued, "I wasn't in contact with him at all until my mom gave me a box of cards and letters from him after I graduated from college."

"What do you mean?"

"After we moved to Detroit, he sent me birthday cards every year and a few letters. But my mom thought it was better if he didn't have any contact with me. She tried to make a clean break so she hid them in a box in her closet. She gave them to me a week after I moved back in with her after graduation."

"Wow. How did you feel when she gave them all to you?"

"I was angry," Paige whispered, looking down at her plate. "I didn't talk to her for a couple weeks. Hid myself in my room as I read and reread every single card. In one of the last cards, Brian…my dad…sorry, it still sounds weird to say. And I'm not sure if I'll ever be comfortable calling him Dad."

Zoe reached over and covered Paige's hand with hers, lightly stroking her thumb along the top. The touch made Paige feel comfortable, safe.

"As far as I'm concerned, that should be all up to you. If you want to call him Brian for the rest of your life, that's your choice. Don't let him or Jake or your mom or anyone else make you feel like you need to do something that you're not comfortable with."

"I know," Paige said, giving Zoe a soft smile. She slowly pulled back her hand and immediately missed the connection with Zoe. But she couldn't take it anymore. The whole needing-to-get-distance thing wasn't exactly working out tonight. "But… um…he put his email in one of the last cards so I reached out to him a few days later. We sent a few emails back and forth. I asked about Jake and found out that you guys had moved here. I didn't really have anything going on in my life. No permanent job. Wasn't sure if I wanted to go to grad school or not. So one day just made the decision to move. And well, you know the rest."

Zoe chuckled. "That I do. I think it's working out pretty well so far."

Paige forced a smile. While things were working out—she was getting to know Jake, had a great job, and felt like she could call Indy her home for a while—Zoe had no idea how hard it was to make it seem like everything was okay. How could things be okay when here she was, sitting across from someone she was falling for but couldn't do a damn thing about it? She had her heart crushed repeatedly anytime she was near Zoe. And that was why she needed to move out.

"I think so too," Paige murmured. Wanting to shift topics, she pointed to her food and said, "This is making me want to go to Greece someday."

"Oh, that's a dream of mine. Do you like to travel?"

They continued eating as they talked about all things travel. Zoe loved relaxing on a beach with a good book while Paige preferred mountains and lakes for hikes and swimming. Paige couldn't help but imagine them vacationing together, taking turns picking their destination. Maybe Zoe could learn to love hiking and then Paige could learn to love sitting in the sand. But Paige closed her eyes briefly at the wistful thought. Those things were never going to happen.

After Zoe finished a story about an awful sunburn on her first trip to California, she sat back and held her hand against her stomach. "That was so good," she said with a satisfied groan. "I am so glad you like Greek food."

"Me too," Paige replied with a chuckle. Paige relaxed with the knowledge that Zoe was clearly having a good time. Every time she smiled or laughed, Paige knew she'd done the right thing in making sure she came out tonight. There was just one more thing that would make it perfect. "I'll be right back. Just going to use the bathroom really quick."

Zoe watched Paige walk away until she was out of sight. And oh what a sight it had been. Until this moment, she hadn't been able to appreciate how beautiful Paige looked tonight. Her green dress had just the right amount of snugness and the low-cut neckline had been distracting Zoe all night. She prayed that Paige hadn't noticed whenever Zoe's eyes strayed to her chest.

Each time she'd snuck a look, she cursed Mia for putting this whole crush idea in her head.

Prior to their chat, Zoe had been blissfully oblivious. Or it may have been denial, but still… Her mind hadn't been so obsessed with how Paige looked or how Zoe acted around her. But then tonight Paige had to go and put her hair up and all Zoe wanted to do was trail her fingers along the smooth skin of her neck.

As she saw Paige walking toward their table, she murmured under breath, "Get it together, woman." She took a sip of water in hopes of cooling down the thoughts that had made her a tad hot and bothered if she were honest with herself.

Paige sat back down and avoided Zoe's gaze as she took her own sip of water. "Sorry about that," Paige said as she bit her lip as if trying to hide a smile.

Zoe narrowed her eyes. "Everything okay?"

But Paige didn't need to answer because just then Zoe watched as their beaming waiter approached the table, setting down an oval plate. Zoe's mouth watered as she took in the dessert. There were two scoops of ice cream drizzled with honey and chocolate sauce and a piece of baklava in the middle with a lit candle perched on it. Zoe didn't think she had room for more but she was proved wrong as soon as this plate of deliciousness was set in front of her.

Surprisingly, the waiter gave her a polite "Happy birthday" before leaving. She expected a song like so many restaurants did.

"I told him not to sing," Paige said, breaking Zoe out of her thoughts. "I wasn't sure if you'd like that."

Zoe let out a breath and smiled. "I wouldn't have, so thank you. This looks so good. Time to dig in."

"Nope. Not yet. You need to make a wish first," Paige said.

A wish. Paige's smile was all she needed, Zoe thought. Still she closed her eyes and blew out a breath. Now to see if it would come true.

She grabbed a spoon and scooped up a little ice cream and a small piece of baklava. Zoe moaned as the sweetness hit her tongue.

She looked across the table and noticed that Paige's mouth was parted ever so slightly and she had a far-off look in her eyes. "Do you not want any?" Zoe asked before scooping up another bite. She held the spoon across the table a few inches from Paige's mouth. "Here. Try it."

Paige's eyes darkened and they moved from Zoe's face to the spoon in front of her. She leaned forward and took the proffered dessert into her mouth.

Zoe's own mouth went dry. She didn't think she'd ever paid such close attention to someone eating. Paige seemed to move the food to the right side of her mouth and after she swallowed, her tongue slipped out and she licked at the corner of her mouth. Heat curled low in Zoe's belly and she wished that she'd been the one to lick that ice cream off of Paige's lips. Zoe felt her cheeks flush and she sat back, using her napkin to wipe at the nonexistent food on her lips in hopes that it would cover up how much she'd been affected by that little movement.

"Oh, that's really good," Paige said.

"Mmhmm," was all Zoe could reply. She took another bite so she had something with which to occupy herself instead of staring at Paige's mouth. Zoe swirled her spoon in the chocolate sauce. *Oh look, I can make a little design. I should look at that and not at Paige. Definitely don't look at Paige.*

Zoe's attention was pulled toward Paige's phone on the table as an alert sounded. Paige picked it up and frowned. "Sorry. I thought I'd turned it off," she said, wrinkling her nose. Paige scoffed as she looked at the screen.

"Everything okay?"

"It's Jake. He's wondering where we are. Said you weren't answering your phone."

"Oh yeah. I guess I forgot to grab it off the counter," Zoe said, shrugging. She looked at her watch before returning her gaze to Paige, a small frown on her face. "I guess we should head home. It's getting late."

Paige set the phone down and with a firm gaze looked at Zoe. "We are only heading home if that's what you want. Not because my brother finally gets his head out of his ass and wonders where you are."

Zoe laughed, reaching her hand across the table to squeeze Paige's hand. So soft. So warm. What she really wanted to do was forget about Jake and spend more time with Paige. The night so far had probably been the best birthday she'd ever had. It even topped her Mickey Mouse-themed party she'd had when she turned six.

Zoe hadn't thought about Jake once. *That should probably tell me something.* But now that he was in her mind again, she felt guilty. How could she let herself have such an amazing time with his sister and not think about him once? Maybe because he'd been a dick and bailed, she thought. Okay, so maybe she was guilty *and* angry.

But it was the guilt that gnawed at her the most. "Let's head home. Stupid work in the morning," Zoe replied, rolling her eyes as if that was the reason to leave rather than her guilt.

"Then home it is." Paige signaled to the waiter for the check, which arrived quickly. Zoe reached for it, but Paige snatched it away before she could grab it. "Your birthday means my treat." She slid in her card and set the bill on the table.

Zoe murmured, "Thank you."

Bill settled, she stood and reached for Zoe's coat, holding it out to her. Slipping her arms inside, Zoe closed her eyes and enjoyed Paige's proximity. Paige seemed to let her hand rest at the small of her back for a moment as if she didn't want to let go.

Wordlessly they walked out of the restaurant to Paige's car. Zoe spent most of the ride staring out her window, mentally kicking herself for letting her crush become so all-consuming. What she needed to do was figure out what she wanted. Did she want to try and work things out with Jake? Or did she want to break things off? Maybe if she did the latter she could see if her crush was one-sided or not. If she was reading Paige correctly, she really didn't think it was.

Inside the apartment building, Zoe stood behind as Paige pressed the button for the elevator. "I'm glad it was you," Zoe whispered.

The elevator door opened and Paige walked through, looking over her shoulder at Zoe, one eyebrow lifted. "What do you mean?"

Zoe followed her in and stood in front of her, not close enough to touch but close enough to see Paige's normally soft blue eyes darken to almost black. "I'm glad it was you that took me out tonight. I had a really great time."

Zoe dropped her gaze to Paige's lips. Full lips that were now slightly open. God if she could just lean in, then she could know what they felt like. What they tasted like. Zoe couldn't deny it anymore—she wanted Paige. Badly.

Paige rested her hand against Zoe's stomach and Zoe took in a sharp breath. "Zoe," Paige whispered.

Zoe found herself leaning in. A little voice in her head tried to stop her. *This isn't you. You don't cheat. Stop.* But it was like she was being drawn to Paige and nothing could stop her.

"I can't," Paige said, her voice hoarse. Then she stepped around Zoe and out of the elevator.

Zoe was left staring at the back wall and her stomach dropped, tears springing to her eyes. She hadn't even heard the elevator ding. She'd been so distracted by Paige. So distracted that she almost cheated on Jake. What the fuck was wrong with her? She took in a deep breath and tried to force the tears away.

Just before the elevator doors closed, she reached out her hand and slipped through them, rushing to meet Paige at the apartment door just as she was putting her key in the lock. "I'm sorry," Zoe forced out.

Paige didn't reply and she pushed through the door as if wanting to get as far away from Zoe as possible and as quickly as possible.

"Happy birthday!" Jake called out.

Zoe walked in and found him holding a small plate with a cupcake on it. He hurried to light it as he began to sing "Happy Birthday."

Zoe looked from Jake to Paige, wanting Paige to look back at her. Paige just stared into the living room, her eyes wide and almost fearful. And was that a hint of tears Zoe saw? But her focus was brought back to Jake as he now stood in front of her, his eyes showing remorse and worry.

"I'm so sorry I bailed. It wasn't my fault this time. I swear," he said in a rush.

"I'll let you guys celebrate," Paige said as she started to walk away.

"Wait. You don't have to go. We can all celebrate together," Zoe pleaded. It wasn't Jake she wanted to spend time with. It was Paige. It was all becoming very clear at warp speed. And she needed to talk to Paige. She needed to know what she was thinking.

"I should get to bed." Paige finally looked at Zoe. Her eyes swam with emotion. The regret was obvious but Zoe also still saw the lingering desire. "Happy birthday, Zoe," Paige murmured.

Before Zoe could respond, Paige was down the hallway and behind her closed bedroom door. Zoe wanted to call to her. Stop her. Anything. They needed to talk. They needed to clear the air. If Zoe wasn't with Jake, would Paige have kissed her? Did Paige actually have feelings for her? She'd never felt so unsettled before. Her stomach was in knots and her mind raced with questions. But she also felt so incredibly exhausted. It was like her body was shutting down for almost crossing the line in the elevator.

"It is late. I think I'm gonna head to bed too." She quickly blew out the candle, not wanting to see it anymore.

"Great idea," he said with a quick bounce of his eyebrows. "I'll shower really quick and then maybe we can celebrate your birthday the proper way." He hurried down the hall, setting the plate on the counter as he passed.

Zoe's stomach dropped as she just stood there. Sex with Jake. The thought made her nauseated and then the immediate remorse made her feel even worse. She was supposed to be excited that her boyfriend wanted to have sex, but the idea now seemed almost repulsive. Even if nothing ever happened with Paige, she couldn't stay with Jake. Not after tonight. Not after she realized that it wasn't just a crush she had on Paige. It was full-blown feelings. And she didn't want to, and obviously couldn't, ignore them anymore.

What a weird and scary realization to have on her birthday—she clearly no longer had feelings for Jake. She had feelings for his sister instead.

CHAPTER TWENTY-TWO

Paige closed her bedroom door and leaned back against it, sliding down until she was sitting on the floor with her knees up to her chest. She tugged out her hair tie and threw it across the room. Hot tears cascaded down her cheeks. Running her hands through her hair, she gripped it hard. Maybe the pain of almost ripping out her hair would overshadow her incredible emotional pain. How could she almost kiss Zoe? What had she been thinking?

But if she was honest with herself, she hadn't been thinking at all. At least not with her head. Paige felt absolutely sick to her stomach. She was almost the cause of Zoe cheating on her brother. But did Zoe have feelings for her? Or was Paige just there at the right place and right time? She shook her head at the thought. It couldn't be that. She'd seen the look in Zoe's eyes. The want. The desire. Paige covered her mouth with her hand as she stifled a sob.

When she heard footsteps coming down the hall, she hurried into bed. She'd seen the look on Zoe's face in the living room.

She wanted to talk. She wanted answers. But Paige couldn't give them. Definitely not tonight. She hadn't even bothered turning on the light so hopefully Zoe would see the room was dark and she wouldn't bother Paige.

She held her breath for what felt like minutes as she listened to the silence. When nothing happened, she let out a breath. But just then another set of footsteps started down the hall and stopped in front of her door.

"Paige?" Zoe quietly called through the door. "Are you awake?" A beat of silence. "Please talk to me."

Paige closed her eyes tightly and gripped the covers over her head. "Please go away. Please go away," she whispered. God, she couldn't do this. She couldn't risk anything happening between her and Zoe. And she couldn't let Zoe see her losing it like she was.

Then she'd for sure know that Paige was in love with her.

Paige's breath caught in her throat at that thought. She didn't know when it had happened, but it was true. She was in love with Zoe. And she couldn't do a fucking thing about it. Only thing she could do now was leave. It was no longer right to stay here. Not for even one night longer.

Paige heard Zoe's footsteps go farther down the hall and the muted thud of her bedroom door closing. She pulled the covers down and let herself take a few deep breaths. Sitting up, she started to think of her plan. First, she would wait ten minutes to make sure Zoe or Jake weren't coming out of their room again and then she would start packing her stuff. Not everything. She couldn't move it all without making a lot of noise. But she'd pack the essentials—her clothes and everything in the bathroom.

As she waited for the time to pass, she grabbed her phone and pulled up her text thread with Tom.

You awake?

She leaned her head back against the wall as she waited for a reply. It would probably be a long shot that he'd be awake at almost eleven at night. After a few minutes without an answer, she knew she wasn't getting one. Then she sent the same text to Vanessa but again got no reply.

Fuck, she thought. Where would she go now? She checked her phone again just to make sure she hadn't missed a text. She also realized her self-imposed ten-minute wait was over. Throwing back the covers, Paige got out of bed and quietly opened her closet door. She pulled her duffel bag out and filled it with clothes from her dresser. She grabbed work shirts out of the closet and tossed those on top.

Work. That was it. She could crash at Craft for the night. There was a couch in the staff room. It would be pretty unprofessional but it beat sleeping in her car. Or staying here for that matter. When Rebecca had assigned Paige as the primary opener a couple of days a week, she'd given Paige a key. Coming to sleep there in the middle of the night probably wasn't what Rebecca had in mind, but Paige would have to deal with that tomorrow.

She changed into jeans and a hoodie. She tossed the dress onto the closet floor as she wouldn't be wearing it anytime soon. Or maybe ever again. It would forever remind her of this night. And that couldn't happen. She needed to start forgetting and move on.

As quietly as she could, she slung the bag over her shoulder and opened her bedroom door. She had never been more thankful for carpet as it muted her careful footsteps. Paige grabbed her toiletries from the bathroom and stuffed them into her backpack.

Passing by the kitchen, Paige stopped. She didn't just want to leave without any word. She turned on the light above the sink and found a small notepad on the counter. She hurriedly scribbled out a quick note to Jake. Closing her eyes as another wave of nausea hit, she almost added Zoe's name to it too but she couldn't bring herself to. Jake could tell her she left. He was her boyfriend after all.

With a flick of the switch, Paige turned off the light and the apartment was in darkness once again. She made her way out the door and shut it quietly behind her. Instead of waiting for the elevator, she slung her bags over her shoulder and hurried down the stairs to her car.

The drive was quick and she arrived at Craft within a few minutes, parking in the back. She unlocked the back door and put in the security code. Paige didn't turn on a light until she walked into the staff room. Squinting at the bright fluorescent lights, she dropped her bags on the floor next to the couch and then she sat down heavily, holding her head in her hands.

When she had started at Craft, she'd been surprised at all the nice touches in the staff room. Of course there was the couch where Rebecca had encouraged folks to nap on their breaks if they were tired. There was also a desk with a computer monitor and laptop dock as well as a table and four chairs. Paige had asked about it all during her first week and Rebecca had told her that since she hired a lot of college and graduate students, she wanted a place where they felt they could study or even chill on breaks or before and after shifts. It was true that Rebecca had treated her staff like family.

Paige set the alarm on her phone and grabbed a blanket from the closet before shutting off the light. She kicked off her shoes and lay on the surprisingly soft and comfy couch, covering herself with the blanket. She was unlikely to sleep tonight. She'd be lucky if she got a few hours before her alarm.

As she curled onto her side, she wondered how things had gotten so messed up. How she had let things get so far that Zoe had almost cheated on Jake. Paige also had no idea where she'd found the strength to stop Zoe. Because she'd wanted to kiss her so badly. She'd been dreaming about it for weeks. But there'd been the smallest whisper in the back of her mind. *Zoe is your brother's girlfriend. She's taken.*

Paige had repeatedly told herself that since she started having feelings for Zoe and it had been the only thing stopping her from making a move. She had come to Indy to reconnect with Jake and she almost betrayed him. Hell, she felt like she had already by developing feelings for Zoe in the first place. She wondered if she should just leave the city. If she messed things up with Jake, there wouldn't be any reason for her to stay. While she loved working at Craft, she could find a similar job somewhere else and maybe figure out her next step.

So many scenarios raced through her mind. She could stick around and continue building her relationship with Jake. She'd just have to make sure to avoid Zoe at all costs. Of course, that would be hard since she was Jake's girlfriend. But she'd just have to try and hang out with only Jake, at least until Paige's feelings for Zoe went away. Not that she thought that would be happening any time soon. But what if Jake found out about the almost kiss? She imagined he'd be fucking pissed at her. Then this whole getting to know him again would've been for nothing. She couldn't see him wanting her to be around him and Zoe if he couldn't trust her.

Closing her eyes, she tried to clear her mind by taking a few deep breaths. Paige needed rest and she hoped her sleep would be uninterrupted by dreams of Zoe or nightmares of ruining things with Jake. Fat chance, she thought.

CHAPTER TWENTY-THREE

When Jake's alarm went off the next morning, Zoe had to stop herself from groaning. Instead, she lay there as still as she could, trying to keep her breathing even as if she was actually sleeping. She didn't want to let Jake know she was awake. She couldn't talk to him. Not after last night. Not after almost kissing Paige.

Zoe didn't even know if Jake would talk to her this morning. When she'd walked into the bedroom the night before, Jake had still been in the shower. As she was brushing her teeth, he had pushed back the shower curtain and told her she should join him. Again, she had used the excuse of being tired and he had huffily closed the shower curtain.

He'd tried to initiate sex again once they both were in bed, but Zoe had turned away from him and mumbled, "Not tonight."

Zoe knew she'd upset him but frankly she didn't care. Just because he was waiting for her at home with a fucking cupcake didn't mean she owed him sex. What she cared about was Paige in the next room. What was she thinking about? Did she hate Zoe? Did she think Zoe was the biggest asshole in the world? If Zoe wasn't with Jake, would Paige have kissed her? That was the question that kept her awake most of the night. She went over the scene in the elevator again and again. The way Paige had whispered her name. The way Paige had rested her hand on Zoe's abdomen. The way that Zoe had almost said "fuck it" to a three-year relationship. There was no denying now that she had feelings for Paige. And they were stronger feelings than she had realized.

Once Jake had dressed and left the bedroom, Zoe had waited a few minutes in hopes that he would have gone by the time she went into the kitchen. She threw back the covers and padded down the hallway, arms crossed over her chest. She stopped when she saw Jake standing at the counter, a piece of paper in his hand.

"What's that?" she asked.

Jake turned, giving her an indifferent glance. "Note from Paige."

Zoe's stomach dropped and she braced herself on the wall. "What's it say?" she choked out.

Jake shrugged as if it was no big deal. "She found a place of her own. She said she'll get her stuff later this week."

This is my fault, Zoe thought. She had made Paige leave and she'd made her so uncomfortable that she left in the middle of the night. Zoe felt like complete and utter shit. She was so stupid and selfish. Paige had come here to reconnect with Jake but what if she'd just ruined that? "Did she say where she moved?"

"No," Jake said, tossing the note to the counter. "That fucking sucks. I liked having her around." Jake looked at his watch before grabbing a protein bar out of the cabinet. He turned to leave, but changed his mind and hesitantly kissed Zoe on her cheek. "See you tonight."

"Y-yeah," Zoe said.

After Jake shut the front door, Zoe quickly sat on a stool and grabbed the note and read it.

Jake,
*   Three's a crowd here so I found an apartment of my own. Sorry to*
leave without saying anything. Had to get the keys before work. Once
I get moved in, I'll have you over to watch a game or something. I'll
probably grab the rest of my stuff later this week. I'll let you know.
*   Paige*

Tears filled Zoe's eyes as she realized that Paige wasn't coming back, not to stay at least. Would she even try to see Zoe again? Or would she make it a point to only hang out with Jake? Zoe was kicking herself for almost kissing Paige. For doing something that made Paige leave without giving them a heads-up or really even saying goodbye.

Zoe didn't know what to do. She still wanted to talk to Paige. Let her know that she didn't mean to put her in that position and that she didn't have to leave. She needed to know that she was safe.

Zoe hurried to the bedroom and grabbed her phone off her nightstand. She pulled up her text thread with Paige and sat on the bed. But she didn't know what to say to make it all better. To make Paige come back. Before she could second-guess anything she just started typing.

I'm sorry.
You didn't need to leave.
Are you okay?

Zoe sat on her bed staring at the phone. Every passing second felt like a minute. And every minute felt like an hour. Each time the screen went to sleep, she unlocked her phone and checked the thread again. Maybe she had missed one come in. But there was nothing. Ten minutes had passed without a word from Paige. At this time in the morning, Paige was probably already swamped with customers and Zoe tried to tell herself that that was the only reason why she hadn't heard anything. But her stomach sank as time continued to pass. Her gut feeling was that she wasn't going to hear. That she had fucked things up so royally that Paige would never reply.

Closing her eyes, Zoe took a deep breath to dispel her nausea. But another thought slammed into her and she quickly opened her eyes—Jake. She had almost cheated on Jake. Hell, she should probably consider she might have already, given she'd let herself develop feelings for Paige. She needed to do something about that. It was clear that neither of them was happy in their relationship. Although that wasn't an excuse for her actions. But she needed to make a plan.

Maybe with Paige out of the apartment they could have more time to themselves and work on getting their relationship back to the way it used to be. But that thought didn't make her happy. It made her almost dread it. And that should be the sign that things should probably end with Jake and soon.

She snuck a glance at her phone but there was nothing. But what Zoe did see was that she was going to be late for work if she didn't leave soon. After a quick shower and some fresh clothes, Zoe was out the door. Maybe work would provide some distraction from all the uncertainty surrounding her at the moment.

CHAPTER TWENTY-FOUR

Bright light brought Paige out of a fitful sleep. She was facing the back of the couch and rolled over to see why the lights were on. She hadn't fallen asleep with them on last night, right? When she turned and was able to open her eyes a bit more, she found Rebecca standing in the doorway with her arms across her chest. *Oh shit.*

Paige opened her mouth and tried to speak but what could she say in this situation? She had hoped to be up and have her stuff put away by the time Rebecca got in. Paige was scheduled to be the opener for the day which usually meant Rebecca didn't get in until seven or so. Why did she have to come in early today of all days?

Paige stood quickly, tossing the blanket onto the couch. "Rebecca. Um…hi. I was just…"

"Sleeping on the couch in the break room?" Rebecca asked, her eyebrows lifted.

"Um, yeah, I guess." Paige looked helplessly between the couch and Rebecca.

"What are you doing here, Paige? Did you sleep here last night?"

Paige opened her mouth and quickly closed it. *What answer won't get me fired?* Fuck, she couldn't take losing her job right now. Then she would have nothing. She'd already lost a place to stay because she couldn't control her feelings. If Jake found out about what had almost happened last night, she'd most likely lose him too. She fought against the sting of tears.

Rebecca grabbed a chair and set it next to the couch and sat down. "Hey," she said calmly. "I can see the panic on your face. Just have a seat, Paige. Talk to me. Why did you sleep here last night? Because it's obvious that you did." Rebecca gestured to the blanket on the couch and Paige's bags on the floor.

Paige dropped onto the couch, resting her hands in her lap. "I just...I couldn't stay where I was."

Rebecca straightened in her seat, her eyes narrowed and there was a deep crease between her eyebrows. "Why? Did something happen to you? Did you need to get away for your own safety?"

Paige lifted her hands and waved her off. "Oh, no. Nothing like that. I..." She wavered on whether to say anything. This was her boss. And while Rebecca was friendly and she did treat her employees like they were family, Paige found it difficult to tell her anything that might make her see Paige in a negative light. But what other option did she have? This was Rebecca's shop and if she thought she couldn't trust Paige, then she could easily fire her. "It's kind of a long story."

Rebecca checked her watch. "I have plenty of time. I came in early to do some paperwork but that can wait until later. You can tell me whatever you need to."

The concern in Rebecca's eyes made the decision for Paige and she decided to lay it all out there. And she didn't leave out a single detail, including how she and Zoe had almost kissed last night. "So there it is. I obviously can't control how I feel about her and I almost crossed an uncrossable line. I felt like I needed to remove myself from the situation. So here I am," Paige said, gesturing to the couch. The next words came out in a rush. "I'm sorry, Rebecca. I know this is totally unprofessional of me. I just didn't know where to go. I...I was desperate."

"You're right," Rebecca replied with a nod. "It was pretty unprofessional."

Paige stared at her hands. "I know," she murmured. "If you need to fire me, I get it."

Rebecca held up one hand. "Now don't go falling on your sword just yet. I like you, Paige. You're a hard worker and a valuable member of the team. And I don't know if you know this, but I not only own the business, I also own the building. That includes the apartment above the shop."

Paige's head shot up. There was an apartment? Paige knew something was up there, but she never thought about what the space was used for. "An apartment?" Paige asked hopefully.

"Yep. And you're in luck. My renters just moved out on the first and my wife and I haven't found our next tenant just yet. It's yours if you want it."

For what felt like the tenth time, Paige couldn't form any words. Rebecca's kindness brought tears to her eyes and she wasn't ashamed when one fell down her cheek. Rebecca didn't even seem to hesitate in offering the apartment to Paige. She couldn't believe it and it felt as if a weight had been lifted from her chest. If this could work out, then that would be one less worry. But her excitement was short-lived when reality crashed down. Would she even be able to afford it? The apartment could be huge and bring in loads of money for Rebecca and her wife, which meant that would be an apartment that Paige could never afford.

Paige swallowed audibly and asked, "How much is rent?"

Rebecca held Paige's gaze as if sizing Paige up. "Can you do eight hundred?"

Paige released a quick breath. That was all? The apartment she was on the waitlist for was twelve hundred and that was only a studio. Was that all Rebecca charged her last renters? Or did she lower the price because she felt sorry for Paige? Not that Paige was going to turn it down for that reason. It was an added bonus that it was cheaper. "I'll take it."

Rebecca smiled. "Did you want to see it first?"

"No. Honestly it could be as big as this room and I'd be fine with it."

"Well, okay then," Rebecca replied with a chuckle. "We just finished all the fixes and the cleaning last week so it's all good to go. You can move in today if you're ready?"

Paige nodded quickly. "Yes, please."

Rebecca slapped her thighs and stood. "Perfect. How about I take you up there and show you around on your break?"

Paige smiled and let out a long, slow breath. "That'd be great."

"All right. I know these lockers aren't big so you can put your bags in my office so they're out of the way. And then it's time to get to work. You are opening after all."

"Will do." Paige stood, folding the blanket and setting it on the back of the couch. Before Rebecca could leave the room, Paige called out, "Rebecca?"

Rebecca turned, her eyebrows lifted in question. "Yeah?"

"Thank you."

Paige hoped those two simple words conveyed her immense gratitude. She had gone to sleep with her world crumbling around her. But now there was a sliver of hope that things would be okay. The thought of leaving the city completely had crossed her mind more than once since last night. Now she didn't think she'd have to. Unless Jake found out about last night and told her that he never wanted to see her again. Then there'd be no point in staying.

"You're welcome," Rebecca said with a soft smile.

Paige took a deep breath and grabbed her bags, following Rebecca into her office and setting them behind her desk. As she started going through the opening checklist, she shifted her focus from the uncertainty of her life to the routine of work. It would be nice to lose herself to the tasks of greeting customers and filling their orders. Paige felt like it would return some control over her life.

When Tom started work in the early afternoon, Paige was ready for someone to talk to. She was on friendly terms with her morning's coworkers, but Tom was the only one she'd grown close to. He walked behind the counter, tying his apron around his waist, and gave her a wide smile.

"Hey there. How's the day going so far?"

"Work, great. Life…" She held out her hand and wiggled it back and forth. "Not the greatest."

"Oh, no. Tell me everything." An older man walked up to the counter and Tom held up one hand. "Hold that thought." He quickly filled the man's order and then turned back to Paige with his hands on his hips. "Tell me everything."

"So, last night was Zoe's birthday."

"Okay, happy birthday to her. What happened?"

"She almost kissed me. Or I almost kissed her." Paige shook her head and looked to the floor. "We almost kissed each other."

"Shut the fuck up!" Tom said, his mouth hanging open. "Now you really need to tell me everything. And I mean it. Every last detail."

Paige took a deep breath and told the story, starting with how heartbroken Zoe looked when Jake bailed on dinner to how tempting it had been to just lean in those last few inches to kiss her, and she wrapped it up with Rebecca finding her sleeping in the break room and offering to rent her the apartment upstairs. Of course, the entire story had been broken up by fulfilling several coffee orders.

Once Tom handed off a latte and a muffin to a young guy in ripped jeans and a hoodie, he turned to Paige and whistled. "You sure know how to cause some drama."

"Me? It's not my fault. She's the one who stood close to me in the elevator."

He gave her a pointed look. "You're the one that initiated contact."

As she opened her mouth to defend herself, her bravado deflated when she admitted he was telling the truth. "I know," she mumbled. "But it was like my entire body was buzzing with the need to touch her. To feel her warmth. To just be closer to her." Paige shook her head. "She was so beautiful last night, man. Like can't-breathe beautiful. And she's so smart and funny and it just feels so natural to be around her."

"And she has a boyfriend," Tom said.

"I know that," Paige ground out. That wasn't something she could forget. Okay, she almost forgot for a moment last night in the elevator but she was able to come to her senses in time.

"Have you talked to her?" Tom asked.

Paige shook her head. "No. She texted me this morning. Probably when she realized I was gone. But I didn't know what to reply. She seemed kinda worried though."

"Maybe you should tell her you're okay."

"I don't know if talking to her is a good idea," Paige said.

"You just need to send one text."

"Nah. I think a clean break is good. I texted Jake earlier, let him know everything was okay and that I got the apartment. He can tell her."

"Okay. That's your call. How are you feeling about things now?" Tom asked.

"Still feel like an asshole. I can't believe I let myself get that close to her." Paige shrugged and wiped at a drop of milk on the counter. "But now that I'll have some distance, maybe I can work on getting over her. Eventually at least," she said with a humorless chuckle.

"Good luck with that," Tom murmured.

Yeah, Paige didn't even really believe it herself. She'd fallen hard and fast for Zoe. It wasn't like she could get over her with a snap of her fingers. If it had been that easy, she would've already done it. Now that she wouldn't be spending every waking hour she wasn't at work with Zoe, Paige could focus on herself and on her relationship with Jake. It was why she'd moved here after all.

"What time do you start work tomorrow?" Paige asked.

"Three. Why?" Tom called over his shoulder as he filled another order.

"Do you have any plans in the morning?"

"No," he replied, drawing the word out and looking at her suspiciously.

Paige gave him her most innocent smile. "Any chance you'd help me get the rest of my stuff out of Jake's apartment and move it upstairs?" She batted her eyelashes at him.

"Do you think that's going to work on me?"

"I don't know. Did it?" she asked.

Tom pursed his lips. "Of course, it did. Yes, I will help you."

"Yay," she said, wrapping him in a quick hug. "Thank you."

"Yeah, yeah. What do I get out of it?" Tom put his hands on his hips and gave her an expectant look.

"My undying love?" Paige asked.

Tom scoffed. "That's it?"

"My undying love and a six-pack of your favorite beer?"

Tom scratched at his chin as if wondering if it was a good trade. He broke into a smile and winked. "Deal."

Paige exaggeratedly wiped the imaginary sweat from her forehead. "Phew. I promise it's not a lot. I just want to get in and out as fast I can, you know?"

"I get it."

"Rebecca said I can take a couple hours off after the morning rush. Meet me here at ten?"

"That works. I'll borrow Steve's truck."

"Any chance you guys have any boxes or plastic bins?" Paige again gave him an innocent smile.

"Anything else, Miss Needy?"

"Hey, I recycled all the boxes I used to bring my stuff here. I didn't think I'd need them for a while," she muttered.

"Yes, we have some. I'll bring them with."

"Thanks," she replied.

Now Paige had one less concern. Then once she was fully moved out of Jake's place, she could work on repairing her heart. That was going to be a much bigger task.

CHAPTER TWENTY-FIVE

Zoe was counting down the final minutes of her workday and she couldn't wait to get out of the office. She had been in knots all day and lost track of how many times she checked her phone in hopes that Paige had texted back. But she hadn't. Zoe at least knew she was okay because Jake had texted her around lunch that Paige would get her stuff sometime this week.

Zoe hoped it would be one night after work where Jake worked late so they could at least talk. She wanted to apologize for making things so uncomfortable and how she didn't mean to put Paige in such a position. Zoe also hoped that she hadn't completely ruined their friendship. Not that Zoe was sure there even had been a friendship. Maybe Paige had just been hanging out with her because she felt sorry for her. Paige had come to Indy to get to know Jake, not Zoe. If Paige had thought spending time with Zoe would help her relationship with Jake, maybe that was all it was. Something to make sure that Paige would have Jake around as her brother again.

Those negative thoughts occupied Zoe's mind all day. But one other positive thought had tried to push its way through—

in the elevator, Paige had started to lean in too. Zoe had seen the want in her eyes. But maybe it had all been wishful thinking and Zoe had only seen what her heart wanted to see.

As soon as the clock on her desktop hit five, Zoe shut down her computer and hurried out of the office. No one had intercepted her to do one last thing and she breathed a sigh of relief as she stepped onto the sidewalk. She drove over to Mia's apartment, desperate to talk to her and tell her everything. She needed guidance or perspective or someone to tell her what a big jerk she'd been. Zoe knew she deserved that last option.

After Zoe's three quick knocks, Mia opened the door, concern etched on her face. "Zoe? What are you doing here? Is something wrong?"

Zoe slid past her without waiting for an invitation. Not that she really needed one. She paced the small living room as Mia closed the front door, standing just inside with her hands by her sides.

"I almost kissed Paige. Now she's moved out and I don't know where she is. And I think I need to break up with Jake."

Mia looked at her with wide eyes. "Okay," she said, dragging the word out. "How about you start from the beginning? I'll grab the wine. And maybe sit?" Mia gestured to her couch.

Zoe nodded. "Sure. Right. Sitting is good."

A minute later, Mia came back into the living room with two glasses of red wine. Zoe took her glass and took a generous gulp.

Mia gave her a placating look. "How about we take our time with that?" she said, gently taking the glass out of Zoe's hand and placing it on the coffee table.

"Sorry. I just didn't really sleep last night and have felt on edge all day," Zoe said.

"Then maybe you should take it easy with the drinking. I'll order us a pizza." Mia pulled out her phone. "Now, tell me what happened."

"I already told you. I almost kissed Paige and now she's gone and I don't know where she is. And I need to break up with Jake."

"Yes. You did tell me all that. But you left out quite a few details. I kinda need to know those to know the whole story."

Zoe shook her head and smiled apologetically. "Right. Sorry." She took a deep breath and tried to start at the beginning, but the only words she found were "I fucked everything up."

"Just tell me, Zo," Mia said softly.

"So Jake bailed again…" She told her how Paige wouldn't let her mope and took her out instead. How amazing the dinner was and how she hadn't thought about Jake all night. How beautiful Paige looked in that gorgeous green dress. How all night, Paige had made her feel important and wanted and like she mattered.

When she got to the part where she almost kissed Paige in the elevator, Mia interrupted her. "Zoe."

Mia was obviously disappointed. Zoe felt like she was crawling out of her skin and she stood to pace the room again. "I know! Okay? I know. I'm a huge asshole and almost cheated on Jake. Fuck! Some people probably think I *did* cheat just because I thought about kissing her. I know I'm a horrible human being. You don't have to fucking remind me." Zoe held the back of her hand to her mouth as she tried to stop a sob from escaping but it didn't help and before she knew it, she was full-on bawling.

Mia stood and pulled her in for a tight hug. "Oh, honey." She held Zoe's head to her shoulder and stroked her hair as Zoe's shoulders shook with her cries. "Shh. It's okay. I wasn't judging."

"Yeah, you were," Zoe mumbled into her neck.

"Okay, maybe a little."

Zoe chuckled quietly and gripped Mia even tighter. "What have I done, Mia? What am I going to do?"

"What do you want to do?" Mia asked, pulling Zoe away and wiping a tear with the back of her finger.

Zoe groaned. "Stop answering a question with a question. Just tell me what to do."

"Not how this works, Zo."

"Well, it should be," Zoe grumbled, resuming her seat on the couch. She sighed. "I know I need to break up with Jake. I think I've known that for a while."

"What about Paige?" Mia asked quietly.

"You were right," Zoe answered, her voice hoarse. "I definitely have feelings for her. Pretty strong ones. Am I allowed to blame you for putting the idea in my head?"

"Not at all," Mia replied with a pointed look.

"Damn."

Mia reached for her wine and took a sip. "What are you going to do about it?"

Zoe shrugged. "I don't know. I need to talk to her. Even just to talk about last night. But I don't even know if she feels the same way."

"I would be pretty surprised if she didn't."

"You think?" Zoe asked, hope tinging her voice.

"She never would have let you get as close as you did."

"Yeah, maybe," Zoe replied, nodding as she stared at the floor. Any thought of Paige feeling the same way brought a warmth and lightness to Zoe that she hadn't felt since the elevator. But that thought was washed away as reality set in. "Why did she have to be Jake's sister? Even if she has feelings for me, I don't know if she'll let herself do anything about it. Jake is what brought her here. I don't think she'd give up the chance to have him in her life again. Not for me at least," she mumbled. Zoe didn't think anything about her was good enough to risk a relationship with family.

"You don't know that. You are one amazing person. And I think you would be worth the risk to have you in her life."

"You have to say that. You're my best friend," Zoe mumbled.

"Yep. But I still think it's true," Mia said with a wink.

Zoe laughed as her distress eased a little. "Thanks."

As a knock sounded at the door, Mia stood and said over her shoulder, "Anytime." She took the pizza and set it on the coffee table. "Time to eat."

"I really don't know if I can," Zoe said, holding her hand to her stomach.

"You can and you will. And while you do that, we'll watch some mindless TV. Not bothering with plates, Mia handed Zoe a napkin and slice of cheese pizza. Once she grabbed a slice of her own, she closed the box and slid it to the middle of the table. She turned on *Below Deck* and sat back on the couch.

As the show played, Zoe took a small bite of her pizza, telling herself that food was important and she needed to eat. When she thought it wouldn't come back up, she took another bite and then another. Next thing she knew, she'd eaten two more pieces and was now sitting comfortably full next to Mia.

They didn't say much for the rest of the evening, watching another episode before Zoe got up to leave. The night had been exactly what she needed. Mia was always there for her with an ear for listening and a sounding board for her thoughts. But Mia seemed to know that sitting in silence with Zoe was just another way to support her. Zoe didn't always need to talk with someone when she was with them—sometimes the closeness was enough.

Once home, Zoe found the light on over the sink, which meant that Jake had left it on for her before going to bed. She turned it off and made her way into the bedroom, moving quickly to brush her teeth and change into pajamas. She slid under the covers and put her glasses onto the nightstand.

Jake was on his side, facing away from her. Zoe hoped this wouldn't be one of those nights where he turned over and tried to cuddle. She lay as still as she could so she wouldn't wake him up. Once she was satisfied he was staying where he was, she rolled away from him and gripped the sheets to her chin.

She knew that breaking up with him was the right thing to do. Let both of them be free from a relationship that clearly wasn't working anymore. But Zoe hated any kind of tough conversation and breaking up with a boyfriend of three years definitely counted as tough. It also didn't help that she still loved Jake for being such a great guy. She just wasn't *in* love with him anymore.

As she closed her eyes for what she assumed would be another shitty night's sleep, she hoped she'd find the courage to end it. Then maybe she'd have a clearer conscience when she could finally talk to Paige. If she'd ever talk to Zoe again.

CHAPTER TWENTY-SIX

Waking up in her new apartment had been a bit surreal for Paige. It probably didn't help that she'd had to sleep on an air mattress, which she panic-bought at seven last night once she'd gotten off work and realized that the apartment was unfurnished. *Way to go, brain.*

Even though Rebecca had shown her the apartment earlier in the day and there clearly hadn't been any furniture, it didn't register that she'd need to find some. She'd be able to take her time acquiring most things, but a bed was her top priority. Getting an actual mattress would be her first big purchase with her next paycheck. Then it would be a gradual process of getting other pieces of furniture which she was certain her bank account would appreciate.

She ate a granola bar as she walked around her apartment in awe. This would be the first place where she'd lived alone which was simultaneously exciting and scary. The apartment was small but she didn't need a lot of space. The kitchen and living room were open with a breakfast bar separating the spaces. Colors and styles ran through her head as she thought about how she wanted to decorate. Biggest bonus of the move was that it would help distract her, something which she was definitely going to need if last night's dreams told her anything.

She'd woken up at least three times, each time because she'd had a dream or a perhaps a nightmare, about Zoe. In two, she'd closed the distance between them in the elevator that night and kissed her. The first of those dreams ended happily and she'd woken up with her hand down the front of her sweats. The other was a completely different story. In the second, Jake had caught them and he'd kicked them both out of the apartment, saying he never wanted to see either of them again. She definitely preferred the happy ending over the other.

Paige started a list on her phone of the bare essentials she'd need to get after work, making sure to include Tom's beer. Since she hadn't needed to put down any deposit with Rebecca, she had money for groceries and kitchen necessities so she could cook for herself.

The morning at work flew by with an unending stream of customers from moment they opened. It helped keep Paige distracted and she didn't look at her watch once. It wasn't until she saw Tom come in through the front door that her anxiety flared. What if Zoe or Jake were at the apartment when she got there? Neither of them should be since it was a Thursday and they'd both be at work. But still, Paige was nervous she'd run into one of them when all she wanted to do was get in and get out with her stuff as quickly as possible.

"You ready?" Tom asked as he stood in front of the counter with his hands in the pockets of his jeans.

"Yep. Let me get my sweatshirt." Paige went back to her locker and exchanged her apron for her zip-up hoodie. She grabbed her empty duffel bag. Paige met Tom back up front and they walked to his boyfriend's truck. "You'll have to thank Steve for me. Once I get my place all set up, I'll have you guys over for dinner or something."

"Sounds like a plan."

When they got to the apartment building, they each took two of Tom's plastic bins and got in the elevator.

"Ah. So this is where it all went down huh?" Tom asked as he lifted his eyebrows.

"Yes," Paige mumbled. "I'd rather not think about that right now if that's okay with you."

Tom raised his hands. "Got it. I won't say another word about the almost lady-loving that went down right here."

Paige nudged him as she exited the elevator. "Shut up." Tom laughed. At the door of Jake's apartment, she stared at it, willing herself to go in.

"You can't get your stuff unless you unlock it," Tom quietly said from over her shoulder.

"I know." Paige took a deep breath, set the bins on the floor, and turned the key.

Tom followed Paige inside and looked around. "Nice place," he murmured.

"Yeah. Um, the guest room is down this way." She led him to the bedroom and turned on the light. Nothing had changed. Not that she really expected it to. It wasn't like Jake and Zoe were going to find a new roommate in two days. And they probably wouldn't get a roommate again anyway.

Paige pointed out to Tom everything that needed to be packed away and left him to it while she went across the hall into the bathroom. As she emptied the drawers and shower of her things, she breathed a sigh of relief that Jake and Zoe hadn't been home. Even though she longed to see Zoe again, she wasn't sure she was ready to face her just yet. She needed to get some perspective and distance.

She took her bin into the living room and looked around for anything that was hers. There was the purple blanket still laid across the back of the couch. The same blanket where she and Zoe had started *Ted Lasso* and Zoe had held her hand. As she tossed the blanket into the bin, she closed her eyes at the memory. Next she grabbed her books off the shelves and set those on top of the blanket. The last thing she saw was her running hydration vest hanging on the back of a stool. She smiled sadly as she picked it up, thinking about all the times Zoe had given her crap for running in the cold. *Maybe I would've gotten her to run with me this spring,* she pondered. She sighed at the realization that that wouldn't be happening at all, tossing the vest into the bin.

The picture frame on the table next to the couch caught her eye—Zoe and Jake on their anniversary trip to Chicago. The picture Paige had held in her hands on her first night here. She reached for it again now and stared at it. Well, she stared at Zoe. With one arm wrapped around Jake's waist and her other hand resting on his belly, she looked so happy. Her smile was wide and her eyes held an excited glint. Tears filled Paige's eyes as she took in the scene. Zoe was with Jake. Not Paige. It would never be Paige.

"I think I got it all."

Paige jumped at the sound of Tom's voice and turned toward him. Paige gently set the photo back on the table and let out a slow breath. "Thanks. Let me just go take one last look around. But I think we've got everything."

She went back into her old room and leaned against the doorframe, trying to stop the tears burning her eyes. She didn't want to cry right now. That could be for when she was home alone at her new place.

Alone. No more nights of having someone with whom to cook dinner. No more random nights out to play mini golf. No more trivia nights. No more bingeing TV with commentary about how cute the actresses were. Paige's evenings were going to be drastically different than they had been over the last months and she felt the pain of what she'd be missing.

Seeing Tom had everything out of the room, Paige took one last look in the closet. She started to slide the door closed when something on the floor caught her eye. She bent down to pick it up—the green dress she wore for Zoe's birthday. Now she couldn't stop her tears. She held her hand to her chest as she took a deep breath and then another, hoping to calm herself before she turned into a full-on sobbing mess. Once certain the tears were under control, she shut off the light and went back into the living room.

"That's Zoe and Jake?" Tom asked, pointing to the framed photo.

"Yeah," Paige murmured, shoving the dress into the closest bin.

"She's pretty."

"Yeah," Paige rasped, her bottom lip quivering. Tom had no idea how pretty. That picture didn't do her justice at all. Paige cleared her throat and turned away, trying to wipe at the tears before they could fall down her cheeks again. "I should leave my key." She reached into her jeans pocket for her set of keys and was about to take off her key to the apartment when she realized she couldn't. "Crap. I can't leave it. I won't have any way of locking the door after we leave."

"Ah. Right. Could be an excuse to see Zoe?"

"That's the last thing I need," Paige mumbled. "I'll text Jake and let him know. I can meet up with him to give it back." She sent Jake a quick text and shoved her phone in her back pocket. "Let's go."

They each took their two bins and set them on the floor outside the apartment as Paige locked the door behind them. She stared at the door for a moment. It wasn't like she wouldn't see the place again. Hopefully she'd still be able to work on her relationship with Jake. She'd just have to try to see him when Zoe wasn't home.

With a sigh, she stepped into the elevator. She'd have Tom drop them off so she could get back to work. She'd worry about unpacking later.

Work. Unpacking. Both just the things she needed to distract herself from the void of leaving Zoe's apartment.

CHAPTER TWENTY-SEVEN

After another long day at work, Zoe unlocked the apartment door. She'd been trying to build up the strength for what she was about to do. Breaking up with Jake wasn't going to be easy. She still loved him, but she just wasn't *in* love with him anymore. And the more she thought about it, the more she couldn't really contribute the impending breakup to Paige. Ever since they had moved to Indy, Zoe realized that their relationship was slowly coming to an end. They just seemed to want different things right now and that was totally okay. But it wasn't fair to either of them to stay in the relationship and there was no point in waiting until the time was right to break up with him. Would it ever be more right than now? She couldn't string him along hoping things would get better when she knew deep down that they never would.

Zoe's eyes were immediately drawn to the couch and the spot on the back where Paige's purple blanket was now missing. Her chest tightened at what that probably meant—she must've come to get the rest of her things. Needing to be sure, she rushed into Paige's room, opening the dresser drawers and sliding open the closet doors. Everything was gone. She walked across the hall and pushed back the shower curtain. No more shampoo, no body wash, no razor.

Zoe forcibly swallowed at the realization that Paige had completely moved out. It wasn't like this was never going to happen. Paige had told them she'd found a place. It was inevitable that she would come get the rest of her things. But Zoe didn't expect such a sick feeling to wash over her as she saw all the empty space where Paige's things used to be. Plus, Zoe would be moving out soon too, probably as early as tonight if she sucked it up and talked to Jake as soon as he got home. Mia had offered Zoe her couch to crash on for as long as she needed.

Might as well start packing some of my things too. Zoe saw it was only six so she figured she'd have at least an hour or so until Jake got home. That meant she'd have enough time to pack a bag of essentials. She knew she wouldn't be able to take everything with her tonight. But most things in the apartment were Jake's. They'd bought their bed and some kitchen items together, but the rest had pretty much come from his last apartment in college or gifts from his parents. So really Zoe just had to make sure to get all of her clothes, bathroom items, and some books and movies. Everything else in the apartment would be staying.

Once Zoe had filled her only suitcase and a small duffel bag, she set them in the living room by the front door and then sat on the couch and waited. Her stomach was in knots and her palms were sweaty. She had never been the one to initiate a breakup. Her partners had done it or things had just fizzled out and they kind of ghosted each other. She really didn't want to hurt Jake, no matter how much he'd hurt her over the past few months.

When a key in the lock drew her attention from her own thoughts, her mouth went dry and her heart started racing. Jake walked in the door and gave her a tight-lipped smile. "Hey," he said. Closing the door, he looked down at the bags. "These Paige's things?"

Zoe swallowed, trying to find her voice. It took her two attempts and a clearing of her throat to hoarsely say, "No. They're mine."

A deep crease formed between Jake's eyebrows as they drew together. He loosened his tie and sat on the opposite end of the couch. "What do you mean?"

His eyes seemed as if he might be relieved but his tone was filled with worry and it made Zoe almost lose her resolve. But no, she had to do this. She needed to put herself first for once. Needed to go for what she wanted. And that wasn't a relationship with Jake. Not anymore. At one time, he'd made her happier than she thought she could be. But that was a distant memory now.

With a quick intake of breath, she finally found the words. "I want you to know that this isn't easy for me, Jake." Zoe picked at a thread poking out from the cuff of her button-up. She struggled to meet his gaze but he deserved to have her look him in the eyes, especially if she was about to break his heart. She looked up at him and cleared her throat. "This isn't working. We aren't working. And there's no reason for us to keep trying to make it work. I'm done. I can't do it anymore."

His lips parted slightly and he looked as if he was trying to find the words. He swallowed and whispered, "Do what?"

"Us. I loved you for three years, Jake, and I'm not throwing us away on a whim. We clearly want different things and that's okay. If I thought we could make it work, I would put all my effort into it. But I think if we're both honest with ourselves, that isn't going to happen. Especially with how things have been going."

Jake moved closer and reached for her hand, grasping it firmly in his. "I'm sorry. I know I can be better. Are you sure you can't give us just one more chance?"

Zoe's eyes watered at the sight of a tear falling down Jake's cheek. She reached up and wiped it away with her thumb, cupping his face in her hands. "You are a good guy, Jake. But I think it's time for us to focus on ourselves."

Jake nodded. "I think I kinda figured this was coming. I wasn't being fair to you. At all. And I am sorry about that."

Zoe gave him a sad smile. "I know. It's okay."

He pulled Zoe's hands away from his face and held them in his lap. "No, it's not. I didn't mean for this job to control my life. Our lives. I never meant to make you feel like shit or that I didn't want you. Zoe, you are such an amazing person and I'm sorry I took advantage of that all these years. You didn't deserve that."

"Thank you for saying that," Zoe murmured as she gave his hands a gentle squeeze before letting them go. "You seem to be taking this surprisingly well. Should I be offended?" She let out a self-deprecating laugh.

Jake opened his mouth as if to say something else, but he just closed it and looked away, wiping his palms on his pants. Jake was clearly nervous, but Zoe had no idea why. It didn't seem like this was necessarily going to shatter him, especially after seeing his reaction so far. Something else had to be going on and Zoe was a little scared to find out just what that might be.

"What's wrong? Why'd you get all nervous all of a sudden?"

"I'm not nervous," Jake squeaked out.

Zoe crossed her arms in front of her chest. "Jake, we have been together a long time. I know when you're nervous." She reached forward and gently squeezed his knee. "You know you can tell me anything. This whole breakup thing doesn't change that."

"Okay. So, um, I also wasn't being fair to you. Because... well...I've been questioning things lately I guess."

Zoe tilted her head and narrowed her eyes. "Questioning?"

"Um, yeah. My identity. I just, um...I don't think I'm as straight as I always thought," Jake replied, turning scarlet and rubbing the back of his neck. "I've been meaning to talk to you for a while. I just didn't know what I was feeling or what was going on."

Well, that wasn't what Zoe was expecting. The revelation kept her silent for a moment as she let his words sink in. Why was he questioning his sexuality now? Was there *someone* that was the motivation behind all this? She sat up straighter as the night of Jake's company party came crashing to the front of her mind.

Ian.

I'm quite certain he'd enjoy it.

Zoe and Jake had talked about that night the day after the party. Zoe was furious and horrified but Jake had shrugged it off as something absurd and that it was just Ian being Ian. He'd apologized and had said he'd talked to Ian about it and that Ian promised he would never say anything like that again.

Ian? Fucking Ian? What in the flying fuck did Jake see in Ian? Zoe's brain couldn't wrap around the idea that Jake could be into Ian. He was such a slimy, disgusting, and disrespectful prick. Zoe scooted back on the couch until her back hit the armrest, keeping her arms firmly wrapped around her torso. "So, what Ian said that night of the party? You would've been into it, us going up to his room?"

"No! At least not a threesome. I know that's not your thing. And I'm not sure it's mine either."

"But you want to sleep with Ian?"

"I...I don't—"

Zoe didn't let him finish as soon as he started to hesitate. "Jesus, Jake. Have you already?" Her thoughts spiraled and she started word-vomiting as she stood to pace the room. "Or anyone else for that matter? Fuck, we only use the pill. We've had unprotected sex. For years. How long has this been going on? Do I need to fucking worry about getting tested? What the fuck, Jake!"

Jake quickly closed the distance between them and carefully took hold of Zoe's hand, softly cradling it in his own. "No. Of course not. I haven't had sex with anyone but you. I wouldn't have cheated on you, Zo. Ever." He swallowed hard and he cleared his throat. "It came close."

Her anger skyrocketed but it quickly dissipated. That would be pretty hypocritical, wouldn't it? Zoe had come within inches of kissing Paige in the elevator so she had no right to be upset that he seemed to have almost slept with Ian. She wanted to confess to her almost indiscretion but it wasn't entirely her truth to tell. Zoe would be "outing" Paige in a sense too. Not in terms of her sexuality as Jake had known for a few years of following Paige on social media that she was a lesbian, but because it would out her as someone who had feelings for Zoe, and vice versa.

"How close?" Zoe asked.

"Ian has come onto me pretty strongly a few times. We've never had sex. Hell, we've never even kissed. But he's been in my personal space a couple of times. And lots and lots of innuendo. Horsing around. Completely inappropriate really. And well...I never stopped it."

"That night you came home smelling different," Zoe murmured.

Jake nodded. "Yeah. I'm sorry. I know I should've told you sooner."

"Why didn't you?"

"Come on, Zo. You of all people should understand that this isn't always a switch that gets flipped on and I totally get who I really am all of a sudden."

Jake was right. Zoe had struggled with her sexuality throughout high school, only realizing she was bi near the end of her senior year when a girl kissed her at a party on a dare. The way she had felt after that kiss had made a few things from earlier in her life a little clearer, like her fascination with Anna Kendrick. She certainly hadn't sought out every movie she'd ever been in just because she had wanted to be like her...

Zoe reached up to cup Jake's cheek in her hand, lightly brushing her thumb along his sharp cheekbone. "You're right. I'm sorry." She then dropped her hand as another realization hit her. "And I'm sorry if I ever made you feel like you couldn't talk to me. You always could and you always will be able to. None of this will ever change that." Had her crush on Paige made her miss any signs? And even if there were signs, would she have even really cared? Obviously her focus hadn't always been on Jake over the past months.

"It's okay. I don't think I've really been ready to talk about it. I think it's taken me longer to wrap my brain around things than I thought it would."

"Well, I'm serious, Jake. If you ever need to talk through any of this, or talk about anything else, I will always be here for you. Always."

"Thank you," Jake replied, his eyes shimmering with tears. "Can I have a hug?"

Zoe smiled. "Of course."

When Jake wrapped his arms around her shoulders and pulled her close, he sighed slowly as he rested his head against hers. Zoe listened to the familiar beat of his heart and could still smell a hint of his cologne. The finality of the hug was what struck Zoe the most and fresh tears pooled in her eyes. She knew breaking up with him was for the best and she was finally doing things for herself and no one else. But no one walked away from a breakup unscathed. Jake obviously understood the reasons for it, but she knew she'd hurt him. But she'd also probably given him a sense of hope and relief. He'd be able to focus on every aspect of himself and find what would truly make him happy.

Zoe broke the hug and stepped back, wiping a finger under her eyes. "But seriously. Ian? What the fuck do you see in him?"

Jake covered his face with his hands and groaned. "Ugh. I know. He can be a total tool but he's so fucking hot."

"Thinking with your dick, huh?" Zoe raised an eyebrow and crossed her arms in front of her chest.

Jake snorted a laugh. "Basically."

"At least you're honest," Zoe replied, joining in on the laugh and shaking her head. She glanced up at Jake and gave him a long look. He looked lighter which would make sense since he'd been holding this truth in for so long. Zoe patted him on the chest. "Now you have the freedom to give all your focus to your job if you want. Go kick ass at it like I know you can. A year from now, I want you to tell me that they love you so much that they gave you Ian's job. Or ya know, say fuck it to the job and switch your focus to figuring out exactly who you are and are meant to be, which might lead to some fortunate or maybe not-so-fortunate hookups, especially if they're with Ian," she said with a teary wink.

Jake chuckled as he shoved his hands in his front pockets. "I'll try."

Zoe took a deep breath, slowly releasing the rest of her tension. Even though it'd been so hard to do, breaking up with

Jake made her feel lighter. She was no longer nauseous and her heartbeat had slowed. And that meant she'd made the right choice. "I think I'm gonna head out. I'm going to stay at Mia's until I can find a place."

"Are you sure? I mean, I know it might be awkward, but you could stay in the other bedroom now that Paige is gone."

And just like that, those knots were back in her stomach. Just hearing Paige's name made her realize that her moving out had been all her fault. And Zoe missed her. It had only been a little over twenty-four hours, but Zoe wished she could see her. They still needed to talk. Zoe needed to explain herself. Let Paige know what she'd been feeling.

Zoe shook her head, trying to clear her thoughts of Paige and focus on Jake. "I'm sure. I'll grab the rest of my stuff this weekend."

"Okay," Jake said.

Zoe slung her duffel bag over her shoulder and extended the handle of her suitcase. As she reached for the doorknob, she looked back at Jake and said, "I'll see you later."

Jake nodded and gave her a little wave but didn't say anything.

Breathing deeply, Zoe was out the door. Even though this was what she wanted, tears filled Zoe's eyes. She was sad that she couldn't make things work with Jake. But she was also feeling a weird nervous excitement. Her life was kind of up in the air and it was a novel feeling. It may have once made her panic, but Zoe felt resolved. It was time for her to concentrate on herself, her own needs. That meant figuring out what she wanted in life. But that meant talking to Paige. Because it was Paige she wanted. She just didn't know if that feeling was mutual.

When Mia opened up her apartment door, she gave Zoe a knowing smile. "All done, huh?"

Zoe nodded and bit her lip, trying not to let herself cry again. "Yep," she said hoarsely.

"Come here," Mia replied with her arms open wide.

Zoe rolled her suitcase inside and then dropped the duffel bag next to it. Stepping into Mia's arms, she held her tightly. Tears soaked into Mia's sweatshirt where Zoe rested her head on her shoulder. "I don't know why I'm so upset. It's not like I didn't see this coming. And I was the one to fucking break up with him. Why am I crying?"

"Maybe because you and Jake were together for three years. And even when we accept the fact that a relationship needs to end, it still hurts."

Zoe nodded but stayed quiet. She just wanted comfort right now and Mia had always been a source of that for her. Zoe had done the right thing, but it still hadn't been fun. She hadn't set out to hurt Jake, and despite his revelation she was sure the breakup had still hurt him, at least a little. She desperately wanted to tell Mia everything, but it wasn't her place to out Jake without his approval first.

"How about you sit down and I get us ice cream? Everything is better with ice cream."

Zoe pulled back and wiped at her eyes. "That is a true statement. I'm just gonna go change. Where do you want me to put my stuff?"

"I cleared out a drawer for you in my dresser and then you can put your bags next to the closet. Then there's a *tiny* amount of room for you in the closet and some empty hangers."

Zoe smiled at Mia's sweet gesture. Mia liked her clothes so to have her clear out some space meant a lot to Zoe. "Aww. Thanks."

Once she put her most frequently used clothes in the drawer and hung up what she needed to keep as wrinkle-free as possible, Zoe changed into sweats and a T-shirt. She removed the hair tie she'd had in all day, running both hands through her hair and scratching her scalp. Just that simple movement drained her of the rest of her energy and she just wanted to crash on the couch. Maybe the ice cream would give her a little boost.

Zoe came into the living room to find three pints of ice cream sitting open on the coffee table, with spoons stuck in the middle and standing like little flagpoles. "Think you have enough ice cream?"

Mia shrugged. "I knew the breakup was going down tonight and what better way to heal the heart than with a shit-ton of ice cream."

"You were always the smart one, my friend. Let's see. What have we got here?" Zoe scanned the containers—cookie dough, strawberry cheesecake, and caramel swirl. She tapped her chin as she tried to decide, although, more than likely she'd be eating some of all three by the end of the night. She reached for the cookie dough and sat on the couch, kicking her feet up onto the coffee table and crossing her legs at the ankle.

Mia sat on the opposite end of the couch with her legs extended toward Zoe. "So how are you doing?" Mia asked before taking a bite of the strawberry cheesecake.

Zoe shrugged and took a small scoop of her ice cream, letting it melt on her tongue before answering, "I'm okay. Being the one to do the breaking up really sucks. But I think even Jake would admit that this had been coming for a while."

"How'd he take it?"

Zoe almost blurted that she thought it had been a relief for him, but she needed to explain as if he hadn't come out to her after she'd broken up with him. "I think as I expected? I don't know. I guess I really didn't know what to anticipate going into it. I think he was just going through the motions with us too. He cried," Zoe said with a groan. "I felt like such an ass when I saw that. Didn't matter that I knew it was the best decision. I never meant to hurt him."

And she never meant to fall in love with someone else. That thought made her feel like even more of an ass. She didn't want to think of everything as if they both had one foot out the door in their relationship so it was inevitable that any bit of attention Zoe received from anyone else she would cling to. And she didn't break up with Jake for Paige. She ultimately did it for herself. It hammered home the idea that Zoe needed to take care of herself most of all. Her people-pleasing tendencies often made her put herself last. Making people happy and making sure they were taken care of did make her happy, but sometimes she wondered at what expense? She knew putting herself first was going to take some practice. It wasn't a change that was going to happen overnight. Breaking up with Jake was just the first step in that process.

"I'm sure he knows that. When do you want to get the rest of your stuff?" Mia asked.

"Sometime this weekend. I'll have to text him."

"Well, I'll be free whenever you need me. I have that small storage locker in the basement. There should be plenty of space in there."

"Great. Thanks. And thank you for letting me stay. I'll have to start looking for apartments I guess," Zoe mumbled.

"You can stay here as long as you need. You should see if there are any openings here. How awesome would it be if you were only an elevator ride away?"

"I certainly wouldn't complain." Zoe smiled. She actually hadn't put much thought into finding an apartment. Jake had done the apartment hunting when they were getting ready to move here and she just went along with what he wanted. But it would be nice to be that close to Mia. "I'll check with them tomorrow."

Mia took a bite of her ice cream and stared at the empty spoon as if it would give her courage for what she wanted to say. "What about Paige? Are you going to tell her how you feel?"

Zoe felt both excitement and dread simultaneously. She needed to talk to Paige, but what if it was all just a big misunderstanding and there were no feelings on her side at all. If the heat in Paige's eyes the other night was anything to go by, Zoe didn't think that was the case. But Paige hadn't said a word to her. She probably regretted ever getting to know Zoe.

Shrugging, Zoe scraped a thin layer of ice cream with her spoon but didn't bring the bite to her mouth. "I don't know. I've texted and called. And nothing. Not one, 'Hey, I'm okay' or 'Hey, we should talk.' Just silence." Zoe shook her head. "I definitely need to talk to her but I'm gonna give it a bit. Even if there's a chance she does like me, I'm not in any position to start something. Not when I just broke up with Jake. That would feel pretty shitty."

Mia nodded. "Yep. Kinda would be."

"So, just wait and see, I guess. She obviously doesn't want to talk right now so I'll give it some time and try again."

"Solid plan," Mia replied.

"But for now, how about we zone out to some TV? I don't think my brain can handle anything else tonight."

"You got it," Mia said as she reached for the remote.

As Mia scrolled through channels, Zoe took another bite of her ice cream. She hadn't eaten dinner and ice cream probably wasn't the best replacement, but it totally hit the spot right now. They spent the next couple of hours in silence watching TV. The only words exchanged were when Mia asked if Zoe was done with the ice cream so she could put it away. Zoe didn't always need to or like to talk about her feelings and so she loved that Mia let her have that mental space while still having the physical closeness and comfort.

After Mia had yawned for the third time, she sat up straight and stretched her arms above her head. "I gotta get to bed. Did you want to sleep with me tonight? It can be like our high school sleepovers all over again," she said with a laugh.

"No. That's okay. The couch will be fine for tonight. Ask me again tomorrow and I might say yes." Zoe had actually slept on Mia's couch a few times before so she knew it was pretty comfortable. Sleeping next to Mia sounded kind of nice too but Zoe wanted some time to herself after her long emotionally grueling day.

"Okay. Well you know where everything is. I'll see you in the morning." Mia kissed Zoe on the top of her head and then went into her bedroom at the end of the hallway.

Zoe brushed her teeth quickly and then made the couch up for sleep. She grabbed a pillow and blanket from the hall closet. As she lay down and pulled the blanket up to her chin, she stared at the stream of light coming through the top of the curtains from the light post just outside the building. She took note of how her body felt and realized how different it was from the night before.

Last night she felt nervous and scared and had a sense of dread knowing that she would be breaking up with Jake. But now as she lay on Mia's couch, she felt calm and even hopeful. That solidified that she'd done the right thing. Now she'd have to think about how she was going get Paige to talk to her and what she was going to say. No pressure.

CHAPTER TWENTY-EIGHT

As Paige finished her shift on Sunday afternoon, she sent a text to Jake.

Wanna come over for dinner?

It had been a few days since moving out and she still needed to give her key back to him. Inviting him over meant she could do that and wouldn't have to see Zoe. Unless he brought her. Shit. She unlocked her phone again and her thumbs hovered over the screen. She desperately wanted to send a follow-up text to say she only meant for the invite to be for him. But that would make her look like a huge ass or that she didn't like Zoe. When liking Zoe wasn't the problem. The problem was that she liked Zoe a little too much. So much that that was why she was now living above Craft.

Although she wasn't entirely upset by that. It was nice to have her own place. It was also nice that her commute to work was walking down a flight of stairs. As she woke for each of her opening shifts, she thanked the universe that living here had given her at least an extra fifteen minutes of sleep.

After leaving through the front door of Craft, she walked around the side of the building and opened the door to a flight of stairs that led to her apartment. She smiled as she took in her apartment and her new couch. Well new to her. Tom's best friend was in the process of moving across the country for a new job and part of that process was getting rid of his stuff. So being the awesome friend that Tom was, he'd convinced his best friend to give Paige first dibs on the couch. She'd paid about a hundred bucks more than she'd wanted to, but having a comfy place to crash after a long day on her feet was completely worth it.

Just as she sat on her couch and toed off her shoes, she received a reply from Jake.

Be there at 6.

Paige let out a breath. Now she just hoped that she'd only be seeing Jake. But she needed to prepare herself that Zoe might come too. Maybe she should go stand in front of a mirror and practice having a blank expression at the thought of seeing Zoe again. Paige laughed quietly to herself as she lay on the couch. As if she could ever have a blank expression at seeing Zoe. Looking at Zoe made her light up and she was certain she wouldn't be able to hide that. And if Zoe had been her girlfriend, she never would hide it because Zoe was the type of woman that should know her partner loved her and that their day was brightened just by being near her.

Paige groaned as she covered her eyes with her arm. "Waxing poetic a little too much there. Aren't ya, Paige?" she mumbled into the crook of her elbow. Zoe wasn't her girlfriend and she wouldn't be. Paige needed to stop wishing she was.

After a quick nap, Paige rolled onto her side and lit up her phone screen. Jake would be there any minute and she needed to start dinner. Okay, she needed to preheat the oven since she still needed to stock her kitchen with basic cooking essentials. Frozen meals and cereal had been her go-to meals since she moved in. Maybe another week or two of extra shifts and she'd make sure she could make meals from scratch again.

Just as she put the frozen pizza on a baking sheet and set the oven to preheat, her buzzer rang. She hit the button and said, "Jake?"

"It's me," he replied.

"Come on up," Paige said as she pressed the second button to unlock the ground-floor door.

Heavy footsteps hurried up the stairs and a knock sounded within a few seconds. Smiling, Paige opened the door. "Hey."

Jake gave her a quick hug. "How's it going?"

"Good," Paige looked behind him as he stepped inside. "Where's Zoe?"

"Ah, right." Jake rubbed at the back of his neck. "We kinda broke up."

Paige's hand slipped from the doorknob as she went to close the door. "What?" Holy shit. They broke up. Paige's mind raced as she tried to take it in. What happened? Who broke up with whom? If Zoe broke up with Jake, did it have anything to do with her? If Jake broke up with Zoe, did he suspect something between her and Zoe?

She mentally shook herself at that last one. He couldn't have suspected anything. He had hugged her when he walked in and had a huge smile on his face. That wasn't the typical greeting if someone knew about the person having feelings for their girlfriend. Well ex-girlfriend now.

"Kinda?" she asked, hoping her voice didn't sound as, um, hopeful as it sounded in her head.

"Well, no kinda about it. She broke up with me."

Holy shit. Again. Her mind couldn't think of any other expletives. All her mental capacity went to taking in the news of the breakup and making sure her face conveyed empathy and not elation. Now wasn't the time to show any hint of happiness. Because even though they weren't together, it wasn't like Paige could all of a sudden get together with Zoe. Paige was Jake's sister and Zoe was his ex-girlfriend. That was a huge no-no regardless of how much she wanted Zoe.

Paige forced herself to shift her focus back to Jake. "Want a beer?"

Jake gave her a surprised smile. "Yeah, sure. And don't worry, I walked."

She went to the fridge, getting his beer and a Pepsi for herself. Living with him, she'd taken a mental note of the beer he drank. Paige wanted him to feel comfortable at her place.

What he just said took an extra moment to process for Paige. "Walk? It's what? Two miles from your apartment?"

Jake shrugged as if it was no big deal. "Needed to decompress a bit."

Paige handed him his beer before taking a seat on the couch. "How come? Because of the breakup?"

"A little," he said, nodding his head from side to side. He twisted the cap off his beer as he sat on the opposite end of the couch, crossing an ankle over the other knee. "Zoe came to get the rest of her stuff this morning."

"Ah. Was it tough?"

"Not as much as I thought it'd be I guess."

"What happened with you guys?" Paige asked quietly.

"As if you can't figure it out," Jake said with a scoff.

Paige sat straighter and gripped her can so hard that she heard the metal crunch and she had to force herself to relax. There was no way he knew that she had feelings for Zoe. Or that Zoe had almost kissed her. That they had almost kissed each other. Paige cleared her throat, wanting her voice to come out as natural as possible. "What do you mean?"

"You're the one that had to bail me out and hang out with her all the time."

Paige relaxed back into her seat. "So it was because of your job?"

"Kinda."

"Again with the kinda?" she asked tentatively.

"Sorry. I think the job had a big part in it. I think it just brought the inevitable forward for her."

"So even if you didn't have a shitty boss, you don't think you guys would've stayed together?"

"Probably not." He took a large gulp of his beer. "In fact, I'm sure we wouldn't have."

Okay, so maybe they weren't as in love as they seemed. Not that it made how she felt about Zoe any better. She'd still crossed the line. "Why do you say that?" she asked.

"I loved her. Still do. She is such a good person. Initially, I think I just liked the idea of coming home to someone. And yes, I was a dick and took advantage of her too much because I liked coming home to a place that was clean and cozy and had dinner ready."

"You think?" Paige said, giving him a pointed look.

Jake held up his hands. "I know. Ever since she broke up with me, I've been realizing more and more that I was a bit of an ass."

"I'll keep my mouth shut on that one," Paige murmured.

Jake barked out a laugh. "Shut up." He grew serious and picked at the label on his beer bottle. "I never made her feel that she was wanted. And I think I got caught up in trying to have the things we're told we should have—a partner, a home, a successful job." He took a deep breath, opening his mouth to speak twice before he said in a quiet voice, "There's something else." Jake looked almost scared.

"What's going on? Is something wrong?"

"No, not wrong. I've just been realizing over the past few months that I'm not exactly straight," he replied, rolling his bottle between his hands.

Okay, not where she thought he was going. "Well, obviously that's not a big deal to me, but of course it is for you," she said with a laugh which Jake thankfully joined in on. "What made you realize it?"

"I know there've been hints in the past that I was also just really good at ignoring. Or, at least I'm recognizing now as I look back on things more that there were hints. But I was sure Zoe and I were truly happy. I adore her. Then I started spending all this time at work and with Ian—"

Paige held up a hand. "Wait a minute. You have the hots for your boss?"

Jake scrunched up his nose and shrugged. "Guilty."

"Isn't he a bossy asshole?" What in the world did Jake see in that appalling jerk?

"It seems that is part of the appeal," Jake replied, giving Paige a pointed look.

The reasoning behind that quickly sunk in for Paige. "Got it. Don't need to explain any more."

"But seriously, he's not that bad. All that trivial bullshit he had me do happened more at the beginning than it does now. He's still demanding and acts like a jerk more often than not, but I just can't help it." Jake laughed but then grew serious. "I never meant for it to happen. But I'm glad Zoe broke up with me. I know it would've happened eventually but I'm happy she figured out that she deserves someone better. And before I hurt her even more than I have already."

As he finished that sentence, he looked over at Paige with a look she couldn't decipher and her breath caught in her throat. *Was he talking about me? Am I the someone better?* He can't know what almost happened in the elevator. How could he know? No way. And how would he know that Paige had feelings for Zoe? Even if they had been blasted across her face all that time, he wasn't around that much to notice. So no way could he know. The beep of the oven pulled Paige from her panic, if only briefly. She popped the pizza in the oven and set the timer.

Before she could more fully respond to Jake's life-altering revelation, he asked with a grin, "Wanna watch the Bulls game?"

Paige lifted her arms as she gestured around the room. "On what TV?" That purchase was definitely going to be one of her last. She watched some TV but not enough to warrant an immediate purchase.

"Don't you have your laptop? We could stream it."

"True. It'll be a bit small. Not that a big screen makes the Bulls look any better."

"Oh please," Jake scoffed. "Detroit probably isn't even gonna make the playoffs this season. We should."

"Yeah yeah," she mumbled, knowing full well that he was probably right.

For the next couple of hours, they ate pizza, talked, and watched basketball. They'd had nights like this when she'd first moved in with him and Zoe. So having this time with just her brother was really nice. Maybe it would happen more often now that she was in her own place.

As the game came to an end and Paige had to begrudgingly congratulate Jake that his team won, Jake stood and stretched his arms over his head. "I should head out."

"Do you want a ride home?"

Jake waved her off as he put on his coat. "Don't worry about it. I'll be okay."

Just as Jake reached the door Paige stopped him with a "Wait." She grabbed her jacket she'd tossed onto the breakfast bar. She found the key to Jake's apartment, slid it off the ring and held it out to him. "Here you go."

Jake waved her away. "Keep it."

Paige furrowed her brows and looked at the key in her hand. "Why?"

"You're my sister," he said with a nonchalant shrug. "You can come by anytime. And hey, maybe I'll finally get a cat and you can cat-sit for me."

"Finally?" Paige asked.

"Yeah. Zoe didn't want one," he said with a sad smile. "She's more of a dog person."

Me too, Paige thought. She squeezed the key in her hand and gave her brother a warm smile and a hug. "Thanks, Jake."

He stepped back and gave her a little wave. "Night, Paige."

"Night."

Paige closed the door behind Jake and listened until his footsteps on the stairs had stopped and she heard the ground-floor door open and close. She took a deep breath as one thing replayed in her head over and over—Zoe was single. Her heart quickened at the thought, but it only lasted until her brain remembered that she was still Jake's ex-girlfriend. It felt like there was no scenario where Zoe and Paige could end up together and Paige could still maintain her relationship with Jake. Feeling defeated, Paige shut off the living room lights and readied for bed.

CHAPTER TWENTY-NINE

A few weeks had passed and as April rolled around Paige was loving her new normal. She'd cut down on her extra shifts at Craft and had become the regular opener for most of the week. Paige found she'd liked the early mornings and could spend her afternoons running or finalizing everything in her apartment. She had scoured garage sales and secondhand furniture shops for a TV stand and a bed frame. Paige let herself splurge on the comfiest mattress she'd ever lain down on. If she was going to be getting up early almost every morning, then she figured she'd deserved a bed that would help her get the best possible sleep. Maybe someday she'd have someone with whom to share that bed. Once she got over Zoe.

As her shift came to an end on late Tuesday afternoon, Paige stuck around to chat with Tom while he worked behind the bar, something she'd also found herself doing once or twice a week. Tom typically came in just before lunch and stayed until close at ten. She went back into the staff room and clocked out. She stuffed her apron into her locker before tugging off her T-shirt and setting it on top of the apron. Paige had splashed some milk on herself earlier and she wanted to get into a fresh shirt. She could have gone upstairs and showered and then come back down, but she didn't plan on staying too long tonight. She pulled a clean, long-sleeve T-shirt over her head, redid her ponytail and went back out front.

Tom had just placed a beer in front of Vanessa, already seated at the bar. Paige took the stool next to her and said, "Hey. How's it going?"

Vanessa gave her a once-over and smiled widely. "Hey, yourself. Can I buy you a drink?" she asked with a wink. Vanessa still tended to come in when Paige was working but also later, like today, on the chance she'd be hanging out after work. It was nice and it was comfortable, even though Vanessa continued to flirt shamelessly with her. That just seemed how their relationship would be. Flirty friends but both understanding it would never go beyond that.

Paige laughed and signaled for Tom. "Are you sure you can afford it? I've got expensive tastes." When Tom came over to them, she said, "A Diet Coke, thanks."

Vanessa playfully cringed. "Ouch. I was just expecting you to go for your usual water."

"Need that caffeine boost," Paige replied with a small shrug.

"Everything okay?" Vanessa asked, her expression switching from playful to serious.

"Yeah. Just rough sleep last night." A night plagued by dreams of Zoe but Vanessa didn't need to know that. Paige had been doing well with her thoughts about Zoe, or lack thereof. Not having to see her every day meant it'd been a little easier to not think of her constantly. Her mind would only conjure images of her maybe every other hour instead of every other minute. Maybe she'd get over her in a year at that rate, Paige thought, not believing it for a minute.

Vanessa nodded but didn't say anything, maybe understanding that what had kept Paige up the night before she didn't want to talk about now. "Well, cheers to that," Vanessa said as she raised her beer to Paige. "I was up until two studying and then up for class at eight. To the joy of shitty sleep."

Paige laughed and touched her glass to Vanessa's. "Cheers. Aside from the grind of school, how's life?"

"Good. I have a date this weekend," Vanessa replied.

Paige gave her an exaggerated gasp and put her hand to her chest. "One failed date with me a month ago and you're already moving on? I'm hurt."

"Oh, please. That would maybe be true if you weren't in love with Zoe."

And with that Paige's playful smile dropped and she let out a sigh before taking a sip of Coke. She couldn't deny it. Vanessa was right. She was absolutely still in love with Zoe. And probably would be for much longer than was healthy.

Vanessa cringed and reached out to cover Paige's hand with hers and gave it a light squeeze. "I'm sorry."

"Sorry about what?" Tom asked as he leaned forward with his forearms on the bar top.

"Nothing," Paige said with a shake of her head. "She just reminded me about how nonexistent my love life is."

"Yeah. It's pretty awful," Tom replied.

Paige laughed. Maybe it wouldn't hurt as much if she laughed about it. "Ouch. I mean, it's true, but still. Ouch."

Tom and Vanessa laughed with her, but a second later Tom straightened up and looked past Paige with wide eyes.

"What is it?" Paige asked as she turned around to look toward the front door. The laughter fell away and Paige inhaled sharply. "Zoe," she whispered.

Zoe stood just inside the door, scanning the opposite end of the room. Her hands fidgeting with the bottom of her white button-up shirt that poked out from underneath her black sweater. She must've just come from work and fuck did she look good. Paige always liked seeing Zoe's outfits when she got home from work. It was even better when she wore glasses instead of contacts, like she did now.

Zoe bit her lip and Paige saw the uncertainty in her eyes as she continued to look around the room. Zoe turned toward her and met her gaze. Paige's heartbeat felt like it tripled in speed. She watched as Zoe's chest heaved and she gave Paige a small awkward wave.

Paige held her breath as Zoe started walking toward her. What was she doing here? Paige knew Zoe had wanted to talk to her ever since the night of Zoe's birthday, but Paige wouldn't let herself reply to any of her calls or messages. It was easier to have a clean break. Or as clean as that break could be when she constantly thought about Zoe.

Nothing else registered to Paige except Zoe standing in front of her looking as anxious as she'd ever seen her. The chatter around her was silent. She no longer registered Vanessa or Tom's presence. Only Zoe mattered right now.

"Can we talk?" Zoe asked.

Paige watched as Zoe's nervous brown eyes drifted down toward the bar counter. She followed her gaze to see what Zoe was looking at. It was Vanessa's hand still on top of hers.

Just as Paige turned back around, Zoe bit her lip again and murmured, "Never mind. I shouldn't have come here." Zoe started to turn away but Paige hopped off her stool and stopped her with a gentle grip on her forearm.

"Please don't go. We can go upstairs to my apartment."

"Upstairs?" Zoe asked.

"Yeah, I'm staying in the apartment above the shop. I'll show you." Paige looked back to Vanessa.

Vanessa held up her hands and said, "Go on. I got this." She smiled softly and gave Paige a little nod.

Before Paige turned back around, she saw Tom give her a thumbs-up. With a quick breath, Paige turned back to Zoe and gestured toward the front door. Her heart raced and her stomach churned as she led Zoe down the sidewalk and to her ground-floor door. It was so good to see her but Paige was nervous. She didn't know what Zoe came to say and was also anxious for her to see her place.

As she unlocked the door, she looked over her shoulder at Zoe and said, "Follow me."

* * *

At the top of the stairs, Zoe waited nervously as Paige unlocked the door. Zoe walked in behind her and looked around. It was small but Paige had made a good use of the space with a couch, coffee table, and small kitchen table along the far wall. Zoe smiled as she saw Paige's purple blanket on the back of her navy couch. Her stomach clenched as she remembered the last time they sat together under that blanket and watched *Legally Blonde*. Back when she tried to deny the feelings for Paige that had been brewing for months. Probably since the very first day Paige had shown up at her door.

Zoe was pulled away from her inspection as Paige asked, "Do you want something to drink?"

Probably should, Zoe thought as she swallowed against her dry throat. But her stomach was a ball of nerves and she didn't think even something as simple as water would sit well right now. She shook her head and rasped out, "No. Thanks."

"So you wanted to talk?" Paige asked as she sat on the couch and folded her arms across her chest. One knee bounced rapidly and Paige started to bite her thumbnail.

"You're gonna make yourself bleed," Zoe said with a soft smile.

Paige chuckled and pulled her hand away from her mouth and shoved it underneath her arm. "You've told me that a time or two."

Zoe sat on the opposite end of the couch. She wanted to pace the room, but was trying to calm down in hopes of finding the words she wanted to say to Paige. "Hasn't sunk in though I see."

Paige shrugged but didn't reply.

Zoe stared at her hands as she trapped them between her knees, trying not to fidget. "You never texted me back," Zoe said, realizing her voice sounded so small. She didn't care. She'd been hurt that she hadn't heard from Paige. Zoe knew it wasn't a simple situation but she still felt like she deserved an answer.

"I'm sorry."

Zoe waited for a fuller answer but nothing came. "But why didn't you? We almost kiss and you basically ghosted me. Could hardly look at me the rest of the night. Didn't talk to me. And then moved out with a fucking note."

Paige stood and forcefully pulled out her hair tie and slipped it on her wrist. She ran a hand through her hair as she paced in front of the coffee table. "Ugh. I couldn't, Zoe. It was too hard. Don't you see that?" she asked, hands on her hips as she faced Zoe.

"What was?" Zoe asked as she stood and slowly made her way to stand in front of Paige, forcing herself to keep at least a couple feet apart.

"Knowing I couldn't have you," Paige replied, her voice hoarse and her eyes shimmering with tears.

Zoe's breath caught in her throat. Did that mean what she thought it meant? Did Paige want her just as much as Zoe wanted her? God, how she wanted that to be true. There was only one way to find out. She took one step forward and heard Paige's sharp intake of breath. "What if you could?" Zoe whispered.

"Could what?"

"Have me," Zoe replied, her voice firm now.

Paige's eyes darkened and her lips parted ever so slightly. "I...I..." Paige started but didn't say anything else.

"I broke up with Jake," Zoe blurted.

"Yeah, I know."

"Oh, right. He probably told you. Duh."

Paige nodded. "He told me about the breakup and *all* of the reasons for it. But, um, did I have any part in why you initiated it?" she asked as she looked away as if she couldn't bear the thought of being the one to cause their breakup.

Zoe reached for Paige's hand in an attempt to reassure her. Plus, she needed the connection. Over a month with no contact, verbally or physically, and she was desperate to be close to Paige. "No." Zoe nodded her head from side to side as she tried to find the words. "Not in the way you're thinking at least."

She took a deep breath and looked down at their joined hands. It was time to lay everything out. The reasons for the breakup. Her feelings for Paige. Everything. "Moving here hadn't even been on my radar until Jake got his job. I was fine staying in Muncie after graduation. But I didn't question it because I saw how excited he was to get the job and I wanted him to go for what he wanted. Even though I liked making him happy, I realized I wasn't happy myself. And I think deep down I knew that. Jake is a great guy and I genuinely like being around him. I started out being in love with him, but then it just gradually shifted to being in love with the idea of having someone. I knew he loved me and he was dependable. Until he wasn't.

"I think his job and his obsession with getting ahead was the ultimate breaking point for us. Or at least for the realization that I wasn't as all in as I used to be or needed to be. And it no longer seemed fair to either of us to continue to just go with how things were. And yes, you showing up on our doorstep and getting to know you after that might've pushed things along a little quicker. But we were never going to work. I knew that and he knew that, especially with Jake now questioning his identity and wanting to explore that."

Paige opened her mouth to say something but Zoe held up her hand. She needed to get everything out before she lost the courage to tell Paige exactly how she felt. "Please let me finish?" Zoe asked.

At Paige's nod, Zoe took another deep breath and chuckled self-deprecatingly. "I don't consider myself very romantic. I rehearse lines in my head and they never come out the way I plan. It's usually ten times shorter and much less mushy and poetic." Zoe opened her mouth again but closed it when the words wouldn't come. This was her problem. She'd have the conversations in her head and plan them out, but when it came time to say the words, they weren't there, at least not there in the exact way she wanted.

So she simply said, "I miss you. I miss you so much. Every night when I came home from work, you were the one I was looking forward to seeing. Not Jake. And maybe that should've been a clue that I needed to end things sooner, or maybe I'm just too oblivious and stubborn to see things clearly.

"But, Paige, you were home for me. You were who I wanted to, and still want to, spend time with. Being around you makes me happy. And it makes me feel safe and like you actually care about what I think and feel. I want you. I want you so badly. You are smart and funny and fucking sexy as hell. I want to date you and love you for as long as you'll let me. Please tell me you feel the same. I want to think you do, especially after that night in the elevator. The way you looked at me. Fuck. I felt like I was gonna melt right then and there. Please tell me I'm not making this all up in my head."

Paige closed her eyes for a moment and took a deep breath. When she opened them again, they were filled with conflicting emotion. Zoe could see the obvious desire and maybe even love, but she also saw a hint of uncertainty and regret. "You're not."

Zoe smiled widely and felt her tears burn. *Yes!* She knew Paige had to feel the same way and that it wasn't just one-sided. Maybe this was it for them. They could start dating and see where that took them. Zoe knew they got along and the chemistry was obviously there. All she needed to do now was ask Paige out. Take her on a date and show her how much she meant to her. And finally fucking kiss her. "So, will you go out with me?"

A tear slipped down Paige's cheek and she let go of Zoe's hand, stepping away and putting a few feet of distance between them. "I can't."

Fuck. Zoe's stomach dropped and she held her hand against it as if she could make the nauseous feeling go away. "What? Why?"

"Why do you think, Zoe?" Paige replied with a scoff.

Jake. Of course. Why did Zoe think that this would be easy and it'd be a happily ever after? But Jake wasn't an asshole. Sure, he probably wouldn't be thrilled at the idea of his half-sister dating his ex, but Zoe figured he'd get over it eventually. It wasn't like Zoe had been the love of his life. He knew they weren't meant to last and he had other things to look forward to now. Jake knew Zoe would want him to be happy and she didn't see any reason why he would want to hold her back from the same happiness.

"Look. I know you're concerned about Jake, but I don't think he'd have an issue with it."

Paige gave her a look that screamed "You can't be serious."

"Okay. So I don't think he'd have an issue with it *eventually*," Zoe added.

"I can't just jump right into something with you, Zoe. As much as I'd very much like to." Paige folded her arms across her chest as more tears streamed down her cheeks.

The sight was heartbreaking. Zoe never wanted to cause pain for Paige and she didn't want to force her to do anything she didn't want to do. But Zoe needed to be completely, one hundred percent honest. Maybe then that would ease some of Paige's hesitation. Plus, Paige not wanting to fight for them kind of made Zoe a little angry and hurt. Paige had had strong enough feelings that she felt she needed to move out of their apartment without warning or a word to Zoe. That meant she couldn't just brush aside those feelings. Zoe needed to make sure Paige knew she felt the same and that they both deserved for them to explore those feelings and see where it would take them.

Zoe slowly closed the distance again and put her hand underneath Paige's chin, lifting her face to meet her eyes. "Tell me you don't love me like I love you. Tell me you don't think we are worth it to try and see if this would work between us. Tell me you don't want to give us a chance."

Paige gasped. "You...you love me?" she whispered.

Zoe replayed the words in her head. *Fuck I didn't mean to blurt it like that.* "I did just admit that, didn't I?" she asked, cringing.

Paige chuckled and wiped her eyes with her shirt sleeve. "Yeah. You did."

Zoe shrugged. "I told you the words don't always come out right. But I was telling the truth. I'm in love with you, Paige. And I have been for a while even though I tried to fight it. Don't you wanna see what we could have?"

"Fuck. I do. Of course I do. I've been so in love with you that it hurt. But I don't know what to do about Jake. He is the whole reason I moved here. Having him as my family again is my priority. I'll try and talk to him because I want us to work more than anything. Well almost anything. If he's not okay with us, then…I just don't see how we would work. And that would absolutely break me more than you know. But I can't in good conscience start something with you without him knowing about it and being okay with it."

"I totally get it. I know your relationship with him is important and I don't want anything to get in the way of that. And if that means we can't be together, then I'll have to accept that. It would fucking suck. But I won't push it."

"Thank you," Paige whispered.

Zoe lifted her hand and gently cupped Paige's face, stroking her thumb along her cheekbone. "As much as I'd love to stick around and hang out for a bit, now that I know you feel the same I'm not sure I trust myself to be around you and not kiss you. Because fuck, it is so tempting to kiss you." Her gaze drifted down and she watched as Paige slowly traced her bottom lip with her tongue. Zoe groaned and dropped her hand. "Okay, that little tongue thing was not fair."

Paige grinned and chuckled quietly. "Sorry. Well not really. But I can pretend to be remorseful."

"Mmhmm. I hope you have a good night." Zoe reached out and squeezed Paige's hand. She held her gaze and didn't want to let go. Not one fucking bit. She could stare at her soft blue eyes for days and not get tired of it. Zoe took a deep breath and forced herself to pull away.

"Text me when you get home. Wait. Where is home?" Paige asked.

"I'm staying with Mia for now. I just got an apartment in her building and I move in in a few weeks."

"That's great."

"Yeah, it'll be fun. But I should head out. Good night."

"Night, Zo," Paige replied as she opened the door.

When Zoe made it down the stairs, she looked back up and found Paige waiting for her to walk out the door. With one last smile and a wave, Zoe made her way outside and toward her car. She drove back to Mia's with a mixture of out-of-this-world happiness and a hefty dose of anxiety. She didn't think

Jake would cause an issue but she really had no way of knowing. It wasn't like there was any rule book for their situation. What if he hated the idea of his ex-girlfriend dating his half-sister? She closed her eyes as she shut off her car and truly hoped that wasn't the case.

The instant she walked through Mia's door, Mia said, "Tell me everything."

Zoe laughed. "Geez. Let me at least close the door and take off my shoes."

"I don't see the problem. You can talk and take your shoes off at the same time."

"Smartass," Zoe mumbled as she sat on the couch next to Mia. "And you need to be patient for one more minute."

"Why?"

Zoe ignored the question and pulled out her phone, sending a text to Paige. *Home! Mia's hounding me for details. So talk to you tomorrow.*

Within seconds, Paige replied. *Of course. That's what BFFs do. Good night.*

Night, Zoe typed and followed it up with a kissy face emoji. Zoe knew she had a goofy smile on her face as she turned to face Mia.

"So I take it that it went well?" Mia asked, her eyebrows lifted.

Zoe let out a small sigh. "Yes and no."

"Hold up." Mia quickly went into the kitchen and poured two glasses of wine. As she handed one to Zoe, she said, "Okay. Now I'm ready. Details. Now."

"So I love her. She loves me. But we don't know if we can be together."

Mia took a big gulp of her wine. "Start talking."

So, Zoe did. And every time she rehashed some part of the story, a little worry wiggled deeper and deeper into her brain. What if after all this they still couldn't be together?

CHAPTER THIRTY

Two days later, Paige knocked on Jake's apartment door. When he didn't answer, she gave two more quick knocks before shoving her hands in her pockets and rocking back on her heels, trying to dispel her nervous energy.

She sucked in a breath as Jake opened the door. "Hey! Sorry I took so long. I was in the bathroom. Commercial break during the game." He waved her inside. "What are you doing here? Did I forget we had plans?" Jake asked, looking apologetic.

Paige shrugged off her jacket and held it tightly, flicking a button back and forth. "Um, no. I just wanted to hang out. Chat."

Jake's shoulders sagged. "Oh, okay. Awesome. I've been working even more lately and sometimes I don't think I'm keeping my head on straight," he said with a laugh. "Want anything to drink? Water? Pop?"

"Just water. Thanks," she replied as she tossed her coat onto the arm of the chair and sat down. Paige sat up as straight as a board and she held her hands between her knees. Relax, she told herself. She didn't want to give away how uneasy she was feeling. Paige rolled her shoulders back and let out a quiet breath. Relaxing back into the chair, she raised her feet and rested them on the edge of the coffee table. Her plan was to hang out a bit, watch the game, and then she could drop her bombshell. She wouldn't know whether that was the best decision or not until she actually mentioned Zoe.

Jake filled a glass of water and then grabbed himself a beer from the fridge. Back on the couch, he said, "I was just watching the Bulls game. We're beating the Clippers by five. You okay with watching?"

"Yeah. Definitely." Not her team of course, but right now Paige would watch anything to postpone the conversation she needed to have with her brother. She was dreading the potentially heartbreaking result. Paige still couldn't guess how Jake might react. She definitely expected him to be somewhat hurt, but she was really hoping he wouldn't feel betrayed. If that happened, she had no idea how she could ever be with Zoe in good conscience.

The game returned from commercial and there were six minutes left in the second quarter. Shit. Did she talk to him at halftime? Or did she wait until the game was over? Paige wasn't entirely sure that she could last until then without giving herself a heart attack. But halftime would be coming pretty soon, even with timeouts and commercials.

She stared at the TV but registered none of the play. Jake commented every now and then and she responded with the expected "Mmhmm" but didn't have the brainpower for anything more than that. Paige couldn't concentrate on who was guarding who or who was about to take a shot. The only thing she could focus on was how weird it was being in this apartment and Zoe not being there. And even weirder that there wasn't a single thing she could find that proved Zoe had ever lived here. She must've been pretty meticulous when she'd come to get her things. Or, in a worst-case scenario, Jake was more broken-hearted than he'd admitted and he'd made sure to remove every single reminder of her. Her stomach was in knots.

He could be hurting more than he had ever let on and Paige was about to tell him that she was in love with Zoe.

"Fuck," she mumbled.

"That was a shitty shot, wasn't it?" Jake said.

Paige whipped her head around toward him, her eyes wide. She didn't think she'd said that out loud. She definitely hadn't meant to. Paige had no idea what shot he was talking about. Was it someone on the Bulls or the Clippers that did it? Why was it shitty? Would she have to elaborate on why it was shitty? She quickly replied with a soft, "Yeah," and relaxed a bit when Jake just nodded his head and continued watching the game.

As the buzzer sounded for halftime, Jake stood, grabbing his empty beer bottle. "Want anything else?"

"No thanks," Paige muttered. She started bouncing her leg up and down as he went into the kitchen. Okay, she could do this. She could tell Jake about her and Zoe. Or at least about her wanting there to be a her and Zoe. And she really wanted there to be one. But ultimately, that was in his hands. Jake just didn't know that. Yet.

Jake threw his empty bottle into the recycling bin under the sink before grabbing another. "So how's life?" he asked.

Well, I guess that's the opening I was waiting for. But fuck, every single negative outcome was running through her head. The worst one being he felt betrayed and never wanted to see her again. For a brief moment, she thought she was going to chicken out. But that would mean there would never be a her and Zoe. No. She needed to suck it up and talk to him. Zoe was too important to her.

She must have stayed silent too long because he nudged her foot with his and asked softly, "Everything okay?"

Paige wiped her sweaty palms on her jeans. It was now or never. "Y-yeah," she said. Paige took a deep breath and met Jake's concerned gaze. "I wanted to talk to you about something."

Jake dropped his feet from the coffee table, reaching for the remote and turning off the TV. He held his beer bottle and rolled it between his hands. "Go for it. What's up?"

"So I know this won't be ideal. And honestly, I never meant for it to happen. It just did and I couldn't really stop it. But it happened and I can't ignore it. I moved here to get to know you and try to have you feel like you were my brother again. You are so so important to me and I never wanted to do anything that would come between us. I don't want to betray you."

"Hey. Slow down. Just tell me what's going on."

"I'm in love with Zoe," she blurted.

Jake's mouth dropped open and his eyebrows furrowed. He looked as if he tried to say something more than once but nothing came out of his mouth.

Paige closed her eyes and silently cursed at herself. She hadn't meant to just come out and say it. She wanted to be a little more delicate with the whole thing. "I'm sorry," she murmured. "I never meant for it to happen. It just…did, I guess."

Jake took a big gulp of his beer and set the bottle on the coffee table. "What? When? How?"

Paige held up her hands. "I don't know. Just a gradual thing. I tried to fight it. I really did. But no matter what I tried, I couldn't stop the feelings. Moving out couldn't even stop them," she said with a small scoff.

"Why are you telling me now?" he asked, staring at the black screen of the TV.

Here it goes, she thought. But he continued to stare at the TV and Paige wanted to see his eyes when she told him. She needed to see what he was thinking. She wanted to see if she was hurting him. "Jake, can you look at me please?" she asked softly. When he turned to meet her gaze, Paige didn't necessarily see hurt but she didn't see his typical happy expression either. "I'm in love with her and I want to date her and see where things go." His eyes slightly narrowed but he showed no other change in his features. "But I needed to make sure you were okay with it first. You are my brother and I love you. I would never do anything to jeopardize that. If you don't want me to date her or even talk to her, I won't. I promise."

Paige waited for him to say something, but at least a full minute went by and he still hadn't said a word. He just continued to stare at her. Was he that pissed off that he didn't know what to say? Had she just hurt him so badly that he'd just throw her out?

Jake broke eye contact as he reached for his beer and took a small sip. As he held the bottle in his hands, he started to pick at the corner of the label. Finally, in a quiet tone, he said, "You know, I think part of me wondered if something was going on between you guys."

Paige's mouth dropped open. No way he could've known. She hadn't done anything. Yes, she almost crossed the line once, but it wasn't like her feelings for Zoe were obvious. Or were they? Had he been able to see it on her face that she was in love with Zoe? Had it been clearly there all along? "Why do you say that?" Paige whispered.

With a small, sad smile, he met her gaze again. "Those nights when I bailed and you two went out instead?" he asked.

Paige nodded. Those were some of the best nights of her life. Paige had selfishly started to hope that Jake would bail more and more.

"She just seemed really happy after you guys got home. Happier than I ever made her." Jake shrugged. "Well, since we moved here at least."

"Why didn't you say anything? Confront one of us?"

Jake turned his head and stared off into the distance. His voice was hoarse as he said, "In the back of my mind, I think I liked that she had someone. Someone who was actually spending time with her. Making her laugh. Giving her the attention that I couldn't. Someone that could show her that she was wanted."

Paige's eyes widened. Fuck, did he think Zoe cheated on him? She couldn't let him think that. She never wanted him to think badly of Zoe. Not on account of her at least. Paige scooted forward until she was sitting on the edge of the seat. She held up her hands. "Nothing happened between us. I swear."

Should she tell him everything? Zoe didn't physically cheat and she didn't want Jake to be pissed at either of them or hate them, especially Zoe. But she needed to be honest. He deserved the truth. "It came close though," she murmured. "The night of her birthday."

Jake met her gaze again and nodded as if things were starting to make sense. "And that's why you left." It didn't come out as a question. He said it as a statement. Things seemed to be falling into place for him.

"Yeah. I couldn't risk it anymore. I never wanted to betray you, Jake. You're my brother and I moved here for you. Our relationship...well, if you still want to see me...that's the most important thing to me."

Nodding silently, Jake stood and paced between the coffee table and TV. He downed the rest of his beer and set the empty bottle on the kitchen counter. He kept his back to Paige for a moment and Paige held her breath the entire time. She didn't think that she could say anything else that would make this situation better. But she sure as shit could probably say something that would make it worse. Paige just wanted to know what he was thinking. She just needed answers.

Jake tapped his knuckles on the counter twice and turned to her as he shoved his hands into the pockets of his sweats. "Okay," he said quietly.

Okay? Okay? What the hell did that mean? Okay as in Paige had his blessing to date Zoe? Okay as in Jake was about to tell her to fuck off? More confused than ever, she asked, "Okay? Okay what?"

"I'm going to be honest, Paige. This is a real shit situation." He took a deep breath and let it out forcefully as if he was gathering the courage to say more. "But I'm not going to stand in your way with Zoe. I'm not gonna lie, it might be hard to see you two together so don't get upset if I don't want to hang out with you guys or hear about how things are going between you for a while. Even though I knew things needed to end, she was a big part of my life for three years. So seeing her with someone else isn't going to be super easy at first."

He walked over and sat down on the coffee table in front of Paige. When he met her gaze, Paige saw tears pooling in his eyes. "I'm not going to let anything come between us though. We lost all those years because my parents were assholes. I can't go through that again." He bit his bottom lip as it quivered.

Paige let out a shaky breath and tears stung her eyes. Relief. Utter relief. That was what she was feeling right now. "Are you sure?" she rasped.

"Yeah. You're my sister and I just want to see you happy. No matter what."

Paige threw her arms around his shoulders and pulled him toward her as tightly as she could. She let her tears of joy and relief and happiness soak into his T-shirt. "I never wanted to hurt you, Jake. I love you."

Jake nodded. "I know. I love you too." They held each other quietly for a beat until Jake whispered, "Be good to her. She deserves it."

"I will," Paige replied as she pulled back and looked into Jake's wet eyes. "I promise."

Jake smiled softly and wiped at his cheeks. He cleared his throat and gave his body a shake as if trying to get rid of the last of his emotions. Looking at his watch, he asked, "The game might still be on. Wanna stick around and watch the rest?"

Paige hesitated for a brief second because she wanted to see Zoe and tell her what happened. But no. That could wait. Right now it was important to hang out with her brother and solidify that things between them would be just fine. "Yeah, of course."

Jake reached for the remote and turned the TV back on. There were ten minutes left in the fourth quarter. He shifted to reclaim his seat on the couch and he patted the cushion next to him. "Have a seat."

Paige moved to sit next to him and set her feet back onto the coffee table. She took stock of how she was feeling and elation was all she could pinpoint right now. Her heart was still racing from the entire conversation and because she was pretty impatient to talk to Zoe. She'd told her she was going to talk to Jake but she never said when. Paige glanced at her watch and realized it was almost eleven. She held back a sigh as she realized that Zoe was probably already sleeping. She would have to wait until tomorrow to talk to her. Knowing that, she shifted her focus back to the TV. Might as well pay attention to the game this time.

Jake broke the silence between them when he said, "I think you dating my *ex-girlfriend* now requires you to cheer for the Bulls."

"What?" Paige asked with a laugh of disbelief. "That doesn't even make any sense." Jake gave her a pointed look as if he was threatening to take back his acceptance of Paige and Zoe together. She could suck it up and root for the Bulls if it meant she could be with Zoe. "Fine. Go Bulls," she deadpanned.

Jake smiled widely. "Now was that so hard?"

"Yes," Paige grumbled. Jake elbowed her and Paige gave him a smile. He really was a dork sometimes.

They finished watching the game in silence. As the final buzzer sounded, Paige stood and stretched her arms above her head. "I need to get going." Normally she'd already be in bed at this time, especially when she opened in the morning like she was doing tomorrow. She shrugged on her jacket and buttoned it up. Before she walked to the door, she turned back to Jake and met his gaze. "Thanks, Jake."

She hoped that simple sentence was able to convey what she was feeling. How happy she was that she'd be able to see where things went with Zoe. How grateful she was that he was willing to accept that she wanted to date his ex-girlfriend. Paige was relieved that his relationship with her seemed just as important to him as it was to her.

Jake nodded but didn't say anything until she put her hand on the doorknob. "Be good to her. Treat her a million times better than I ever did. Zoe shouldn't have anything less."

"I will. I promise."

"Good," he said with a nod. "I'll see you later."

With a wave, Paige walked out and softly closed the door behind her. Her shoulders sagged. It felt as if all the energy had drained from her body. She hadn't realized how tense she'd been. Now that it was over, she just wanted to get into bed. Plus, going to sleep meant talking to Zoe would come even sooner and that was the best thing about it all.

CHAPTER THIRTY-ONE

As Zoe hit send on her last email of the day, her phone chimed with an incoming text. A smile instantly formed as she saw it was from Paige.

Come over after work?

Her heart skipped a beat. Zoe had confessed her feelings to Paige two nights ago, but hadn't heard much from her since. Had Paige talked to Jake? Was that why she hadn't heard from her last night? And if she did, was it good news? Was it bad news? Zoe didn't really expect him to be a hundred percent on board with them. But she also didn't think he'd be a complete butthead and make Paige choose him over ever being with her. But what if he did? A wave of nausea came over Zoe at the thought. After laying everything on the line, she really thought she and Paige would have a chance. She would be absolutely crushed if that chance never came.

I'm leaving in 5 min, Zoe sent back. Then she immediately called Mia. With every ring, Zoe whispered, "Pick up."

"What's up? Want me to grab dinner on my way home?" Mia asked when she answered after the fourth ring.

"Paige asked me to come over." Zoe blurted. "Do you think she talked to Jake? What if he hates the idea of us being together?"

"Whoa. Let's calm down there. You won't know anything until you see her."

"Ugh I know. But what if Jake said he has a problem with it? Or what if she decided I'm just not worth it and didn't even try to talk to him?" Zoe asked, knowing she sounded more and more defeated with every word.

"Zoe Elizabeth Tyler. Stop coming up with scenarios that probably won't happen. Get your ass over there and talk to her."

Zoe took a deep breath and let it out slowly. "Okay okay. You didn't need to break out the full name," Zoe mumbled. She knew Mia was right. She shouldn't be coming up with every worst-case scenario but she couldn't help it. She wanted to be with Paige so badly that she was scared it would never happen.

"It was necessary," Mia said, her voice firm. She sighed and then continued in a softer tone, "Just talk to her, Zo. You won't know what she wants to say until you do."

"I know. I just really love her and want to be with her more than anything."

"No shit, pal," Mia replied with a chuckle. "I hope you know you will be telling me everything when you get home tonight."

"I wouldn't have it any other way," Zoe answered with her own laugh.

For the entire drive to Paige's apartment, each worst-case scenario replayed over and over in her mind again. Zoe didn't think she'd ever believe things would work out with Paige until she heard from her that Jake was good with it.

She pulled into a parking space a block down from Craft. Nervous energy flooded her body as she got out of her car and waited to cross the street. She bounced from foot to foot and speed-walked across the street when free to do so. Zoe pressed Paige's buzzer and anxiously waited to hear her voice.

"Zoe?" Paige asked a second after Zoe had pressed the button, as if she'd been waiting by the door.

"Yeah, it's me."

"Come on up," Paige replied.

Zoe hurried up the stairs. Not quite a sprint, but close. Paige opened the door. Zoe smiled as she took her in. Paige was so so pretty, especially when she wore simple leggings and a T-shirt like right now. Zoe tried to read her expression, but Paige's face gave away nothing.

"Hey," Zoe said.

"Hi. Come on in." Paige opened the door farther and stepped back, waving Zoe inside.

Zoe could smell Paige's floral shampoo as she passed. She stood in the living room, wringing her hands together. *Please tell me what's going on. Please tell me Jake's okay with us. Please. Please. Please.* But she said that all in her head. Outwardly, she tried not to seem as anxious as she felt. Paige's expression still wasn't giving anything away.

When Paige moved to stand in front of her, Zoe couldn't breathe. Paige's blue eyes held a hint of mischief and the corner of her mouth was quirked up in a grin.

"So I was wondering if I could take you out for dinner?" Paige asked, shrugging as if what she'd just said was no big deal.

But it was a big deal. A huge deal in fact. Because if Paige was asking her out, that meant Jake had to be okay with things. Right? Blinking rapidly, Zoe stared at Paige as she tried to process what she'd just asked her. Holy shit. Did that mean what she thought it meant? Jake was fine with them being together. He wasn't going to stop Paige from seeing her. He didn't make Paige pick her relationship with him.

"Like a date?" Zoe whispered.

"Like a date," Paige replied, her smile widening.

Zoe wrapped her arms around Paige's waist and pulled her in for the tightest hug she could without hurting her. "Yes. A thousand times yes," she replied. Zoe felt like her heart was going to beat out of her chest. Or maybe it was Paige's. They were so close Zoe couldn't tell where she ended and Paige began. "Jake is okay with us?" Zoe asked.

"For the most part, yeah. He said it might take him a while to be comfortable with the idea, but he just wants us to be happy."

Zoe pulled back and cupped Paige's face in her hands. "I promise to spend the rest of my life making you happy."

Paige gripped onto Zoe's hands with her own. "No. We will make each other happy. This isn't a one-way street for you anymore. If something is bothering you, I need to know about it. If I'm ever making you feel less than, I need to know about it. The only way this is going to work is if we talk with each other. Okay?"

Zoe swallowed hard. Talking had always been an issue for her, but she'd never wanted something to work so badly. She'd do anything to keep Paige around. "Yes. Of course. I promise."

"Good," Paige replied with a grin. "I think the only thing left to do is for us to kiss."

Zoe sucked in a breath. "God. I've been waiting so long for this," Zoe whispered.

"Me too."

Zoe leaned forward and Paige's lips parted. She wanted to close the distance so badly. Touch her. Taste her. But she also wanted to take her time. Savor her. Tease her. Instead of kissing Paige's lips, Zoe lightly pressed her lips just below Paige's ear and she trailed soft kisses along her jaw. With each kiss, Paige's breathing quickened and her grip on Zoe's hands tightened.

"Please kiss me," Paige ground out.

"My, my. Impatient?" Zoe asked as she released one of Paige's hands so she could cup Paige's cheek. She traced Paige's bottom lip with her thumb.

Paige responded by giving the tip of Zoe's thumb a light bite. "Yes. I've been waiting for this for months. I—"

Zoe cut her off as she pressed her lips firmly to Paige's and she was absolutely and utterly lost. She didn't think she wanted to do anything for the rest of her life except kiss Paige. Her soft, responsive lips had Zoe ready to melt there on the spot. Paige slipped her tongue inside Zoe's mouth, and Zoe groaned as she sucked and nipped at her tongue. Gripping Paige's hips, Zoe pulled her close as she walked backward until her legs hit the couch. She collapsed back onto it and let Paige fall into her lap and straddle her hips.

Paige unbuttoned Zoe's shirt, tossing it aside. Zoe couldn't be the only one shirtless so she pulled off Paige's T-shirt and whimpered when she saw that Paige wasn't wearing a bra. Now in front of her were perfect breasts begging to be touched. Zoe traced her fingertips along the curve of Paige's breast before taking the nipple between her thumb and forefinger, rolling it between her fingers until it hardened. Paige hissed as Zoe then took that nipple into her mouth and grazed it with her teeth. Zoe's hand traveled down Paige's stomach and hit the waistband of her leggings.

Before Zoe could slip inside, Paige stopped her with a firm grip on her wrist and she lifted Zoe's head until their eyes met. "Wait," Paige rasped. Her chest heaved with every breath and it took every ounce of Zoe's strength to maintain eye contact and not let her gaze stray back down to Paige's breasts.

"Are you okay? Did I hurt you?" Zoe asked.

"Not at all." Paige bit her bottom lip. "I hate to ask because it's super awkward. But, um, are you clean?"

Zoe shook her head to get rid of the lust-induced brain fog but she still wasn't comprehending. All she wanted to do right now was get her hand inside Paige's pants. To feel the wetness. To make her come. God how she wanted to hear the sounds Paige made when she came. "Huh?" Zoe asked, the one word she could form.

"STDs," Paige replied.

"Oh, right. Don't worry. I just had a check-up last month. And Ja...well we..."

Paige held up her hand. "You don't need to explain. Just knowing you're clean is good enough."

"No. I do need to explain." Zoe rested her hand on Paige's stomach, wanting to feel her warmth. "I haven't had sex since New Year's. It never felt right again. Because I wanted you. I wanted you so badly, Paige. Even if I didn't let myself understand that." Zoe took a deep breath and slowly released it. "Are you? Clean?"

"Yep."

"Good. Now where was I?" Zoe said as she nipped at Paige's neck. "Oh yeah. I was going to make you come."

And with that Zoe slipped her hand inside Paige's leggings and her fingers met wet heat. *Fuck me.* She wasn't wearing underwear either. Paige whimpered and rolled her hips forward when Zoe slid her finger through her folds, gathering wetness and bringing it up as she circled Paige's clit.

"You're already so fucking hard," Zoe rasped as she continued peppering Paige's neck and collarbone with kisses and soft bites. "Tell me what you want, Paige."

Paige was breathing heavily into Zoe's ear and she had a tight grip on Zoe's hair at the back of her neck. "Right there," she rasped. "Stroke it. Please. I'm already so close."

Zoe put a finger on each side of Paige's clit and gently squeezed, stroking faster and faster as Paige's moans came quicker and quicker. The grip Paige had on Zoe's hair tightened and Zoe let out a groan at the pleasurable pain. She could feel her own wetness soaking her underwear and she desperately needed some attention but she tried to keep her focus on Paige. Zoe needed her to let go. She needed to hear Paige come.

That need was fulfilled only a few seconds later when Paige let out a guttural moan as she came. "Oh my god. Oh my god," she whispered as she lazily rolled her hips into Zoe's hand. Her hot breath warmed the side of Zoe's face. "I didn't think I would come that fast."

"Fuck. That was so hot," Zoe said into Paige's neck. She lightly kissed Paige's shoulder before lifting her head so she could see Paige's eyes. Her eyes still weren't completely focused and Zoe had never seen them darker than now. Zoe brought Paige's head down so she could kiss her. This kiss was slow and unhurried. Paige had released the grip on Zoe's hair and now gently held Zoe's face in her hands.

Paige pulled back and whispered, "I love you."

"I love you too."

Zoe slid her hand out Paige's pants and she instantly missed that connection and was counting down the seconds until she could feel her again. But first she wanted to get Paige completely naked and have her sprawled across her bed. Zoe also had an urgent need of her own. Her clit throbbed and she almost stuck her hand in her own pants to take care of it. But she didn't want relief from her hand, she wanted it from Paige.

"How about we take this to bed? I need to see you. All of you," Zoe said, resting her hands on the warm skin of Paige's sides. Paige stood and stumbled backward a bit until Zoe reached out to steady her. "You okay?"

"Yeah," Paige replied, her voice shaky. "A little wobbly. Can you blame me?" Paige grinned at Zoe and winked.

Zoe let out a small laugh. "Not at all."

Zoe had all intentions of being the one in charge as she led Paige to the bed but Paige seemed to have other plans. Paige quickly undid the button on Zoe's pants, forcefully shoving them down her legs as they made their way over to the bed. Next she unhooked her bra and let it fall to the floor. As Zoe's legs hit the back of the bed, Paige pushed her gently on the shoulders until Zoe fell back onto the bed.

"Move up," Paige said, her voice firm.

Paige didn't have to ask her twice. She would obey her willingly. Zoe pushed herself up on her hands and shifted up until she could rest her head on Paige's pillows. Paige stripped off her leggings and then removed Zoe's underwear, licking her lips as she stared at Zoe's naked body. Seeing Paige kneel on the bed and crawl toward her was the sexiest thing Zoe had ever seen. Zoe's hands itched to reach out and touch Paige but before she could, Paige gripped her wrists and pinned Zoe's arms above her head.

As Paige's thigh met Zoe's center, Paige grinned and said, "You're ready for me?"

"Fuck yes. I have been since we first kissed. I need you to touch me so bad."

"Mmm. Soon." Paige bent down and kissed Zoe fiercely. She pressed her leg harder into Zoe who moaned into Paige's mouth.

Zoe needed more. She needed to feel Paige touch her. She ground her hips up as much as she could, hoping to get some relief. Zoe just wanted to come. Paige must've sensed her desperation as she slowly trailed her fingers down Zoe's stomach, tracing light patterns along Zoe's hipbone.

Paige broke the kiss and looked down at Zoe. "I have a strap if you want that."

"No," Zoe rasped. "Your fingers. Inside. Now. Please."

Without hesitation, Paige slipped one finger inside Zoe's heat and Zoe gasped at the contact. Paige slowly began to pump her finger in and out, but it wasn't enough. She tried to rock her hips in hopes of directing Paige to go faster, but it was like Paige was trying to torture her. The slow movement was agonizing and Zoe let out a frustrated groan.

Zoe pleaded, "More. I need more."

"How many do you want?" Paige asked, her voice husky.

"Three. Please," Zoe replied with a whimper. She never knew she could sound so desperate.

Paige pushed three fingers inside and Zoe screamed, "Paige!" As Paige's thrusts increased, Zoe felt like she couldn't breathe. She couldn't think. All she could feel was the tension building between her thighs. Paige brushed her thumb over Zoe's clit with the next thrust and it immediately pushed Zoe over the edge. White lights flashed in front of her eyes and she let out a loud moan. Zoe arched back as Paige slowed the pace of her fingers. As her orgasm faded, Zoe relaxed into the mattress and she opened her eyes, seeing the satisfied smile on Paige's face.

Chuckling, Zoe asked, "You seem pretty proud of yourself, huh?"

"Oh yeah," Paige replied. "I'm gonna pull out now."

Zoe nodded as Paige slowly slid her fingers out and she sucked in a breath at the empty feeling. Zoe reached out and held Paige's face in her hand, gently tugging her forward for a soft kiss. Paige rolled over and pulled Zoe with her until Zoe was curled into her side.

As Paige trailed her fingertips along Zoe's spine, Zoe felt her eyes grow heavy. She rested her head against Paige's shoulder, breathing in the familiar scent of her skin. Zoe had never felt anything like this before—the peace, the pleasure, the love.

Just as Zoe's eyes began to close, the sound of Paige's stomach growling pulled her out of near-sleep. She lifted up, resting her weight on her elbow as she smiled down at Paige. "Hungry?" Zoe asked with a laugh.

"Maybe a little," Paige murmured, a faint red dusting her cheeks.

Looking down at Paige and her delicious body, Zoe craved more than just food. She moved to straddle Paige's hips and she traced a path up Paige's sides with her fingers until she cupped Paige's breasts in her hands, stroking her thumb over hardening nipples. "Did you want to order something?" Zoe asked before she bent down and licked the side of Paige's neck, nipping just below her ear.

"Fuck," Paige hissed.

"Was that a yes, Paige?" Zoe whispered.

Paige rested a hand on Zoe's chest and gently pushed as she blew out a slow breath. "Yes. Are you hungry?"

"I could definitely eat." Zoe grinned as she slid down Paige's body. Zoe kissed the inside of one thigh as she spread open Paige's legs. "How about you call for some Chinese? I bet you can't order without letting on that you're getting fucked."

When Zoe nipped her skin, Paige sucked in a sharp breath. "What do I get if I stay quiet?"

"I'll fuck you with that strap you mentioned." Zoe slowly slid her tongue between Paige's folds.

Paige whimpered. "And if I don't?"

"You get to fuck me," Zoe murmured. In her mind, they'd both come out as winners either way.

"Deal." Paige grabbed her phone off the nightstand and called. "Any preferences?"

"As long as it tastes as good as you, I'm game," Zoe replied, dipping her tongue inside Paige.

"Holy fu…Yes, hi. I'd like to place an order for delivery." Paige's voice had developed a high-pitched breathiness and she rattled off her address.

Zoe delighted in the effect she was having on Paige, but she needed to make this more of a challenge for her. She circled Paige's clit with her tongue, loving how quickly it hardened.

Paige pulled the phone away for a moment, covering her mouth as she let out a deep moan. "Sorry, I'm still here," she said as she brought the phone back to her ear. "Can I get an order of edamame?" Paige took in a shaky breath when Zoe wrapped her lips around her clit and gently sucked. "Shrimp fried rice." Then she let out a soft whimper. "Beef and broccoli." Paige pulled the end of the phone away from her mouth and looked down at Zoe. "Do you want white or brown rice?"

Instead of answering, Zoe slipped two fingers inside as she sucked on Paige's clit even harder. Paige immediately reached down with her free hand and gripped onto the back of Zoe's head. The pain of her fingernails digging into Zoe's scalp sent a shock of arousal straight to Zoe's clit and she fought back a moan of her own.

"Oh my god," Paige said. She probably tried to whisper but she definitely failed and Zoe was certain the person on the other end of the phone had to have heard. "White, please. No, that's it. Twenty minutes? That's great. Thank you." Paige ended the call and abruptly dropped the phone to the floor.

The call over, Zoe gave it to Paige more intensely. She sucked harder and pumped her fingers faster. Every time Zoe bottomed out, Paige let out an increasingly louder whimper. Just as Zoe felt Paige clench around her fingers, Paige pulled Zoe's face even tighter to her body and she let out a scream as her back arched, causing Zoe to hold onto her hips with her free hand. Paige didn't drop her hand from Zoe's head until the rest of her body relaxed into the bed.

After a soft kiss to Paige's clit, Zoe wiped her mouth on Paige's thigh and slowly extracted her fingers. She moved up on the bed and laid her head against Paige's stomach, trying to calm her own breathing. Once she felt like she could talk, she rested her chin just above Paige's bellybutton and gave her a smirk. "Sounds like you lost."

Paige laughed. "I don't fucking care. I will lose every time if you do that me. Jesus, Zo. I still have tingles going all the way down to my toes."

Zoe shifted until she covered Paige's body with hers and she leaned down for a kiss, letting out a low moan as her hips settled between Paige's legs. "I think I should pat myself on the back for that," Zoe replied as she tapped her left shoulder with her right hand.

"You're oh so modest," Paige said, giving Zoe a wide grin as she rolled her eyes. "So looks like we have some time before the food gets here."

"Hmm. Whatever will we do?" Zoe lifted her eyebrows in question.

Paige summoned her forward with the curl of her forefinger. "Get up here. I'm sure you're dying for some attention."

Zoe didn't think she had ever moved faster as she shifted until her legs were on either side of Paige's head. As she lowered herself down and Paige got her first taste, Zoe knew there was no better way to pass the time.

CHAPTER THIRTY-TWO

Paige hurried to put on her robe as a knock sounded at her door, grabbing her wallet from the kitchen counter. With the bag of Chinese food in hand, she headed back to bed.

Zoe fluffed a pillow behind her and sat back against it, the sheet covering her from the waist down. "You're not keeping that on, are you?"

"The robe?" Paige asked, looking down at the maroon fabric.

"Yeah. Not allowed. It's a naked-only zone."

With a chuckle, Paige disrobed and tossed it on the end of the bed before getting under the sheet and setting the bag of food between her legs. "How silly of me." She handed the shrimp fried rice to Zoe while setting the beef and broccoli on her lap and the small container of edamame on the bed between them. With chopsticks in hand, they opened their containers and ate, famished from their night so far.

They sat together, swapping containers to share the meal. Paige wanted to devour everything but she also didn't want to make herself so uncomfortably full that she couldn't make good on her bet. With a sigh, she tossed her chopsticks into the carton of shrimp fried rice and set it on her nightstand. She leaned back against the headboard and turned her head toward Zoe, smiling as Zoe licked up a spot of sauce at the corner of her mouth.

"You know, when I invited you over here I actually meant for us to go on a date. I wasn't expecting sex and then dinner in bed." Zoe raised her eyebrows and gave Paige a pointed look. Paige raised her hands in surrender and laughed. "Okay. I was definitely hoping for sex, but that wasn't my main reason when I texted you. I just needed to see you."

"Well, no matter the reason, I'm so happy you texted me. Although I will admit that I had a bit of a panic because I didn't know if it was going to be good news or if you were wanting me to come over so you could say we would never be a thing and you wanted to let me down easy."

Paige reached for Zoe's hand as she saw in her eyes just how true that was. Zoe had been scared, and if Paige was being honest with herself, she had been scared too. Still was. Just because they both wanted to try this and they had amazing chemistry in bed, it didn't mean they would work out. They could end up just like Zoe and Jake had. Well, except for the unexpected outing since they were both out already.

"Hey. You okay? You looked like you zoned out."

Zoe squeezing her hand brought Paige back to the present. "Sorry. Yeah. I guess I kinda did."

"How come? You aren't regretting anything about tonight, are you?" Zoe asked, her voice small.

Paige immediately turned to fully face Zoe, kissing the palm of her hand. "No. Not at all. I just never expected this. Never expected you," Paige whispered. Out of nowhere, her eyes burned and she swiped her cheek as a few tears fell. "I moved to Indy to be near Jake. I didn't even have the guarantee that he would want to see me or even remember me. Then imagine my surprise when I not only develop a great relationship with him, but I also fall madly in love with his girlfriend."

"*Ex*-girlfriend," Zoe reminded her.

"Yes, I know. *Ex*-girlfriend." Paige took a deep breath, trying to stop her bottom lip from quivering, and failing. "Zoe, I had given up hope of ever having anything with you other than friendship. And I was even scared of having that because it was so hard to be around you and not want you every single second of every single day. Leaving the apartment on the night of your birthday was the most painful thing I have ever done in my life."

Zoe reached up to wipe the additional tears on Paige's cheeks. She leaned in for a short, soft kiss. That was enough for Paige to feel centered and calm.

"Now to have you here and then after this incredible night so far, it feels a little overwhelming. Like the rug is going to be pulled out from under me at any second. I never thought I could be this happy," Paige finished, giving Zoe a watery smile.

"I'll admit I'm scared too. I spent so long fighting these feelings for you that I still can't believe this is all real." Zoe gestured to everything around her. "Here I am, naked in bed with you. And you love me." Zoe's voice broke on that last word and tears fell just as freely down her cheeks. "I think we both know how important this is to each other. I am never going to take you, or us, for granted. I love you so much, Paige."

They leaned toward each other and met in the middle for an unhurried, heated kiss. Paige could still taste a hint of beef-and-broccoli sauce on Zoe's lips. When Paige moved closer, she stopped when she heard the rustle of the food bag as it was crushed by her leg. She broke the kiss, a little breathless and a lot turned on.

"Let me get rid of all this." She shoved the containers in the bag and tossed everything into the trash in the kitchen. After quickly washing her hands, she returned to the bed and opened up the nightstand. She pulled out a purple dildo and black leather harness. "Now I think we've done enough talking. You are naked in my bed and I think it's time you collected on our bet."

Zoe groaned. "Oh yes, please."

Paige knelt on the bed, trailing her fingers between Zoe's breasts until just above her pubic bone. She grinned when Zoe's hips arched into her touch. "Turn over."

CHAPTER THIRTY-THREE

Paige grumbled as the alarm on her phone went off and she rushed to turn over and silence it. If there was ever a time she hated mornings, it would have to be right now. Zoe had reached for her not long after she'd fallen asleep and they went round after round until they finally passed out around three. Paige was fucking exhausted. And as she sat up on the side of the bed, she realized she was also deliciously sore. It was so unfair that she had to leave the warmth of Zoe in her bed and head downstairs to work. So unfair.

She stood, stretching her arms above her head and trying not to wake Zoe. Paige was sure she smelled of sex. After a quick shower, she ate a granola bar as she got dressed.

Ready to head downstairs, she sat on the side of the bed where Zoe was sprawled out on her stomach with her arms above her head and a sheet covering her from the waist down. Paige licked her lips as she took in the sight of Zoe's naked back. God how she wanted to just say "fuck it" to work and get back in bed with her. But she had responsibilities and all that. While cuddling Zoe and giving her a ridiculous amount of orgasms was also now her responsibility, she couldn't skip work to do so. Especially since Zoe had to work too.

Crap. Zoe had to work which meant she needed an alarm to wake her up. Paige went into the living room to look for Zoe's phone. She hadn't seen her use it last night so it was probably in her coat pocket. Paige held up the coat to check and let out a silent cheer when she found it.

Paige almost dropped the phone as it started vibrating as a series of texts came in. She looked down at the phone and saw message after message come in from Mia.

I woke up and you're not home.
Are you alive?
Are you still at her place?
Did you guys fuck?
Can't wait to hear how good she is.

Paige snorted and covered her mouth with her hand, hoping she hadn't been too loud. She sat back down next to Zoe and finally let herself indulge for a moment as she trailed her fingertips lightly between Zoe's shoulder blades and down until her fingers hit the sheet. Zoe shifted slightly but didn't waken.

Paige bent down and whispered in Zoe's ear. "I got your phone. Is your alarm set?"

"Maybe," Zoe mumbled.

"Can I check? What's your passcode?"

"My birthday."

Paige smiled as she remembered that day. The day things seemed to change for them. The day she knew her heart was gone and she couldn't do a damn thing about it. Guess the universe had other plans, she thought. She quickly pulled up the clock app and checked the alarm. Good thing too because the alarm for seven was toggled off. Paige hit the button and put the phone to sleep, setting it on the nightstand next to Zoe.

She leaned down again and whispered, "I have to go to work. I love you." She kissed Zoe on the cheek.

Just as she started to step away, her hand was tugged back by Zoe who now had one eye open and was looking at Paige. "Love you too," she rasped.

The small tug almost melted Paige's resolve. Instead of completely breaking down and getting into bed with Zoe, she bent down and Zoe lifted her head as they met for a short but sweet kiss. "See you later."

"Mmhmm," Zoe replied as she gripped the pillow and pulled it closer. Within seconds, Paige heard her quiet, deep breaths as she fell back to sleep.

Paige quietly slipped out of the apartment and down the stairs, walking around the building until she unlocked the back door. She flipped on the lights and turned off the security system as she made her way down the hallway and into the staff room. Opening her locker, she reached inside for her apron. As she started tying it around her waist, she got lost in the memories of last night. The kisses. The touches. The screams. Her stomach tightened as scenes replayed in her mind and she knew she'd be counting down the hours until her work day was done and she could see Zoe again.

She jumped and let out a little yelp as someone smacked her arm. Paige turned and found Tom stepping around her and going to his locker. "Holy shit. You didn't have to scare me."

Tom held up his hands. "I thought you would've heard me. The back door slammed shut and I wasn't exactly quiet as I came in here. Why are you so distracted?"

Paige felt her cheeks warm and she averted her gaze to knot the front of her apron. "I'm not. What are you doing here?" she asked.

"Nice to see you too, Paige," he replied as he opened his locker and shoved his coat inside. "Emily wasn't feeling good so she called me and asked me to cover. But seriously what's going on?" He gently gripped her arm and turned her toward him. Tom looked at her from head to toe and then his eyes widened. "Paige! Did you get laid last night?"

"I have no idea what you're talking about," she mumbled.

"Oh please. Red cheeks, bags under the eyes...wait...is that a hickey?" he asked, his voice higher than she'd ever heard it.

She immediately slapped her hand over her neck and pulled at the collar of her button-up. *Shit.* Had Zoe given her a hickey?

Paige knew Zoe had paid a lot of attention to her neck but she never thought it would've resulted in a hickey.

"Why don't you get your ass moving and work on opening up the shop?"

Paige walked behind the counter, working almost on autopilot as she got everything ready for the morning. Maybe if she ignored Tom, he'd eventually give up and not ask her any more questions.

That hope was dashed about ten minutes later when he slapped a stack of paper cups on the counter and asked, "Did she stay the night? Is she still upstairs?"

Paige groaned. "Can't you just focus on getting the shop ready instead of butting into my sex life?"

"So there was sex? I knew it!" Tom said as he threw his hands in the air. "How was it? Amazing? By those huge bags under your eyes, you stayed up pretty late I'm guessing."

"You're impossible," Paige replied. Instead of answering him, she focused on the rest of her tasks. Looking at her watch, there were just a few minutes until she could unlock the front door. She hoped customers would start coming in immediately so she could avoid answering Tom's questions.

Tom seemed to get the hint that she wasn't going to give him any details and he concentrated on what he had to do. Paige quickly finished up with the last remaining items on her to-do list. Her mind drifted to the sexy woman still in her bed and how badly she wanted to sneak away and see her.

This day was going to take fucking forever.

CHAPTER THIRTY-FOUR

When Zoe's alarm went off, she lifted her head from her pillow and groaned. She looked around, trying to find the source of the noise and found her phone on the nightstand beside her. As she tapped to screen to stop the high-pitched sound, she glanced around the room and was briefly confused as to where she was. It only took a quick look to the other side of the bed and a sight of rumpled sheets for the memories of last night to come flooding back into her groggy brain.

Zoe rolled over onto her back and stretched her arms above her head. Mmm last night, she thought. God it was fucking fantastic just like she knew sex with Paige would be. But fuck, they had stayed up too late. Not that she was necessarily regretting it. She didn't think there would ever come a time that she would regret staying up late to have sex with Paige.

She reached for her phone and slowly opened her eyes until they got used to the sunlight streaming through the windows. She had five texts from Mia. She laughed and rolled her eyes. Typical Mia.

Zoe sent a quick reply to Mia. *I'm alive and yes I stayed the night.*

Wine and details tonight? Mia replied within seconds.

Wine, yes. Details, no.

Mia replied with an emoji with a stuck-out tongue.

Zoe tossed her phone onto the bed and threw off the sheet. She needed to get moving if she was going to have enough time to get back home to shower and get dressed for work. Zoe searched for her clothes, donning each item as she found them. Her underwear had been bunched up in the sheets. Her bra had been on the floor at the foot of the bed. Her pants were on the floor halfway between the bed and the living room. Finally she found her button-up shirt partially stuffed between the couch cushions.

Good thing she had just enough time to go home for fresh clothes. She quickly used the bathroom, stopping in front of the mirror to give herself a once-over. Her hair was a mess and she tried brushing it with her fingers but the right side still stuck up at all angles. She left the bathroom and searched around Paige's apartment. "Yes," she whispered as she found a beanie sitting on the kitchen table.

She shrugged into her coat and checked her watch. If she was quick, maybe she'd have just enough time to head down to Craft for a cup of coffee. She was in desperate need of caffeine. And if she got to see Paige again and maybe even got another kiss, then that wouldn't hurt either.

Zoe hurried downstairs and into the café. The jingle of the bells above the door seemed to grab Paige's attention and she met Zoe's gaze even as she handed a coffee over to a customer. Zoe loved how Paige's face lit up from just the sight of her. She took her place in line and waited until it was her turn to order.

"Good morning again," Paige murmured, giving Zoe a once-over. "I don't believe that's your hat, Ms. Tyler."

Zoe shrugged. "Someone gave me a serious case of bed head. I had no other option but to steal her hat."

Paige laughed. "Right. Totally my fault. What can I get you?"

"Large double mocha please. Someone kept me up too late so I need all the caffeine in the world."

Paige leaned forward and whispered, "You weren't complaining when you were screaming my name."

Zoe felt the heat rush to her cheeks. "You weren't either."

"I could hear that every day and I would never complain." Paige gave her a wink and a grin. "Let me make your coffee."

A guy in his late twenties took Paige's place and he smiled at Zoe. She recognized him from the other night when she came to talk to Paige. Zoe read his nametag and it said "Tom."

"Nice work," Tom said to her with a wink.

Zoe furrowed her brows and looked to Paige for an explanation as she came back to the counter with her mocha. "Nice work?" she asked.

Paige curled her finger in a "come here" gesture and Zoe leaned forward. "You left a little mark," Paige whispered as she pulled down the collar of her shirt, revealing the hickey at the base of her neck.

Oh shit. And were those teeth marks too? Zoe covered her mouth with her hand. "Oh my god. I'm so sorry," she mumbled around her hand. "At least your shirt covers most of it?" Zoe cringed and hoped she looked as remorseful as she felt. But could Paige really blame her? Paige's skin was so soft and so warm and so unbelievably lickable. She can't blame a girl for getting lost in certain spots for a little too long.

"You guys are too cute," Tom said. His smile widened as his eyes lit up. He turned to Paige and said, "Why don't you take today off? Go back upstairs and take this pretty lady with you."

"No way. You'd be alone down here."

"It's not that busy right now and I am acting manager for the day. Plus, Scott is coming in at nine. I can take care of things alone until then."

Zoe saw the uncertainty in Paige's eyes but she had to admit she was begging with Paige in her mind to take Tom up on his offer. She'd give anything to have a few more uninterrupted hours in Paige's bed.

"Are you sure?"

"Yes. Go. If it makes you feel better, I'll text you to come back down if we get slammed. Or if you start screaming too loud," he said with another wink.

Paige gently shoved him. "Shut up. And thank you." Paige started to untie her apron but stopped and looked at Zoe. "What about your work?"

Zoe coughed into her elbow and gave her voice a hint of raspiness as she said, "I think I'm coming down with something. Guess I'll just have to call in sick."

Paige grinned. "Let me go toss this in back."

Zoe watched her walk away and her cheeks started hurting from smiling so widely. She quickly pulled out her phone and emailed her boss saying that she needed to take a sick day. Thankfully she'd only taken one since she'd started so her boss would have no reason to think she was lying. She'd just have to make sure she didn't go out anywhere near her office building in case she ran into someone from work. But she didn't think that would be a problem as she planned to stay in bed all day with Paige.

When Paige came back to the front of the shop, Zoe grabbed her coffee off the counter and held out her other hand toward Paige. They walked hand in hand together out of the café and up the stairs to Paige's apartment. As Paige closed the door, Zoe set her coffee on the kitchen counter and shrugged out of her coat, toeing off her shoes as she walked backward to the bedroom.

"Don't you want your coffee?" Paige asked as she followed Zoe. "I thought you needed caffeine."

Zoe reached for Paige and held onto her waist as she pulled Paige close. She brushed a few strands of hair behind Paige's ear and met her darkened gaze. Zoe leaned forward, her lips a breath away from Paige's and she whispered, "I have all I need right here."

EPILOGUE

Zoe rushed up the stairs and unlocked the door to the apartment. "Hey, babe. I'm home," she called out as she set a grocery bag on the coffee table. She had been in charge of bringing the pumpkin pie to Thanksgiving dinner. And she'd had every good intention of making it the night before, but it was all Paige's fault that the pie had not been made.

Last night, Zoe had arrived home from work at her usual time and had just been about to take out all the ingredients when Paige walked through the door after a run. She'd been out of breath and sweaty. And how in the world was a girl supposed to just ignore that and make a pie? So instead of baking, Zoe had taken Paige into the bedroom and had her way with her for a few hours. By the time they were finished, it was too late to bake, so store-bought it was. Zoe was just thankful that there was a store open and they still had pies.

"Paige?" Zoe called out since she hadn't heard a reply. It wasn't as if Paige couldn't hear her since their apartment above Craft wasn't very big.

She found Paige standing in front of their full-length mirror inside their walk-in closet. Well, walk-in-esque. When Zoe had moved in last month, they had convinced Rebecca to put up a couple of walls to make a closet in the far corner of the bedroom space to replace the curtained-off area where Paige had hung her clothes.

Zoe stepped behind Paige and wrapped her arms around Paige's waist, resting her chin on Paige's shoulder. "You okay?"

Paige had been staring blankly at herself, seemingly checking and rechecking her Thanksgiving outfit. In Zoe's mind, the cream sweater with red and blue plaid scarf on top, jeans, and brown boots looked great.

Paige seemed to snap out of it at the contact and she met Zoe's eyes in the mirror. "Yeah. Just nervous. I mean it's my first Thanksgiving with Br...my dad. It just feels so bizarre."

"I know," Zoe whispered. She gave Paige a wide smile. "But just think, Jake's bringing his new boyfriend so most of the focus will be on him."

Zoe and Paige had hung out with Jake a handful of times since they'd been together. The awkwardness dissipating a little more each time. Not long after the breakup, Jake had had an intense but short fling with Ian. A fling he freely admitted had been a very poor decision, much to Zoe's relief. He had started casually dating and he would be introducing his new boyfriend, Trent, to them at dinner later.

Zoe lightly trailed her fingertips up and down Paige's side and kissed her neck. "This is going to be a low-key day with just the five of us. And if ever you feel overwhelmed or uncomfortable, just say the word and we can leave. We can be back here in fifteen minutes, cuddling on the couch and eating your favorite chocolate chip cookies that I also picked up today."

Brian had started the process of divorcing his wife and had moved to the north side of Indy a couple of months ago. Today was going to be the first time Paige had seen him since she was a little kid.

Paige turned in Zoe's arms and wrapped her arms around Zoe's shoulders. "You spoil me."

"I love you. There's a difference."

"I love you too," Paige murmured as she gave Zoe a soft kiss. "You ready to go?"

"Are you sure I look okay?" Paige asked, giving herself another glance in the mirror.

"You look absolutely gorgeous and if we weren't running late, I would slip my hand down and—"

Paige stopped her by pressing her hand over Zoe's mouth. "Nope. You have to stop. That is not what I want to be thinking about all day."

"Might put your mind at ease," Zoe mumbled around Paige's hand.

"Might put my mind at ease but certainly not other body parts," Paige replied as she removed her hand. She took a deep breath and shook out her arms. "Okay. Let's get going before I chicken out and we stay here."

Zoe held out her hand, smiling as Paige's naturally fit into hers and they intertwined their fingers. She grabbed the pie on their way out and led Paige to her car. The ride to Brian's was quiet and Zoe quietly hummed along with radio, leaving Paige alone with her thoughts.

As they stood in front of Brian's front door, Paige took a deep breath before knocking. Within seconds, Brian greeted them with a wide but hesitant smile. "Paige," he whispered. "It's so good to see you." He stood to the side and waved them in. "Come on in. Jake and Trent are already here."

With anxiety-filled eyes, Paige looked back at Zoe. She completely understood it but she would take it all away in an instant if she could.

Zoe held out her hand to Paige. "Together?" she asked.

Paige placed her hand in Zoe's and gave it a firm squeeze. "Together."

Bella Books, Inc.

Women. Books. Even Better Together.

P.O. Box 10543
Tallahassee, FL 32302

Phone: 800-729-4992
www.bellabooks.com

CPSIA information can be obtained
at www.ICGtesting.com
Printed in the USA
JSHW020817091022
31428JS00001B/1

9 781642 473858